PAUL GAMBLE

THE MINISTRY OF SUITs

FEIWEL AND FRIENDS

NEW YORK

A Feiwel and Friends Book
An Imprint of Macmillan

Our books may be purchased in bulk for promotional, educational, or business
use. Please contact your local bookseller or the Macmillan Corporate and
Premium Sales Department at (800) 221-7945 ext. 5442 or by e-mail at
MacmillanSpecialMarkets@macmillan.com.

Library of Congress Cataloging-in-Publication Data is available.

ISBN 978-1-250-07682-3 (hardcover) / ISBN 978-1-250-08682-2 (e-book)

Book design by Liz Dresner

Feiwel and Friends logo designed by Filomena Tuosto

First Edition: 2016

10 9 8 7 6 5 4 3 2 1

mackids.com

To my parents

PROLOGUE

THE SHOE'S THE CLUE

In the middle of the street lay a single shoe, an unmistakable warning that there was an escaped pirate somewhere nearby.

And yet people walked past, ignoring it. Even those who looked at the shoe didn't realize that it signaled danger and the possibility that they could have been run through by a cutlass at a moment's notice.

In fact, most of the people in the street thought it was just a lost shoe.

But think! Who loses a single shoe? Possibly someone might lose both shoes—but why would anyone ever leave a single shoe behind? You'd notice the minute you realized that you were slightly taller on your left leg than you were on your right.

To the educated, those who know how to look at the world

properly, the answer is clear: Only a pirate would leave a single shoe behind. Because pirates, who all have a wooden leg, *have only one shoe to lose.*[1]

But where do these pirates come from? Well, obviously they escape from a Piratorium—a specially built prison for pirates. Then while they are running away from the guards, their shoe falls off; and, being in a hurry to evade recapture, they generally don't turn around to pick it up.

The uneducated mind would ask: Why are pirates particularly prone to having their shoes fall off? Well . . . anyone with an ounce of sense could explain to them that pirate's shoes are always falling off because pirates are notoriously bad at tying their laces. After all, it's incredibly difficult to tie a neat bowknot when one of your hands has been replaced with a metal hook.

It is this state of affairs that caused Captain Buck Steerhawk to say the second-wisest thing that a pirate has ever uttered.

"Lad, if you want to be a pirate, remember this: Get yourself a pair of slip-on loafers."

Coincidentally, Captain Buck Steerhawk is also responsible

---

[1] Generally pirates lose their legs while on board their ships in the heat of battle. While on board a galleon they don't have access to a full set of modern, plastic, molded prosthetic limbs. Therefore the wooden legs tend to come off the nearest piece of furniture available. And it's hard to fit a sneaker or a Doc Marten boot on the end of a wooden leg off a Queen Anne sideboard. Therefore pirates generally don't need two shoes. They just need one shoe. And possibly a caster if they want to go roller-skating.

for the first-wisest thing ever uttered by a pirate: "It's vitally important that you always think very carefully about which hand you're using the toilet paper with."

Uneducated people believe that pirates no longer exist in the world. But how could pirates have just disappeared overnight? Pirates haven't really disappeared any more than the dinosaurs just vanished one day. These days all pirates are locked away in Piratoriums, where they are well looked after, given a daily supply of grog, and allowed to sing sea shanties and screech "A'hr Jim Lad" at each other to their heart's content.

Occasionally a pirate may escape during transportation to or from a Piratorium, and hence you may see a single shoe lying in the road. But this happens rarely, as pirates are securely transported around the road network in sealed tankers. What is truly strange about this world is that no one ever notices this, despite the fact that the tankers are clearly marked with a skull and crossbones. What would a tanker marked with a skull and crossbones be carrying other than pirates?

The question is, are you one of the people who sees how unusual the world really is? Or do you think that the single shoe lying in the road is just a lost shoe? If you look closely at the world, you will quickly realize that there are signs of strangeness everywhere. And if you can see the signs, maybe you're ready to join the Ministry.

All you have to do is open your eyes.

Unfortunately, as our story begins, Jack Pearse's eyes are firmly closed.

PIRATES
FAMOUS ESCAPES OF

The most famous pirate escape to occur in recent years was the notorious French pirate Jacques le Magiste. Jacques was a pinup amongst pirates. He inspired everyone he met. He never took any prisoners, never spent his treasure—always choosing to bury it instead—and further boasted that whatever any other pirate did once he would do twice. Of course this made Jacques rather easy to capture as he had no hands, just two hooks; no legs, just two wooden pegs; and no eyes, just two patches.

1

A LONELY SHOE
MONDAY

It was morning and Jack's head was still hidden under his duvet. It wasn't that Jack didn't like mornings. It was just that he would have preferred them if they happened slightly later in the day. Maybe half past eleven. Possibly even later on the weekends.

"Jack! Time to get up," Jack's mother yelled from down-stairs. "You don't want to be late for school."

It was a strange thing for his mother to yell. After all, being late for school was something that didn't worry Jack in the slightest.

Rubbing his eyes with both hands, he crawled from under the duvet and peeped out of his curtains. The sun was beaming down through a cloudless sky. Jack found this annoying, as it meant that P.E. would be outside today.

Getting sweaty and tired was bad, but getting sweaty and tired and muddy was even worse.

As Jack looked out the window he noticed a single shoe lying in the middle of the road.

"How did that get there?" he wondered. To Jack, a shoe lying in the middle of the road was annoying. There was no sensible or reasonable explanation for it, and Jack hated unexplained mysteries. When reading detective books he almost always found himself flipping to the last few pages to find out who the murderer was. An unexplained mystery felt almost physically uncomfortable, like an unscratched itch or a crumpled sock inside a shoe.

By the time Jack got downstairs his cereal was getting soggy. Jack's father's mustache appeared over the top of his newspaper. As always, Jack's father's face quickly followed the mustache. Jack's father's face and Jack's father's mustache had a sort of double act going in that way. You rarely saw one without the other.

"Morning, Jack," said the mustache.

"Morning, Dad."

"Eat your cereal," said Jack's mother.

Jack poked his cereal with a spoon and frowned. Why did parents always make you do things that you didn't want to do? In Jack's books heroes were almost always orphans, or their parents had been kidnapped, or they just didn't seem to feel the need for parents at all. After all, Peter Pan probably would never have defeated Captain Hook if his parents had been around. They would never have let him use a pointed sword, for a start. And it's almost impossible to kill a maniacal pirate with a pair of safety scissors.

Jack thought that maybe people only ever became heroes because they didn't have parents.

The mustache looked at its watch. "You'll have to get a move on if you want to catch your bus."

"Here's your P.E. kit." Jack's mother handed him a bag. "I washed it."

Jack looked halfheartedly at the bag. It made him wonder about heroes again. If heroes didn't have parents, then who did their laundry? As far as he could remember, Peter Pan never found himself wrestling with an enchanted washing machine and a pair of magically dirty pants.[2]

"Mum," Jack said in his nicest voice, "I don't suppose you could give me a note to get out of P.E.?"

His mother sighed. She had heard this before. "What is it about P.E. that you hate so much?"

"Partly getting muddy, but mainly P.E. teachers."

"Not a good enough reason. So, no note."

It was Jack's turn to sigh as he picked up his schoolbag and P.E. kit. As he was walking out the door he stopped and turned around to his parents. "Mum, how hard is it to do your own laundry? Would it take me a long time to wash my own clothes?"

She arched an eyebrow as she looked at him. "Well, the

---

[2] Magically dirty pants are widely regarded as the worst type of dirty pants.

ironing might take you a while. You wouldn't have much free time if you had to do it."

"I'm glad I'm not a hero, then," Jack said as he left to catch his bus.

The mustache looked at Jack's mother. "That boy gets stranger all the time."

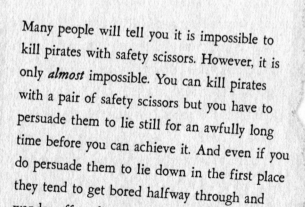

MINISTRY OF S.U.IT.S HANDBOOK

PIRATES
Killing with Safety Scissors

Many people will tell you it is impossible to kill pirates with safety scissors. However, it is only *almost* impossible. You can kill pirates with a pair of safety scissors but you have to persuade them to lie still for an awfully long time before you can achieve it. And even if you do persuade them to lie down in the first place they tend to get bored halfway through and wander off to dig up some treasure or pillage a Caribbean island.

2

AN UNEXPECTED BEAR

Jack ran out the front door with his shirttail flapping inelegantly behind him, making it to the corner just in time to catch the bus. As he walked down the aisle he caught sight of David Sacher, his best friend.

David and Jack had been friends since they met as five-year-olds on the first day of school. So, when it came to going to middle school they had both decided to go to the same one.[3]

---

[3] For those of you who need to know, Jack and David live in Northern Ireland. It's the north end of the island of Ireland. For years people argued over who owned Northern Ireland. Jack and David didn't ever really know why. But it seemed dreadfully important to a lot of people. However, you will be glad to know that politics have nothing to do with our story....

They made a strange pair. Jack was about average height for his age with jet-black hair. The odd thing about Jack was that he was always thinking. Whether it was wondering about heroes or wanting to know how a single shoe could get abandoned in the middle of a road, Jack just wanted the world to make sense. Which was, in many ways, a bad thing to want. Because although the world made many things, sense was rarely one of them.

David was generally a lot more relaxed about such things. He didn't particularly care if the world made sense. If David woke up one morning and found a bacon sandwich tree in his back garden, he would not wonder what could have caused such a botanical anomaly. Largely because he would have been looking for a glass-of-milk bush in order to wash his bacon sandwich down.

David was thin and all angles and points. In many ways he resembled a human erector set. It was never a good idea to wander too close to David when he was walking because you never knew when a stray elbow or knee might come popping out of his body and clatter into a soft and fleshy part of you. It wasn't so much that David was excessively clumsy, it was just that he seemed to have been born with a few extra joints in his arms and legs. Whereas the girls in their junior school had exchanged friendship bracelets to show their devotion to each other, Jack's friendship with David was marked with a series of accidental bruises and numbed limbs.

The top of David's head was home to a scraggly shock of

dirty-blond hair that unfortunately made him resemble a rather badly constructed scarecrow.[4]

"Hey," said Jack as he sat down beside his friend.

"P.E. today," said David.

"You remembered your kit?"

"I will never forget my kit."

Both David and Jack shuddered at the thought of forgetting their kit. Something truly horrible happened to the children who forgot their kit. Something neither Jack nor David wanted to think about.

⚬⚬⚬⚬⚬⚬⚬⚬⚬⚬⚬

There was a loud screech of brakes and the bus jerked to a stop. Everyone on board rocked forward in their seats. On a normal bus this would have thrown the passengers into chaos with people shouting, screaming, and hurling abuse at each other. This, however, was a school bus, and it was already quite chaotic with a fair amount of general abuse being hurled back and forth. Therefore the sudden stop had actually stunned the bus into silence.

Of course, the silence lasted only for a second before chattering broke out again.

"So, did you watch any TV last night?" asked David.

"The bus has just suddenly ground to a halt and you want to ask me what I saw on TV last night?"

---

[4] It should be noted that most scarecrows are badly constructed. It's part of what makes them scarecrows. If they were constructed more adequately, they wouldn't be scarecrows. They'd be store mannequins.

David nodded. "Yes."

"Aren't you the least bit curious as to what's going on?"

David thought about this. "Not really. I mean, if it's important, someone will let us know. Right?"

Jack sighed and looked around the bus. Paper planes were being thrown, mobile phones were pinging, and geeks were being tormented by popular kids. Jack wished he could have gone back to his conversation with David, but his natural curiosity forced him to stand up.

Jack's mother had always said that curiosity killed the cat. Jack would then normally point out that a feeling couldn't possibly kill a cat. Jack's mother then normally said Jack thought too much about things, that he had to know everything and that he might very well be obsessive-compulsive. Jack thought about this, decided he needed to know what obsessive-compulsive meant, and looked it up in the dictionary. As far as he understood, an obsessive-compulsive was someone who worried about things all the time. From that moment on, Jack spent a good part of every day worrying that he might be an obsessive-compulsive.

"I can't just sit here and not know," said Jack. "I'm going to see why the bus stopped."

"It might be dangerous," said David.

"I'd rather be in danger than not know." Jack stood up. "Are you coming with me?"

"Might as well. Danger is always the most fun."[5]

---

[5] This is the kind of thing that your parents lie to you about. Danger is fun. You know it. Your parents know it. Politicians know it. It's just that

At the front of the bus the driver had already opened the door and got out. A line of halted traffic blocked their progress.

"You kids had better get back on the bus," said the driver.

"We will get back on the bus . . . just not yet." Jack always obeyed adults . . . eventually.

Jack walked along the line of cars. He was on his tiptoes, straining his neck trying to see what was happening. He'd been expecting an accident, but when he got to the front of the queue it was something rather different. David was shocked by what he saw and started hyperventilating. He briefly fumbled in his pocket for his inhaler before he remembered that he wasn't actually asthmatic.

There was a large bear on all fours in the center of the road. It was enormous, almost the size of a horse, and had a shaggy black coat. It roared and its open mouth looked like a cave with ivory-white stalactites for teeth. Drool fell from its maw in a most unbecoming way.[6]

Looking at the bear's razor-sharp teeth, Jack suddenly became aware of how tasty his arms and legs might look. For a brief moment he had a stunning

---

no one can actually admit it. (At least no one ever admitted it until chapter twelve of this book.)

[6] It is hard to drool in a becoming way. In fact, it's almost impossible to be charming and erudite while drooling. Which is why St. Bernard dogs are so rarely seen being interviewed on the red carpet at the Oscars.

psychological insight into what it must feel like to be a Gummy Bear.[7]

"What is a bear doing in the middle of the city?" Jack whispered.

"That isn't the right question to be asking," said David. "The question you should be asking is: Can we get away without being eaten?"

"All right, don't panic. We'll just move toward one of the cars and they'll let us inside. We'll be safe."

The bear reared up onto its hind legs and let out a roar that made the hair on the back of Jack's neck stand up. After the roar, David and Jack heard a chorus of clicks as the doors of the surrounding cars locked.

"All right," said Jack nervously, "now that all the cowards in the cars have locked their doors we're going to need another plan."

He looked around. The people in the cars had stopped looking at the bear and had started looking at the two boys. At first Jack was confused. He thought that they should have been watching a bear. Frightening as the bear was, it was an interesting and unique thing to look at.

Then he realized.

A grizzly bear was a frightening and unique thing to look at. However, an even more frightening and unique

---

[7] People think that Gummy Bears seem happy and jolly, but generally their short, wobbly lives are spent in abject terror of having their limbs ripped off and eaten.

thing to look at was two twelve-year-olds who were just about to be eaten alive by a grizzly bear.

"I say we try and make a run for it," said David.

"Remember that documentary we saw about bears on BBC 2?" asked Jack. "They can run at about thirty miles an hour. Do you think you can outrun him?"

David shook his head very slightly. "I wasn't planning on outrunning him. I was just planning on outrunning you."

"Oh," said Jack. Then he realized what his friend meant. "Oh great, and then I get eaten."

"If you're lucky, he won't eat all of you. He looks quite well fed. He might just chew on one of your arms for a while."

"Hopefully the right one," said Jack. "I just got this watch for my birthday and Mum would kill me if I lost it."

"How about we both run in different directions and hope that confuses him," David suggested. "On three."

"Okay," Jack agreed. He didn't have a better plan.

David started counting. "One, two . . ."

Suddenly Jack noticed movement behind the bear. "Wait a minute."

There was a man lying on the ground behind the bear. He was dressed in a black pin-striped suit and had an umbrella lying beside him. His chest was rising and falling, although only very slightly. That meant he wasn't dead yet, but if they left him, Jack had no doubt he would be. The man had already been attacked by the bear and his clothes were torn and covered in bloodstains.

"There's a person lying behind the bear."

"Good," said David. "Hopefully he'll eat him instead of us."

"We have to help him."

David let out a little groan. "Jack, do you have to be a hero? You do this all the time. Remember the time you tried to defend that little kid from the gang of bullies?"

"We saved him, didn't we?"

"Well, yes, but we ended up being thrown into the trash bins. Jack, you're my best friend. But you aren't a hero!"

"I know I'm not a hero, David; I don't do my own laundry."

The bear roared and took two lumbering steps toward the boys. Jack looked around to see if there was anything he could use to defend himself. Ideally a tranquilizer gun.

The road was deserted. Everyone had fled into the local stores or was safely locked inside their cars. It should be noted that the people inside their cars were not quite as safe as they thought they were. Bears have been observed in the wild smashing windows to get to food inside cars. Essentially the people in the cars looked to the bear a little bit like the way baked beans in a tin look to humans.

There was a building site to Jack's right. The builders had abandoned all their tools and clambered up the scaffolding, from where they safely watched the unfolding drama. A large nail gun was lying on the ground where a builder had dropped it.

Jack looked at the other side of the road. There was a small French-style café with a few tables and rickety chairs outside.

He took a deep breath and a feeling of certainty came over him.

"Right, David, I've got a plan. The minute I move you start running in the opposite direction." Without any further hesitation, Jack sprang into action.

MINISTRY OF S.U.IT.S HANDBOOK

BADLY CONSTRUCTED SCARECROWS
Job Prospects

Secretly all scarecrows wish to improve their construction slightly and get a better job as a store mannequin. The work is similar (standing about all day), the hours are similar (again...all day), but there are two important differences between the job of scarecrow and store mannequin. Firstly, a store mannequin gets to work indoors, which is a huge benefit in our uncertain climate. Secondly, store mannequins get to wear all sorts of delightful new clothes whereas scarecrows end up with a variety of hand-me-downs that are inevitably full of holes and patches. Shabby though they may be, scarecrows still have a sense of self-esteem.

3

THE CHAIR OF DESTINY

Jack leapt forward and David took off running in the opposite direction. Out of the corner of his eye Jack saw David running. Many of their school friends had discussed what David's body had been built for. It certainly wasn't running. Watching him run was a bit like watching an episode of *You've Been Framed*. You knew something was going to go wrong, you just weren't sure of exactly when. Predictably enough, David fell over in a heap of flailing arms and legs.

Now Jack's plan had to work; otherwise they would both end up as a bear's breakfast.[8]

The builders who were watching from the safety of some

---

[8] This was, of course, assuming that the bear had not already had something to eat for breakfast. If the bear had already eaten, the risk would have been of becoming a bear's brunch.

scaffolding had expected Jack to leap into the back of their tool van and grab something from there. Maybe a sledgehammer to smack the bear with. Maybe he would go for the dropped nail gun to try and shoot the bear.

But Jack didn't go for the tool van. Instead, Jack leapt toward the café. One of the builders wondered if maybe he just wanted a croissant.

Jack did not want a croissant.[9]

The bear let out a final roar and moved toward him like an enormous, foul-smelling, furry carpet. Jack grabbed one of the rather rickety wooden chairs that was sitting outside the café.

The bear took a swipe at Jack with one enormous paw, its claws glistening with blood. Jack swayed backward. The claw swished the air past Jack's face. A drop of bear sweat landed on the tip of Jack's nose.

The builders watching from the safety of their scaffold cheered, but Jack didn't feel elated. He knew that he had avoided death, but if his next move didn't work, then he would be in serious trouble.

---

[9] Jack never wanted a croissant. It was always unclear to Jack why adults, who could eat what they wanted for breakfast, would opt for a croissant over a bacon sandwich. Personally he felt that adults who opted for muesli at breakfast should be locked up in an asylum until they admitted it tasted awful. Bacon tasted wonderful and Jack felt that if pigs did not want to be eaten they wouldn't make such an effort to taste so nice. Of course now that Jack was facing the prospect of being eaten by a bear he was concentrating very hard on not tasting nice himself. It felt like it was working, but he couldn't be sure.

Jack raised the rickety chair and yelled, "Yah!" He'd seen it in a circus once. A man had kept a lion at bay with a chair. Jack thought the same might hold true for bears.

"Unless that bear really, really wants to have a sit-down, that young boy is going to die," muttered one of the builders unhelpfully.

The bear had pulled its massive paw back to take another swing at Jack, but suddenly its eyes focused on the four legs of the chair. There seemed to be a look of fear on the bear's face.

The people in the cars were surprised. The builders on the scaffold were stunned. But Jack was probably the most shocked of all. A large part of him had expected the bear to smash the chair with one enormous paw. Instead the bear seemed strangely unnerved by the chair.

"Yah!" shouted Jack as he poked the bear in the midriff with his chair. "Scram. Or I'll . . . I'll chair you, I suppose."[10]

The bear gingerly lowered itself down onto four paws. It sniffed the chair cautiously and took two steps backward. For a moment Jack and the bear locked eyes, then the bear turned away and bounded off down the street.

Jack put the chair down.

Then he sat on it.

---

[10] Jack made a mental note to check with his English teacher if the word *chair* could be used as a verb. He knew it was a noun, but he was unsure if the sentence "Just before the bear killed the young boy, the young boy had chaired him," would be grammatically correct.

"That," he said, "was unexpected."

David came over and stood in front of Jack.

"I fell over," said David.

"I saw that," said Jack. "I scared off a bear using a chair."

"Everyone saw that," said David.

All the people who had locked themselves in their cars were opening the doors now. One of them started clapping and before long Jack was the recipient of a hardy round of applause.

"Oh yes, clap now. A few minutes ago you were perfectly happy to lock your doors and let us get eaten!" shouted David.

The people looked slightly sheepish and the clapping petered out. They wandered back to their cars and switched on radios to try and drown out the sounds of the shame they had echoing in their ears.

"Let's see if he's okay," said Jack, indicating the man in the pin-striped suit who had been attacked by the bear.

The man was conscious now and was sitting up. There was a large gash on his right temple where the bear must have hit him. His suit was ripped and covered in blood, but most of the wounds seemed relatively shallow.

"Are you all right?" asked Jack, helping him up.

"Mmmm. Can you count my limbs for me?" asked the man.

David did the necessary mathematics and answered the man. "Four limbs in all."

The man looked down at himself. "Four limbs. Good. Two

of the arm variety and a corresponding number of the leg variety—and they seem to be in the correct sockets.[11] All present and correct. In which case, the answer to your question is yes. Yes—I am okay."

"You were attacked by a bear," said David helpfully.

"Yes, I noticed that too," said the man with more than a hint of sarcasm. "I was tracking the bear. Unfortunately he seems to have escaped."

"You're a bear hunter?"

"A bear hunter?" laughed the man as he picked up his umbrella. "Good gracious, no. And if I was, I wouldn't make a very good one, would I? No—I work for . . ."

The man paused. "Well, let's not talk about who I work for at the moment. Now, what are your names?"

"Look, we'd love to stay and chat," said David, "but we've got to get on the bus and go to school."

The bus driver beeped his horn and leaned out of his window. "Are you getting back on?"

The man with the umbrella waved the bus driver on. "Carry on, sir; I shall walk these two young gentlemen to school."

"Right you are," said the bus driver as he drove off.

"I can't believe you did that," grumbled David.

"Don't you want to know why you managed to defeat the bear?" asked the man.

---

[11] Many people would wonder why a man would check that his limbs were in the correct sockets. The reason for this and for much else will become clear later on, in chapter thirty.

Jack's eyes lit up. It was exactly what he wanted to know. "Yes. I'd really like to know that."

"You are either a very bright or a very lucky boy," the man said.

"Brave but stupid, I'd say. If it had been me, I would have grabbed that nail gun and tried to shoot the bear," said David.

"In which case the bear would have eaten you. You see, our young friend here chose the one thing in the vicinity that could save him from a bear attack. A wooden chair. Bears are terrified of wooden chairs."

Jack thought about when he had grabbed the chair. He had known it was the right thing to do, but he hadn't been sure why. If he hadn't found out why, it would have irritated him all day. "So tell us, then, why are bears afraid of wooden chairs?"[12]

[12] Some of you will have been wondering why this chapter was called "The chair of Destiny." You will have expected there to be some mystical chair that told Jack what his future would be. It was just an ordinary chair, as it turns out. But the woman who owned the café was called Destiny. She owned several things that weren't chairs. There was a hairbrush of Destiny, a car of Destiny, a nice pair of high heels of Destiny, and so on. Very few of these items had any significant magical powers. (For those of you who love your grammar, this is why the word *Destiny* was capitalized [proper noun] whereas the word *chair* wasn't [ordinary noun].)

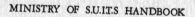

BEARS
FATALITIES CAUSED BY NAIL GUNS

There are no records anywhere in the world of a bear being killed after being shot by a nail gun. If you shoot a bear with a nail gun, you aren't going to end up with a dead bear. You're going to end up with a very annoyed bear. Although it will be a very annoyed bear that you'll be able to hang a picture on.

4

A DANGEROUS UMBRELLA

For the first time Jack really looked at the man in the pin-striped suit. Despite having been recently attacked by a bear he didn't have a hair out of place, and although his shirt was torn it was still neatly tucked into his trousers. His eyes were a steely color and they fixed on Jack, making him feel slightly unnerved. The man looked exactly like a spy would look if he was trying to infiltrate a top-class, Savile Row tailor.

"Normally bears live in the woods," the man began to explain. "In many ways they are the king of all they survey. There really isn't another animal in the woods that could defeat a bear."

"What about a lion?" asked David.

"Well, the one time I saw a bear and a lion fight, the bear definitely won. Anyway, as I was saying . . ."

"Wait a minute," interrupted Jack. "You saw a lion fight a bear once?"

"Yes, it was an office party that went badly wrong."

Jack was about to ask another question, but the man headed him off. "Look, do you want to know why bears are afraid of chairs or not?"

"Sorry for interrupting," said Jack.

"Mmmm. You are a very impetuous boy ..." The man waited for Jack to supply his name.

"I'm Jack; this is David."

The man shook both their hands vigorously. "Very good. My name is Grey. Now, we were discussing bears. In a forest the bear is king. Top dog, or rather top bear. Except for one thing."

David's eyes lit up. "There's a bigger animal that lives in the forest?"

"Not an animal," said Grey. "It's a ..."

"A tree," Jack said.

Grey tilted his head to one side and looked at Jack. His eyes narrowed, as if he was looking at a very hard math equation. It made Jack squirm.

"Quite right, Jack. The only thing that the bear isn't king of is the tree. Trees are bigger than bears. Did you know that bears scratch and bite trees with their teeth and claws? Now, biologists[13] will tell you that they're sharpening their claws.

---

[13] The proper name for a person who studies bears is an ursinologist. Grey clearly doesn't know this word. It is vital never to mistake this word for the word *urologist*, which is the word for a person who studies

But think about it. That's a ridiculous explanation. Have you ever used a knife against a tree? It won't make it sharp, it makes it blunt."

Jack nodded at this. When he was seven years old he'd tried to make a tree house in the garden. In order to get wood he had tried to cut down a cherry tree with a kitchen knife. His mother had been furious when the knife was returned with an edge that was as dull as a double math class on a sunny day.

Grey continued, "So if they aren't sharpening their claws on the trees, why are they doing it?"

Something popped into Jack's head. "Because they're attacking the trees?"

Grey took a step backward. Jack had read about people taking a step back in surprise, but this was the first time he'd ever actually seen it happen in real life. "How did you know that?" asked Grey.

"Jack's always thinking about things like that. He thinks too much if you ask me," said David.

"Thinks too much?" Grey mused to himself. "Jack, I think I should speak to you by yourself."

"And how will you do that?" asked David. "I'm right here."

Grey opened his black umbrella. "Here, hold this." He thrust it into David's hands.

---

wee. A urologist ursinologist would be a person who studied the wee of bears. The world is so unbelievably diverse that there is almost certainly a urologist ursinologist in it somewhere. His scientist friends probably bully him mercilessly.

"What?" David said. "But it isn't raining."[14]

"Oh," said Grey, "I don't suppose it is, is it?" Grey snapped his fingers and the umbrella abruptly closed up again. Unfortunately as David was holding it, it snapped closed on his head, also half pinning his arms to his sides.

"Mmmmphhhh," said David as he frantically ran around trying to free himself.

"What have you done?" Jack cried.

"I just want to talk to you without your friend interrupting us."

David was running up and down the street and making muffled yet indignant noises.

"The umbrella won't hurt him. He's perfectly safe," Grey reassured Jack.

David chose this point to run slap-bang into a lamppost. The noise of his nose crashing against the metal rang out.

"Perfectly safe?" asked Jack.

"To be fair, I said the *umbrella* wouldn't hurt him. Which is true. It was the lamppost that hurt him. But let's move him away from the traffic just in case."

Between the two of them they escorted David into a chair outside the café. David sat in it silently.

"There you go," said Grey, smiling. "He seems to be a lot quieter now . . . Well, either that or he's concussed."

---

[14] Remember this point; it becomes vitally important in chapter nine. It's a pity that Jack can't read the footnotes, as they would make his life considerably easier. One of the major problems in trying to live life is the lack of helpful footnotes.

"Concussed!"

"He's probably not concussed. It really is a very high-quality umbrella. Thick material, frightfully waterproof."

Jack thought to himself that wasn't really a recommendation. Most umbrellas were waterproof. It was their role in life to be so. However, relatively few umbrellas were lamppost-proof.

"Okay," said Grey, "so *why* do you think bears attack trees?"

Jack shrugged. "I don't know . . . Umm, bears are bullies?"

"Eureka!" yelled Grey, who was doing a little dance around Jack. The dance was frankly ridiculous. Jack felt embarrassed for the both of them. Normally Jack did not feel embarrassed for other people. However, Grey looked as if he was too busy dancing to be embarrassed, so it seemed the polite thing to do.

Grey stopped dancing. "You got it in one—bears are bullies. And bears attack trees because trees are the only thing that's bigger than them in the woods. Of course after attacking half a dozen trees, a bear realizes that a tree is much tougher than he is. Trees don't flinch, don't bleed, don't scream. Trees seem invulnerable to the bears."

Jack shook his head. "Still not getting it. So why are bears scared of chairs?"

"Easy!" said the still-jubilant Grey. "Bears know that trees are tough. And yet you appeared to the bear as if you were a man who could not only kill a tree, but one who could bend and shape a tree's body into the shape of a wooden chair. You had power over a tree!"

Jack thought about this. It sounded ridiculous, but also completely logical. If the best a bear could do to a tree was leave a few claw marks, it would be terrified of anyone who had taken an enormous piece of timber and turned it into a chair.

"Wow," said Jack. "So that's why lion tamers use chairs as well."

"Precisely, most woodland and forest animals are scared of a person holding a chair, because it shows that they can kill trees. Jack, my boy, you are quite brilliant."

Jack smiled. He had always wondered why lion tamers used chairs. Now he knew. He loved explanations because they made the world slightly more organized, slightly more sensible.

"We could use a boy like you, Jack," Grey said. "If you're interested, come and visit me at my work." He walked over to David and, with a flick of his wrist, freed him from the umbrella. David sullenly rubbed his bruised nose as Grey turned sharply on his heel and strode off.

"Wait a minute," Jack called after him. "You could use me for what? And anyway, how do I know where you work?"

Without breaking stride Grey shouted over his shoulder. "Jack, if you're half the boy I think you are, you'll be able to figure out where I work without much trouble."

Jack watched as Grey walked into the distance. With most other boys that would have been the last that they saw of Grey, but Jack was far too curious to allow that to happen.

JUNGLE AND WOODLAND ANIMALS
FEAR OF CHAIRS

Anyone with any level of education is clearly aware that most woodland-, forest-, and jungle-dwelling animals are scared of chairs.

However, it is important to state that not all animals are afraid of chairs. Elephants aren't, for example. Elephants are big enough to push over trees and therefore aren't even vaguely scared of them. However, elephants are scared of pianos as they think the white keys are all made of ivory. This is the reason why you never see an elephant at an Elton John concert. Which is a shame, really, because elephants love touching, romantic ballads.

Incidentally, elephants are wrong about the white keys on pianos being made from ivory.

5

A GIRL CALLED TRUDY WHO
HAS A REPUTATION FOR MOODINESS

Jack and David ran through the school gates and sprinted into the main building in a desperate bid to avoid being late. David had been trying to move more quickly than was sensible and ran smack into a girl. They both tumbled to the ground in a flurry of limbs.

Jack started over to help them up, but before he had even completed a single step the girl was already on her feet. She had moved almost impossibly fast, so quickly she almost seemed to blur.

David was on his feet again and he dusted himself off. However, he had barely been on his feet for five seconds when he fell down again and curled himself into a tiny ball.

"Umm, what are you doing?" asked Jack.

David untucked his head from the ball he had curled

himself into. He looked rather like a tortoise wearing a school uniform. "I could ask you the same thing."

"Well, you could," agreed Jack, "but it wouldn't make any sense."

David unfurled an arm and pointed at the girl he had run into. For the first time Jack really looked at her. It was Trudy Emerson.

Trudy was about the same height as Jack and was in the same year. She had fair hair, which would have been shoulder length if she didn't always have it pulled back into a tight ponytail. Half a dozen strands of hair at the front were dyed red and had a tendency to fall across her face, obscuring her dark blue eyes.

But Jack wasn't worried about how she looked. He was worried about her reputation. A reputation that had led her to gain the nickname "Moody Trudy." In Trudy's first year at the school she had already broken several records for detentions, general tellings-off, and suspensions.

What made Trudy really terrifying was that she did all this completely by herself. Most of the bad kids hung around in gangs. By themselves they would have been too scared to break the rules. But nothing seemed to scare Trudy. She didn't *break* rules. She *shattered* them into little, tiny pieces, jumped on the pieces, and then dropped them around a "no littering" sign. Quite possibly hoping that a passing squirrel would try and eat a piece of the rules and then choke.

Jack looked at Trudy and smiled. "Sorry about David; he's just..."

Trudy said nothing. She just stared.

"We'll just be . . ."

Trudy continued staring.

Jack noticed that a group of kids from his class were walking past and heading into the assembly hall. This was very confusing. Assembly should already have been over. It wasn't that Jack stopped being afraid of Trudy at that moment. It was just that his sense of curiosity needed to know what was going on. If curiosity had been an airborne virus, any cats within a five-hundred-foot radius of Jack would have dropped dead.

"Why is everyone going into the hall?" asked Jack. "Shouldn't assembly be over for the day?"

Trudy stopped staring and snorted. "They're having a special assembly," she snapped. "Some stupid company coming to sponsor the school or something. Give us free stuff."

Trudy's fists were curling into balls. If Jack had been a normal boy, he would have thanked Trudy for her time, wished her well in future endeavors, and run away in the opposite direction. However, his curiosity gland was pumping madly.[15]

"Why would you be angry about someone giving us stuff? Isn't it good getting stuff?"

---

[15] Are you wondering if there is really such a thing as a curiosity gland? Of course there is. Otherwise there would be nothing making you curious about whether or not there is such a thing as a curiosity gland.

For those of you thinking that you weren't actually curious about whether there is such a thing as a curiosity gland, that probably just means you have an overactive apathy organ.

Trudy spoke through gritted teeth. "We have P.E. this morning. I was going to use the assembly hall for my gymnastics."

"Oh. Right."

Jack had heard about Trudy's gymnastic ability. When they had first started at the school people were amazed at her ability to tumble, somersault, and spring. There had been talk about her joining one of the senior gymnastics teams. She had been so good that a shelf of the trophy cabinet had been cleared out and dusted down in anticipation of the medals she would win.

But although Trudy was great at individual gymnastics, teamwork clearly wasn't her forte. Trudy's ability to work as part of a team was somewhat compromised by the fact that she didn't talk about clothes, boys, and bands all the time. Millicent, the leader of the popular girls, had sensed weakness in Trudy and had made fun of her mercilessly.

Then one day, when Trudy was meant to catch Millicent coming out of a back flip, she had just wandered away. "There was no one to catch Millicent," the P.E. teacher had screeched at her.

Trudy had shrugged. "The floor caught her, didn't it?"

The floor had caught Millicent, but it had been less than gentle in its approach. Millicent walked with a distinct limp for several weeks afterward. She never made fun of Trudy again and Trudy was asked to leave the team.

There had been a suggestion that Trudy should be allowed to stay on the team for the sake of school pride and the medals she would generate. However, one of the math teachers had put together a spreadsheet estimating what Trudy's presence would cost in sprain liniment, bandages, and increased personal-injury insurance premiums. The numbers didn't lie, and Trudy left the team. She was still allowed to practice gymnastics, but only by herself, in the school hall, away from the other pupils.

Almost everyone in the school was terrified of Trudy. Jack was too, but part of him still wanted to ask Trudy why she was angry all the time. Jack looked at her and thought about asking the question.

From his tortoiselike position on the ground David glanced up and saw the look in his friend's eyes. David had known Jack long enough that he knew when he was going to ask a question that would get them both into trouble. David sprang to his feet in the same way that a tortoise would if you fitted it with a pogo stick.[16] "We'd better get into the assembly," he said while grabbing Jack's arm and pulling him away from Trudy.

Trudy shook her head and walked away.

---

[16] You may be wondering why you would ever consider fitting a tortoise with a pogo stick. After all, if Aesop is to be believed, a tortoise can beat a hare in a race. Of course the answer to this is that a tortoise could never beat a hare in a race. The true story about the legendary race between the hare and the tortoise is that the tortoise cheated the hare in two separate races. However, Aesop, like all good children's authors, believed that all children's stories should provide a moral lesson to their readers and so he didn't report the actual facts.

I'm not a very good children's author.

Make sure you eat five pieces of fruit and vegetables a day. . . .

Or not. Whatever. It's not like I'm going to tell on you.

TORTOISES
The Myth of the Tortoise and the Hare

Although Aesop claimed that the hare lost the race with the tortoise, he didn't actually tell the whole story. There were, in fact, two races. In the first race the hare said that he would race the tortoise to any location the tortoise chose.

"Then let's race to my house," said Mr. Tortoise. He quickly pulled his head and legs inside his shell. "I win!" he yelled triumphantly.

On the second occasion the hare insisted that the location they would race to should be an actual physical location. The tortoise took the hare up a long, winding mountain path.

"Now I will race you to the bottom of the mountain."

The hare dashed into a lead as he ran round and round the mountain, along the twisting path.

The tortoise went to the side of the mountain, tucked himself inside his shell once more, and launched himself straight downward. Naturally the gravity-assisted tortoise made it to the bottom of the mountain much quicker than the hare managed using the circular mountain path.

Unfortunately, at the bottom the tortoise, neatly tucked in his shell, had gained so much speed and energy that he accidentally crashed into a badger, fatally injuring it.

* * *

The reason Aesop never told this story was that the moral he wanted to illustrate was *"Slow and steady wins the race."*

The real story would only have been useful if the moral he had wanted to illustrate had been *"Sometimes when you try really hard to win a race a badger is going to die."*

And that isn't as universally useful a moral.

The moral of this section of the handbook is that if you want to write a series of moral tales to instruct children, you're going to end up telling a lot of lies. A lot of lies.

6

CHAPEAU NOIR ENTERPRISES

Jack and David sneaked quietly into the assembly hall and squeezed into two seats in the back row. The headmaster was just finishing talking.

"... So after last week's accident in chemistry class, all sixth formers will be required to attend a seminar dedicated to explaining that the words *flammable* and *inflammable* mean the same thing. But that was not why I have asked you here today. Rather I wish to introduce a very special person to you all. Our new school sponsor ..."

"How do you sponsor a school?" David asked Jack. "Is the building going to go on a walk to raise money for charity?"

Jack elbowed David in the ribs to stop him from speaking.

The headmaster continued. "... So without further ado, I will introduce you to Mr. Teach from Chapeau Noir Enterprises."

A man with a sinister beard walked onto the stage.

Beards were one of those things that Jack had spent much time thinking about. Jack had a theory about beards. A beard wasn't an indicator of evil in itself, but it was if you shaved it into neat shapes. The simple proof of this was that babies were the most innocent of all creatures on earth. Babies rarely had beards. And if they did, people were rightly suspicious of them.

A full beard that wasn't shaved, trimmed, or sculpted in any way could be all right. Santa Claus had a full beard and he was a nice man. But the more that you shaved or sculpted a beard, clearly the more evil you became. When you saw drawings of devils and demons, they always had goatees. And the most evil people on earth, dictators like Saddam Hussein and Adolf Hitler, had shaved their beards down to practically nothing, in Hitler's case a mustache so small that it barely existed.

Mr. Teach's beard was very sinister indeed. It looked like someone had taken a marker and drawn a goatee on his face using thin black lines.

David leaned over to whisper in Jack's ear. "I don't like the look of this guy."

Jack nodded in agreement.

Mr. Teach was a large man who looked to be in his forties.[17]

---

[17] He was actually in his fifties; the reason for his youthful appearance wouldn't become clear until much later on. However, if you want a clue as to the reason why, one of his arms was slightly longer than the other....

He wore a black velvet suit and had black leather gloves. In his left hand he carried an ebony cane topped with a straight silver handle.

The headmaster beamed at Mr. Teach and reached out his arm to shake hands. Mr. Teach flashed an enormous smile at him but didn't lift up his right hand in response. Instead he set his ebony cane on the lectern and slapped the headmaster on the back with an enormous left hand.

Jack assumed that this was meant to be a friendly gesture, but the force of the back-slapping propelled the headmaster off the stage and into the first row of pupils.

There was a brief moment of panic when it seemed as if someone had been hurt. However, after a few seconds they realized that although someone had been hurt it had only been the craft teacher, so it didn't really matter that much.

Mr. Teach leaned over the side of the stage where the headmaster had fallen. "Dreadfully sorry about that. Here, let me help you."

Using only his left hand, Mr. Teach reached into the front row of the audience, caught the headmaster by his collar, and lifted him effortlessly onto the stage.

Although slightly disconcerted, the headmaster asked the pupils to give Mr. Teach a round of applause.

"Thank you, thank you for welcoming me to your beautiful school." Mr. Teach's voice was deep and booming. "Now, some of you may know who I am. I run Chapeau Noir Enterprises. We're a large company that undertakes a variety of activities. We manufacture various products, we have a financial services arm[18] and a consultancy business,[19] and we also work in the area of energy provision. Over the years my businesses have made me a very rich man indeed. And now I have decided to give something back to the local community."

David leaned over to Jack. "Maybe he's going to buy us all bikes."

Jack admired David's optimism, but he knew that in situations like this, pupils never were given anything directly. It would be a new plumbing system, or computers for the staff room.

There was a loud noise of banging and clattering outside. The pupils looked out the large windows that lined one side of the hall. A huge crane and a long flatbed truck had arrived.

"I see the first of my gifts has arrived." Mr. Teach smiled from the stage.

---

[18] A financial services arm is essentially a bank. Years ago when people worked in financial services they said they were bankers. Then the world decided that bankers were all evil. So bankers decided to change their names to financial services. In due course people will decide that financial services are evil and the name will change again to something else—like economic operation providers. This happens in all parts of life. You may notice that these days politicians have a tendency to no longer refer to themselves as politicians. Rather they tend to use the words "public representative." This changing of names to protect images happens throughout history. Rat catchers became pest control. Toilet cleaners became lavatory attendants.

[19] No one really knows what management consultants do—surprisingly, least of all, management consultants.

David stood up slightly and tried to get a better look at what was going on outside the school. "Why would they need such a large crane for some bikes?"

"I really don't think it's going to be bikes," Jack muttered.

Mr. Teach banged his left fist on the podium to regain everyone's attention. "Power!" he said loudly. His eyes seemed to glitter when he said the word. "My gift to you is power. Outside is a truck that carries the Chapeau Noir 3000. The world's premier wind turbine."

The wind turbines were enormous white poles at the end of which a large set of blades would be affixed. Mr. Teach carried on talking. "The system that I will set up outside will generate enough power for your entire school. The savings achieved will allow your teachers to buy even more books."

"Great," said David, "more books. That's what I wanted. Can't wait until I can go to the park so I can ride round the BMX track on my new book."

"But that isn't all I'm going to give to the school," Mr. Teach continued.

"Oh, good," said David, "now maybe he's going to give us manacles to put on the pupils during detention."

"This is going to be a present for each pupil."

David's eyes lit up with excitement. "Maybe we are going to get bikes after all! Or even better, a games system."

Sometimes Jack wished that he could be as optimistic as David. Of course he wouldn't want to be as stupid as David was, just the optimistic bit.

"What I am going to give you all is . . ." began Mr. Teach.

David had his fingers crossed and had screwed up his

eyes as if he was wishing very hard indeed. It was either that or he needed to go to the toilet *really* badly.

"... new school uniforms."

David's face changed. Either he was very disappointed or he had accidentally gone to the toilet. Theoretically it could have been a combination of both. After all, if he had just gone to the toilet in the middle of the assembly hall, he was likely to be slightly disappointed in himself.

Mr. Teach spread his arms out, indicating both sides of the stage. From the right-hand side came one of the sixth-form girls and from the left one of the sixth-form boys. The girl was wearing a green skirt, white shirt, green jumper, and a striped green, blue, and white tie. The boy was wearing black trousers, a white shirt, and a black blazer, his tie the same as the girl's.

"Wonderful new uniforms, stylish and cool. And more importantly, made of polyester, so they're entirely machine washable! I bet your mothers will be pleased about that." Mr. Teach and the headmaster chuckled onstage. No one else in the assembly hall found the joke funny.

The headmaster walked up beside Mr. Teach. "I'm sure we'd all like to thank Mr. Teach and his company, Chapeau Noir." The headmaster started a round of applause that was gradually picked up across the hall. "But Mr. Teach is being far too modest. In addition to the new uniforms and the wind turbines, he has agreed to spruce up the school. We'll be getting new carpets for all the corridors, new door handles, and a lick of paint around the place! Pretty soon you won't recognize the school."

David whispered to Jack, "We can use that as an excuse next time we're late. We'll just say we didn't recognize the school and walked straight past it." Jack wasn't sure whether David was being serious or not.

The headmaster explained to the assembly that they were all to line up and get their new uniforms immediately. Jack and David shuffled into line.

"There's something suspicious about this." Jack was thinking again. "Why would they give us new uniforms that look exactly the same as the old ones?"

CONSULTANCY BUSINESSES
What They Actually Do

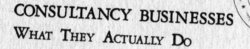

Essentially consultancy firms are hired when a business has a problem they are not sure how to solve. The consultancy firm is called in to help. The conversation then goes as follows:

Business: We have a problem. Here it is.

Consultancy: Well, we can tell from our expertise that is indeed a problem.

Business: Well, yes, we know that it's a problem. We just told you that. Now we need a solution to that problem.

Consultancy: (Thinks for a minute) From our experience we think that you need a solution.

Business: Didn't we already say that?

Consultancy: Have you any idea how you are going to solve it?

Business: Well, we have a few ideas, but we were hoping that you'd...

Consultancy: If you tell us the ideas you have, we'll take them away, write them down, and then give them back to you with a nice cover on the front.

Business: But isn't that just telling us the same ideas we've told you?

Consultancy: Y-eeesss. But we're also going to charge you £20,000.

Business: Twenty thousand pounds! For telling us our own ideas back to us?

Consultancy: Well, yes, but the report will have a *really nice cover*.

7

THE BOX OF SPARES

Unfortunately, although the special assembly had taken up more of the morning than normal, it still hadn't taken up enough time for Jack and David to miss P.E.

It wasn't that Jack especially disliked physical activity. It was more that he especially disliked P.E. teachers.

When Jack's parents had taken him to visit Madame Tussauds Wax Museum[20] in London, they had walked through the Chamber of Horrors. There had been wax figures

[20] Madame Tussauds is very proud of its waxworks and claims they are *identical* to many famous celebrities. If they are identical, this means that many famous people are made almost entirely of wax. Therefore if Benedict Cumberbatch or Tom Cruise pops into your house for a visit, it is vitally important that you do not let them stand next to the radiator for any significant length of time.

of masked torturers doing unspeakable things to poor, unfortunate wretches. Sticking things where things shouldn't be stuck. Placing unbearably hot things onto parts of the body that definitely weren't heat resistant.

"I bet you're glad they don't have those kinds of people around anymore," said the mustache that passed for Jack's father.

Jack had thought to himself that the problem was that people like the torturer still existed. It was just that there were fewer job opportunities in the torturing industries these days. So the kind of people who used to become torturers applied to become P.E. teachers instead.

Jack and David were getting changed with the rest of the boys in their class when Mr. Rackham, the P.E. teacher, walked in. He was a large, barrel-shaped man with thick forearms and legs that bulged like a pair of over-inflated pink balloons[21] out of his regulation blue running shorts.

He was missing a hand, which he said he had lost in a particularly vicious rugby scrum many years ago. His

---

[21] David said that he always felt slightly sad when he saw Mr. Rackham's legs. Overinflated ballons are the saddest of all states for long balloons. Because you know that they will live and die as a balloon. Underinflated balloons have enough give in them to be twisted and folded. This leads to a great deal of excitement in their lives as at any stage a balloon modeler may grab them and turn them into a dog. Or a giraffe (dog with a long neck). Or even a poodle (dog with a slightly different kind of tail).... Balloon modelers have a limited repertoire and they are fooling no one.

hand had been replaced with a pair of steel pincers that he used to crush cans of fizzy pop when he was finished with them.

Jack found it slightly bizarre that a man who had lost his hand playing rugby would want to encourage small children to take up the sport, but the viciousness of P.E. teachers clearly knew no bounds.

Mr. Rackham was completely bald, but still sported an enormous, bushy beard. This had led to Jack once asking him, "Mr. Rackham, why have you put your head on upside down?" Following this incident Jack was made to run twenty laps of the rugby pitch, until he thought he was going to throw up several of his internal organs. Jack later told his classmates that to see the look of rage on Mr. Rackham's face he would gladly have run another twenty laps. We have no information about how Jack's internal organs felt about this proposal.

There was a horrendous screeching noise. Jack's nerves jangled and the hair on the back of his neck stood on end. Jack looked up to see that Mr. Rackham was signaling for silence by pulling the fingernails on his one remaining hand across the small rectangular chalkboard that he carried with him at all times.

This was further proof, if it was needed, that P.E. teachers were evil. Whereas all other teachers had switched to using computer projectors and modern technology, Mr. Rackham still carried a small chalkboard with him. It was about the same size chalkboard that people used in kitchens to write lists on. He claimed that he used it to keep score in football matches, but that clearly wasn't the reason—he could have used a clipboard or even a mobile phone to do that. Mr. Rackham clearly just liked making the ghastly nail noise when he wanted the boys' attention.[22]

Jack always wondered why he found the sound of nails being dragged across a chalkboard so unpleasant. He wasn't scared of chalkboards and he wasn't scared of a person's nails (no matter how badly they were manicured). Therefore why was the combination of those two things together so nerve-wrenchingly unpleasant? He supposed he would never find out.[23]

"All right, ladies,"[24] said Mr. Rackham. "Today it's going to be football. I trust you all brought your kits."

---

[22] Mr. Rackham also used the chalkboard and his nails instead of a whistle while the boys played football and rugby. Bizarrely enough this had a rather positive effect. All the boys hated the screeching sound so much that they tried to avoid fouling another player at all costs. Perhaps if professional sporting organizations wish to ensure more fair games, they should consider replacing all referees' whistles with chalkboards. Although this would require referees to be professionally manicured as part of their training regime.

[23] Wrong, wrong, wrong . . .

[24] Mr. Rackham called all of the boys in P.E. "ladies." The boys assumed that he meant this as a joke. The problem was when the boys were having a joint lesson with the girls, he also called the girls "ladies."

Jack once suggested that his calling them "ladies" wasn't meant as a joke at all and that Mr. Rackham just had an incredibly shaky grasp of biology. Although many people agreed with Jack that this was a possibility, so far no one had discovered any empirical evidence to back it up.

Jack smiled and thanked the heavens he'd remembered his kit. The fate for a boy who forgot his kit was horrific. As Jack pulled up his navy blue socks and began tying his laces he realized the changing room was uncharacteristically silent. He looked up and realized why.

Over in the corner John Andrews had raised his hand.

Rackham noticed the hand and a sadistic smile played across his face, "Yes, Andrews, what is it?"

Andrews gulped. "I've . . . I've forgotten my kit, sir."

"Have you indeed? Well, maybe one of the other boys has brought a spare P.E. kit with them?" Rackham looked around the room at the boys. "No?" Rackham faked astonishment. "How disappointing. And how selfish that none of the boys here thought to bring a spare kit for you."

Rackham walked back into the little cubbyhole room at the bottom of the changing area that he referred to as his "office." He came out carrying a cardboard box. A simple brown cardboard box, and yet it struck fear into the hearts of all the boys present. As always in situations like this, Jack felt extremely sorry for Andrews, but also extremely glad that it wasn't him who had forgotten his kit.

Mr. Rackham smiled so widely you could see every single one of his glistening, brown teeth.

"Looks like you'll just have to pick your kit out of the box of spares."

John Andrews looked as if he was going to cry as he slowly crept toward the box. What followed was something horrific . . . appalling . . . disgusting. Something that no one wanted to behold . . .

David and Jack watched as John Andrews ran around the pitch trying to tackle other players. All the other players passed the ball before they let Andrews get anywhere near them.

The box of spares contained the worst pieces of P.E. kit known to man or boy. Shorts that were too tight, stained T-shirts, socks that smelled of death.[25] Few of the boys who had looked inside the box wanted to talk of its contents, but one had claimed that most of the pieces of kit were covered in moss and that he saw something moving at the bottom of it. Something that was a cross between an insect and a snake.[26]

It was horrifying to watch someone reach inside it. They always reached in as if they were scared that something inside the box of spares was going to bite their hand. The box of spares in its small cardboard heart held as much terror as any medieval torture chamber or modern-day battlefield.

Currently Andrews was running around the pitch wearing a pair of shorts that were far too tight for him. You could

---

[25] Some of you may be asking, "What does death smell like?" Well, if you want the answer to that question, just go to Jack's school. Because there's a pair of socks there that smell exactly like it.

[26] It is hard to imagine what this would have looked like. An insect has many legs, a snake none. Therefore the suggestion seems to be that the creature that was spotted had a reasonable amount of legs. Although it's hard to imagine why a creature with a reasonable amount of legs would inspire such terror.

see marks around his waist where they bit into his flesh. They also had a rip in the back where his underwear poked through. The T-shirt managed to be too baggy for him, and yet at the same time too short, only covering half of his belly button. Finally, as if that was not embarrassing enough, the T-shirt bore two stains. One on the front and one on the back.

The front stain was a kind of orangeish-red. It was also quite textured and small pieces flaked off it as Andrews ran. The stain on the back was a dull green in color and, thankfully, flatter. For some reason it seemed to be in the shape of an elephant.

Andrews was putting a brave face on having to wear the kit from the box of spares, but David and Jack both knew that inside he would be crying.

It wasn't just the social embarrassment of the whole thing, although that was bad enough. It was also the possibility of disease. Simon Jenkins had been the last boy who had worn a kit from the box, and he had died of liver failure. They'd held a special assembly for him and the headmaster had said that it was a tragedy that one so young had died. Apparently the doctors had no idea why Simon's liver had failed at such a young age. However, everyone in his P.E. class had known why—the hateful box. But it wasn't something you could tell your parents. They would just have laughed.

"I'm glad my parents never bought me a P.E. kit like that," David said sadly.

"Me too," Jack agreed. But it made him think. He had never seen any of the other children in his class wearing clothes like those that appeared in the box of spares. So . . . where exactly did they come from? And for that matter, how did they get left in the changing room?

"You think we should actually try and kick the ball or something?" David asked Jack.

"Yeah, might as well," agreed Jack.

David ran up the pitch and made it almost all the way to the halfway line before he fell over and managed to get his limbs tangled. From this distance Jack thought that they'd plaited themselves into a reef knot, but it was hard to tell.

THINGS THAT ARE HORRIFIC, APPALLING, AND DISGUSTING
THINGS THAT NO ONE WANTS TO BEHOLD

It is interesting to note that, anytime someone says, "No one wanted to see that," it is something that people always pay close attention to. So, for example, after a car crash, people are always slowing down to see any gore as they pass. Television programs that show particularly gruesome films of medical procedures always have sky-high ratings. People watching these shows always say, "Oh, this is horrible, this is horrific, this is the worst thing I have ever seen"... and then they look around for their Sky Plus or Tivo remote control so they can rewind it and watch it again.

There are a lot of theories as to why we watch such awful things with such absolute joy. However, it is generally accepted that a large part of the reason that we do it is because it is somewhat reassuring to note that in life, worse things do happen to other people.

8

THE ODD KIDS

Jack spent all morning thinking furiously. He had realized that there was something very odd indeed about the box of spares and tried to explain his ideas to David at lunchtime.

"Okay, I'm really trying to keep up with you here," said David. "Explain to me again why the fact that there's a box of spare P.E. kits means that someone is kidnapping children?"

Jack sighed. "It's simple. Where would clothes like that come from? The ripped clothes? The stained clothes? They'd be thrown out, right? I mean, if your mum bought you a T-shirt that was the wrong color, what would you do?"

David shrugged. "Get her to buy a new one. I'd tell her that I'd get made fun of."

"Right, but who would keep a T-shirt like that?"

"Well, a weird kid."

"And what do you mean by a weird kid?"

"Jack, you know exactly what I mean by a weird kid. One with funny hair, who doesn't have the right schoolbag, or watch the right TV programs. An oddball."

Jack nodded. "Exactly! All the clothes in the box of spares are the kind of clothes that odd kids wear. What's the other thing that we know about odd kids?"

"Ummm..."

"Look, we just watched what happens when someone wears a kit from the box of spares—no one talks to them."

"Well, of course no one talks to the odd kids. There's a very fine line between talking to an odd kid and having other people start to think that *you're* an odd kid." David shuddered at the thought.

"So, would you notice if an odd kid went missing?"

David thought about this for a minute. "Well... of course I would."

"Would you? You don't speak to them. They don't speak to you. One day they aren't there; how would you know?"

"Maybe I wouldn't..."

"So the box of spare kits exists because someone is taking those kids away and leaving their kits behind. No one notices because no one cares if an odd kid goes missing."

David looked at Jack. "Do you really think odd kids are going missing from our school?"

"It's the only thing that makes sense of the box of spares. Think about this, David: Who's the oddest kid in our class?"

David looked around the playground as other members of their class ran by. He *ummm*ed and *ahh*ed for a while and then came to a rather unpleasant realization. "I'm the oddest kid in the class, aren't I?"

Jack put his hand on David's shoulder. "I'm afraid you are. But you aren't even that odd. There must have been more odd kids at the start of the term. But they've gone missing. Their parents may notice, but no one in the school does."

David gulped. "You'd notice if I went missing, wouldn't you?"

"Of course I would," said Jack. "But if other kids have gone missing, we've got to try and track them down."

"How?" David asked. "And more to the point, why?"

"Aren't you curious about anything?" Jack asked.

"Not particularly."

"I've got an idea. Remember this morning, that guy Grey? He seemed to be at the center of very odd things. And what we need at the moment is a man with experience in dealing with very odd things indeed. I'm going to try and find him."

ODD KIDS
How to Identify Them

Many people have asked if there is a simple way to test whether someone is an odd kid or not.

The test is simple. Ask the kid in question if they have ever wondered if they are an odd kid. If they answer anything other than "No. Never," then they're almost certainly a bit of an odd kid.

* * *

In short. Odd kids—you know who you are.

9

MULTITASKING WITH
AN UMBRELLA

It was the end of the school day and Jack waved as David got on the bus home. Then he realized that waving at someone on a bus made him look stupid and stopped.

Jack liked buses because they reminded him of dinosaurs. Any time someone was describing a dinosaur they would never tell you that it stood thirty feet high, or weighed fifteen tons. Instead they always told you how big it was compared to a double-decker bus. Jack knew that a *Triceratops* was the size of a double-decker bus, a *Tyrannosaurus rex* was taller than a double-decker bus, and a *Brontosaurus* weighed the equivalent of fifteen double-decker buses.

Jack had no idea why dinosaurs were always compared to double-decker buses. It seemed odd to compare one to the other as they didn't seem to come in contact. Generally speaking, dinosaurs rarely used public transport.

Jack wasn't riding the bus today. He'd decided to take Grey up on his offer. Although Jack hadn't said it in so many words to David, he was more than a little nervous. If Jack was right about the box of spares, it meant his best friend could be in danger. If odd kids were being kidnapped, it would only be a matter of time before David disappeared. And there was no way that Jack was going to let that happen. He would find Grey and figure out what was happening with the box of spares.

Jack had one clue as to where Grey might possibly work. Grey had said that he had seen a lion fight a bear at an office party and there was only one place in town where you could find both a lion and a bear together.

A lot of people would have assumed the zoo. But there were two problems with that theory. The first was that it was hard to see how zoo animals could get out of the cages. The entire point of zoos was to keep animals separated from each other and the general public. The second problem was that zoos were pretty open-plan. There weren't "offices" to have parties in.

So where was the one place in town where you could find a bear, a lion, and some office space?

The museum.

Of course a lot of people might have pointed out to Jack that the animals in the museum were stuffed. But with the strange things that had been going on today, Jack wasn't going to let an explanation like that stop him.

The nearest museum to where Jack lived was the Ulster Museum, right in the center of the city. He'd already phoned his parents and told them he'd be late for tea as he was joining the school choir. They'd been surprised and he knew he would be quizzed on this when he got home, but he could think about that later.

The museum was an enormous building that sat on top of a small hillock in the city's botanical gardens. The entrance was an old mansion house with enormous white pillars and large cross-latticed windows. It had been expanded years ago and the extension was made up of a series of large concrete rectangles. From the outside it looked confusing—just like every good museum should.

Jack walked through the sliding entrance doors and up to the information desk. Sadly no one there seemed to have heard of a man called Grey who wore a business suit and carried an umbrella. Jack wandered past Viking longboats, native American teepees, and historical flags while wondering what to do next.

Grey had been wearing a suit. That meant that if he did work at the museum, he didn't work on the floor with the exhibits. People who wore suits worked in back rooms and offices. Jack ran to the elevator and looked at the buttons. He had expected to see a button marked "Private" or "Staff Only," but there was nothing like that.

The buttons showed there were two basement levels (marked B and LB) and three ordinary floors. Then out of the corner of his eye he noted a button that was right up near the roof of the elevator. It didn't have a number or a letter on it but instead was marked with a tiny symbol that looked like a suit jacket and tie.

Normally elevator buttons would be within easy reach. Why would someone put one so far out of reach?

Jack realized it wasn't the button that he needed to think about. Buttons were inanimate objects. What he really wanted to think about was the person who pressed them. Once more Jack found himself thinking about what he knew about Grey.

Grey was a very strange man. A pin-striped suit, a sharp side part, and a furled umbrella. Jack could still see Grey in his mind's eye. Standing there. With the sun just over the horizon, beaming out of a cloudless sky. A cloudless sky . . . *a cloudless sky*!

Jack cursed himself for being so stupid and started rummaging around in his schoolbag until he found a ruler. Grey had been wandering around on a bright and sunny day with an umbrella in his hand. There hadn't been a cloud in the sky. Why would someone carry an umbrella when it clearly wasn't going to rain?

The answer was simple. He carried an umbrella because he had to press a button high up on the wall of an elevator. No one could ever have reached the top button in the elevator . . . *unless* they had an umbrella to poke it with. The fact that the button was so high up on the wall would stop people from pressing it by accident, and therefore Jack assumed it would take him to the most secret part of the museum. A man as mysterious as Grey was bound to work in a secret and strange location.

Standing on his tiptoes and using the ruler he had taken from his schoolbag, Jack just managed to click the button. The doors of the elevator closed and it started rumbling ominously. Jack couldn't tell whether the elevator was going up or down. It might even have been moving sideways. It seemed to be moving at considerable speed, making a "ding-ding-ding" sound as it rattled past floors.

Then, without warning, the elevator shuddered to a stop and the doors slid open. Jack cautiously poked his nose outside the door. In front of him was a long corridor, but it didn't look like he was in the museum anymore. The corridor looked as if it had been tunneled through solid rock. The walls were covered in patches of a greenish mossy substance. Jack suspected that the greenish mossy substance might well be green moss. But unfortunately he hadn't paid enough attention in biology classes to be sure.

Jack took a step out of the elevator and nervously walked down the corridor. Behind him the doors of the elevator *schlicked* closed. Jack turned and panicked—how would he ever get out?

"I'm going to be trapped down here forever. How will I ever ..."

Then he realized that this was what elevators always did—you stepped out and the doors closed. Jack pressed a button in the wall beside the elevator doors and they popped open again. "That's handy."

Feeling reassured that he wasn't trapped, he walked down the long corridor. It was dimly lit; however, Jack couldn't figure out where the light was coming from. He was surrounded by a sort of dull glow.

Jack leaned against the wall to contemplate where the light could be coming from. When his shoulder touched the wall there was a sudden burst of bright light. It was as if his shoulder was suddenly on fire. Jack jumped away from the wall and slapped his shoulder to put it out. He was glad, but curious when he realized that his shoulder wasn't actually on fire. In fact it wasn't even warm. Jack extended his best poking finger and pushed it into a lump of moss. When he poked the moss a bright light shot out from the wall. It wasn't hot and didn't burn him like a lightbulb might have.

Jack realized that the moss was the source of light in the corridor. He slapped a piece of the moss hard and was dazzled as a puff of light exploded outward. Jack wondered how it worked and peeled a piece of it off the wall and put it in his pocket, deciding to think about it later.

The corridor widened into a cave that would have been large enough to fit a cathedral inside. At the far end of the cave was a set of ten-foot-high double doors made of dark brown wood, banded across by rusted, black metal. The doors were flanked by two giant statues with squat arms and legs and crudely carved heads.

There was something quite frightening about the statues. Anybody else might have stopped and turned around, but Jack had come too far now. He *needed* to know what was behind those doors. He needed to find Grey and make sure that David wasn't the next odd kid to go missing.

Jack walked toward the statues and the door. "I know what's going to happen next," he said to himself.

When Jack was within ten paces of the doors there was a deep grinding sound from the statues and they slowly hauled themselves upright.

One of the statues turned its dark, hollow eye sockets toward Jack and boomed at him in a voice that sounded like the sea rattling up and down against a pebble beach.

"Halt! You are not known. Leave now or we shall crush you."

"Yeah," said Jack, his eyes widening with fear, "that's pretty much what I thought was going to happen."

INTERESTING PLANTS
GOLDMOSS

Goldmoss is often used by the Ministry to light underground passages and caves because it is environmentally friendly and also saves a fortune on the electricity bills.

Goldmoss is an unusual plant in that it generates light. Like all plants, goldmoss is afraid of the dark. Anyone who knows anything about botany can tell you that plants are afraid of the dark. During the day daisies, sunflowers, daffodils... all flowers, in fact, are perfectly happy. That's why they look so pretty and turn their faces to the sun. But if you ever look at plants, you will know that at night they close their petals. Some scientists were confused by this and came up with elaborate reasons why. They even went as far as to talk about photosynthesis and how plants can turn light into food. Of course this is patently ridiculous. If you could turn sunlight into food, then people with tans would always be fat. But quite often the opposite is the truth. People with tans tend to be thin. Which is absolute proof that sunlight can't be turned into food.

The real reason that plants close up at night is that they are terrified of the dark. They scrunch themselves up and hide until the morning comes.

Goldmoss is so frightened of the dark that it actually produces its own light. Therefore when you poke it, it panics and lets out a burst of light.

Most plants are afraid all the time. Which is why they never go anywhere. If they were brave, they might go for a walk and see what was around the corner. Generally plants don't do this as they are paralyzed (literally) with fear.

Occasionally a really old tree that has grown very tall will be brave enough to go for a wander. But this rarely happens. When Ministry Operatives notice that a tree has gone for a walk they will put up a sign to warn people, lest they get crushed beneath its enormous roots. You may have occasionally seen these signs—they say "Heavy Plant Crossing."

10

VANITY, THY NAME
IS STATUE

"I really don't want to leave," said Jack. "But equally I don't want to be crushed." Jack knew he had to get past the statues. His curiosity always seemed to get worse when someone wanted to stop him from finding out things. If he had to choose between a hundred pounds or a mystery box, Jack would pick the mystery box every time.

"We are the door guardians," said one of the statues. "If we allowed people to get through the doors, we wouldn't be doing a very good job, would we?"

"Can we at least talk about it?" pleaded Jack.

"Oh," said the statue as its hands dropped back to its sides. "I, uhh, I suppose we don't have to smash you straightaway."

"Yeah," said the second statue, "didn't we learn something about that in the customer-care seminar the management made us go on?"

"I'd rather not be smashed," said Jack. "I'd just like to go through the door. That would be excellent customer service."

"I think that would be a step too far," said one of the statues.

"Yeah, I mean if door guardians let people through doors, then what use are they?"

Jack pondered this. "Well, you really do make a pair of splendidly beautiful statues."

The statues laughed. "We know we aren't attractive. Look at our barely carved heads," one statue pointed out.

The other statue chortled along. "Exactly, and look at our teeth. They're just stalactites and stalagmites."

Jack felt that flattery was the route to try. "I disagree; in fact the both of you look very noble. Maybe you should forget about guarding the doors and just try looking decorative. That's what most statues do, isn't it?"

The statues looked unconvinced. Jack would have to try harder.

"Look, we're all friends here, aren't we. . . ." Jack realized that he didn't know what the statues' names were. "Umm, what should I call you?"

"I'm Kevin," said the second statue. "And that's Barry."

Jack's eyes widened. "Kevin and Barry? Really?"

"Yeah," said Kevin. "What's wrong with that?"

Jack shrugged. "I suppose I expected that you'd have names like Rocknar the Destroyer and Grogat the Mighty."

Barry laughed. "Who has names like that?"

"You'd never get a job as a door guardian if you had a name like that," said Barry. "I mean if you got a job application from a guy called Rocknar the Destroyer, would you accept him for an interview? Can you imagine interviewing someone like Grogat the Mighty for a job as a cashier in a bank?"

"You have a point," said Jack, who really wasn't sure whether Barry had a point or not. "Although I suppose I might give a cashier job to someone called Grogat the Destroyer if I were a Viking."

"Aha," exclaimed Kevin, "but how many bank managers do you know who are Vikings?"

Jack had to admit that he didn't know any bank managers who were Vikings. Although this doesn't really prove anything. Jack may not have known any bank managers who were Vikings, but as he was only twelve he didn't know any bank managers at all. "Look, if you let me through the door, I can help you look decorative and noble. Then that could be your purpose in life instead of focusing on smashing people."

"How could you make us look decorative?" scoffed one of the statues out of its badly carved mouth.

"Being a statue isn't about being gorgeous. I mean, let's be honest: The Statue of Liberty isn't going to win any beauty contests. But what Lady Liberty is really good at is accessorizing. What you guys need is a flaming torch or something like that. It'd make you look truly noble and dignified. Maybe help you meet some lady statues." Jack winked at the giant stone figures.

Barry looked suspicious. "And you have a flaming torch to give us?"

"Not exactly," admitted Jack, "but I can improvise."

STALAGMITES AND STALACTITES
TELLING THE DIFFERENCE

Stalagmites go up from the ground. Stalactites hang down from the ceiling. The way to remember this is that if a stalagmite gets big enough it MIGHT one day touch the ceiling. And a stalactite has to hang on very TIGHT or it will fall and smash on the ground.

If you ever see stalagmites or stalactites, it's generally easier to do what I do and yell "Wow, look at those pointy rocks."

It is also interesting to note that despite what geologists try and tell you, stalagmites are generally man-made. For more information on this please refer to the section "Dinosaurs," subsection "Trapping and Care of."

STATUES
Vanity

Generally speaking, statues are very vain indeed.

This is why you see those statues of Greek men standing around totally in the buff. Frankly, they should be ashamed of themselves.

A lot of retirees go to museums. So maybe it's not the statues that should be ashamed. Maybe the retired people should be ashamed for spending all their time hanging around in museums and looking at naked statues and naked paintings. Either way it's fairly certain that someone should be ashamed of something.

11

WEIRDEST INTERVIEW EVER

The enormous doors that Kevin and Barry had been guarding swung open. Jack walked through feeling proud and perhaps even a little bit smug.

"Thanks for this," said Kevin.

Jack hadn't had a flaming torch; however, he had his school ruler and, with the judicious application of some sticky tape, had secured a large clump of the goldmoss to the end of it.

The effect of this was to create an organic flaming torch. Kevin and Barry were now taking turns to hold it above their heads and strike Statue of Liberty poses. They had never felt so dignified before.

They had thanked Jack for his invention and had opened the doors for him.

Jack walked through the enormous doors and into a large white room. It looked like a cross between an old-fashioned bank and a Greek temple. The floor was made out of white marble, and fluted columns were placed around its edges. In the center of the room Grey stood, smiling. "Congratulations, Jack! You made it through the interview."

"That was an interview?"

"Well, of course, I mean we wouldn't let just anyone join the Ministry of Strange, Unusual, and Impossible Things."

"The what?" asked Jack.

"The Ministry of Strange, Unusual, and Impossible Things. That's who I work for. I knew you were a smart lad when I met you earlier, so that's why I offered you a job. You figured out that we were based in the museum?"

"Well, yeah. Where else would you get a bear and a lion in the same place? But what I don't understand is that the animals in the museums are stuffed. And that bear we saw the other day was most definitely alive."

"Yes, it was," said Grey, smiling. "But all the animals in museums are alive. None of them are actually stuffed."

Jack was stupefied. He had just walked through the museum and had seen a dozen animals standing stock-still. Could Grey be telling the truth?

"Think about it, Jack. How could you stuff an animal? It would be full of cotton wool or sawdust. That would never stand up, never mind look as lifelike as museum animals do. So we don't stuff animals; we use real animals."

"But why don't they move around and escape, then?"

"Well, before we bring them in we teach them to play

musical statues. You know the game where you're allowed to move when the music is playing, but you have to stand still when the music stops."

Jack remembered the game from birthday parties when he was little. "And it's as simple as that?"

"Animals are very competitive. So they all remain still when there isn't any music. That's why museums are the one place that never has any background music—unlike restaurants or supermarkets."

"So how did the bear escape today, then?"

"That was annoying. Someone came into the museum with their phone turned on. It had a Katy Perry ringtone[27] and when that started playing the bear stopped pretending to be a statue. It bolted out of the museum and I was sent to recapture it."

"Do the animals ever get to move?"

Grey nodded. "Oh, yes, we play music for a few hours throughout the night, let them stretch their legs, get a bite to eat, and so forth. We only make sure that it's turned off during the day when there are visitors in the museum."

"That makes sense," said Jack, even though it didn't. "Anyway, here I am—and I've got a mystery that I need to solve. I thought you might be able to help me...."

"Hold your metaphorical horses, Jack—before we could even think about helping you with a mystery, you'd have to be actually employed by the Ministry."

---

[27] If you're wondering what Katy Perry song it was, it was "Roar"—rather appropriate, really.

Jack shook his head. "I just came here to try and find out exactly what was going on—I think odd kids are being kidnapped from my school. And that means my friend David could be in danger. I need answers."

Grey rubbed his chin thoughtfully. "Well, if you want answers, what are your questions?"

Jack started trying to think of a question. "Who is . . . Is there a . . . Why am I . . . This morning there was a shoe and . . ." He quickly gave up. "Look, I just want to know what's going on. That's it—What's going on?"

"Aha!" said Grey, waving his umbrella. "That's the question, isn't it? And I have an answer to that."

"Oh, good."

"And the answer is, no one really knows."

"Mmmm," said Jack. "Not a great answer, is it?"

"I never said I had a *great* answer. Anyway, the Minister can explain all this to you."

"Does the Minister know what's going on?"

"Probably not," said Grey. "But he will at least make you confused in a different way. Now follow me."

Grey led Jack through a door that led to a rather shoddy and scruffy-looking office corridor. As the corridor twisted and turned, the floors, ceilings, and walls bulged and sagged alternately. Occasionally a piece of plaster fell from the roof. Jack winced when some fell on his head. "Don't worry about that; you'll get used to it," said Grey as he hurried along.

"It's a bit of a rubbish building," Jack said, looking around.

Grey nodded. "Part of the problem is that the architect was a fan of *Doctor Who*."

"And that's a problem because . . . ?" asked Jack.

"Well, he wanted to make the building like the Tardis, bigger on the inside than on the outside. But he didn't have any of the technology to actually do that. So he just ended up stuffing more into it than he really should have. It makes it kind of bulgy and very unstable."

Grey stopped in front of a door with a large white plaque on it that read "The Minister."

"This is the office of the Minister, the most powerful man within the Ministry. The only people who aren't scared of him are those who don't know he exists."

Jack felt his stomach knot.

"Now, he's a very nice man; just don't say anything about the way he dresses."

"What's wrong with the way he dresses?"

"Well, he wears a long black cassock and has a white dog collar."

"So he really is a minister, then?" asked Jack.

"Well . . ." considered Grey, "you know the way some people are slightly eccentric?"

Jack nodded.

"The suspicion is that the Minister has fallen off the edge of eccentric and into a big vat of totally mad."

"And they still let him be in charge of the whole organization?"

"Yes. Being strange in the Ministry isn't necessarily a bad thing. In fact, it's probably a prerequisite for success."

"I'm beginning to realize that," said Jack as he raised his right hand and rapped hard on the door. From inside, a voice called out for him to "come in."

Pushing the door open, Jack found himself in a very ordinary-looking office, with an ordinary-looking desk. Sitting behind the ordinary-looking desk was an ordinary-looking man. Or at least he would have been ordinary-looking if he had been a clergyman, for as Grey had warned Jack, he wore a full set of vestments.

"You must be young Jack. Come in, sit down."

Jack walked through the door and took the seat that the Minister indicated.

"I imagine you have a lot of questions." The Minister smiled at Jack. Or at least Jack assumed it was a smile. It was hard to tell because the Minister had no teeth at all. He didn't look old enough to have lost them due to decay. Indeed the Minister looked like a middle-aged but vigorous man. His hair was cropped close to his head and his eyes shone.

"So, Jack, this is your time to ask questions, and you may not get such a good opportunity to ask them again—so . . ."

Jack didn't need the offer to be made twice. "What happened to all your teeth?"

The Minister suddenly looked angry and for a moment Jack thought that he had made an error in judgment. The Minister saw the look of fear on Jack's face and his own face softened as he tried to smile again. "Don't worry, Jack," he said, "I'm not angry with you. I was just remembering how I lost them. You see, one night last week I fell asleep with my head under the pillow, and the Tooth Fairy came and took them all. Not a thing I could do about it either. Any teeth left under the pillow are his legal property. Fair and square—he had the contract to prove it. But there's a lesson to be learned. The Tooth Fairy may have a silly name, but he's as hard as nails and ruthless with it."

Jack was used to hearing all manner of strange things by now, but there was something in the last sentence that caught his attention.

"The Tooth Fairy is a he?"

"Of course he's a he! Didn't you know? A nasty piece of work as well. Take my advice, Jack, give him a wide berth and always sleep with your head above the pillow. Otherwise you're just asking for trouble."

This didn't make any sense to Jack. He'd heard of people collecting thimbles or stamps. But why would anyone collect teeth? Apart from anything else, if you tried to glue teeth into an album, the pages would never close properly. "What does he actually do with the teeth?"

"Makes the white keys for pianos."[28]

"Really?"

"Of course. I mean, you don't think that he leaves money under pillows out of the goodness of his heart? He makes a fortune by using them to make piano keys. A shrewd financial mind, an evil heart, and he looks ridiculous in that pink tutu he wears. Still—incredibly rich. But never mind the Tooth Fairy. Surely you have some more questions about the Ministry?"

---

[28] Hence elephants are wrong about the white keys being made of ivory...

Jack thought. "Well, I know you're offering me a job, but I don't really understand what you actually do. That would be a good place to start."

The Minister scratched his head. "Well, at the simplest level we do what we say we do. We are the Ministry of **S**trange, **U**nusual, and **I**mpossible **T**hings. Or M-SUITs, as we call ourselves for short. We deal with things that no one else is prepared to deal with because they don't believe they exist. You know the kind of thing—pirates, dinosaurs, zombies, vampires, and the like. M-SUITs deals with all the things that the average person in the street doesn't want to know about—the Loch Ness Monster, all the Yetis, Bigfoot, although in the modern political climate we can't call him that. Apparently he regards his big feet as a disability. So we have to call him the Sizularly Challenged Bipedal Simian. To be honest, I wouldn't mind, but he can't even spell it correctly so I really don't see why we should bother."

Jack was quite excited about the fact that strange creatures really existed, especially vampires, which had always seemed incredibly cool to him. He hoped that they were the drink-your-blood type vampires and not the wander-around-looking-slightly-glum-wearing-hoodies-reading-poetry-and-falling-in-love type vampires that had become so popular recently. "So what do you do with all these creatures?"

"Mainly we keep them out of everyone else's way and do our best to straighten out any problems that arise. That's the thing you'll find, Jack: Our work can deal with anything and anyone."

"But why employ me? I'm only twelve."

"Only twelve, ha! I joined up when I was eight. The problem with this work is that it is so varied that it takes a long time to learn the ropes. So we start you young. The crucial thing is that you have the mind for it. Our best weapon is curiosity. Most people spend their lives being afraid or amazed of strange things. But you want to know more. Curiosity! You managed to find your way here without Grey giving you a map and that shows promise. In our work there aren't any maps, there aren't any answers upside down at the back of the book, and X rarely marks the spot. Learning isn't all about taking courses and getting qualifications. We throw you in at the deep end straightaway. Anything that doesn't kill you is classed as training."

Jack looked at the Minister. "So you picked me for this job because I'm smart, right? You picked me because I'm smarter than the other kids in my class?"

"Well . . ." the Minister began. "There are two ways I can answer that question. I can either answer it truthfully or I can lie to make you feel good about yourself."

Jack and the Minister stared at each other in silence for a few minutes. Jack knew that lying was wrong but . . . "Lie to me," said Jack. "Lie to me like you're a tabloid journalist."

The Minister inhaled through his nostrils deeply and fixed Jack with an intense stare. "The reason we picked you, Jack, is that you are the most important person in the world. Although you get only average marks in school you are possibly the brightest person ever. You are the strongest and fastest, and if there were a world championship in tiddly-winks, Jack, only a fool wouldn't back you as the winner. That is how important you are."

The Minister stopped talking.

Jack took a deep breath. "You see, what you did there," he said, "was you went too far with the lies and flattery."

"Did I?" asked the Minister.

"Oh yes, definitely. It stopped sounding like you were flattering me and it just became sarcastic."

The Minister's face stopped looking so intense and crinkled into a grimace. "I was worried that it would come off that way."

"It did, it did."

"Should I just tell you the truth, then?"

"I think that's probably for the best."

"We don't pick the smartest kids to work in the Ministry. After all, a lot of the people who work for us get killed. It really is very dangerous work. Squashed by a *Diplodocus*, attacked by a harpy, drowned while trying to deliver a parking ticket to a squid. And we don't want the smart kids to die like that. We need the smart kids to be doctors, architects, engineers, and lawyers. Well, not lawyers, never really seen the point of them myself. But we do need the doctors, the architects, and the engineers."

"I'm not sure I like the sound of this job," muttered Jack.

"You say that, but let me ask you a question," said the Minister. "Would you rather be squashed by a dinosaur or work in an accountancy firm?" The Minister looked very pleased with himself.

Jack tried to figure out if this was a trick question. "Ummm, I'd rather work in an accountancy firm."

The Minister opened his eyes wider. "Really? Really?"

"Well, yeah," said Jack, "I mean, a boring job or death by dinosaur? It isn't a hard choice."

The Minister thought about this. "Mmmm, I suppose you're right. This is why they don't let me attend the recruitment fairs anymore. And you're right! I mean, who wants to be squashed by a dinosaur?"

"Look, if I do join up, can you help me figure out a mystery at my school?" asked Jack.

The Minister seemed to be muttering to himself under his breath. His hands were fiddling with pens and papers on his desk. Jack could only make out half of what he was saying.

"...Squashed by a dinosaur...never really thought about it before...I don't want to be squashed...why did I ever say yes to this job...someone else can be the Minister...wearing these ridiculous clothes."

Jack got up out of his chair and went over to the door. Grey was standing outside.

"So have you decided to join up, then?" asked Grey enthusiastically.

"Umm, I'm not sure that I'll be allowed to. I think I may have broken your Minister."

Grey poked his head around the door and saw the Minister muttering to himself. "Oh, don't worry about that. He gets that way at least four or five times a week."

"You all seem slightly unbalanced to me. And when I say slightly, I mean extremely and dangerously."

"We'd better move on before the Minister starts throwing things." Just as Grey said this, a red-and-green-glass paperweight sailed through the gap in the door, zoomed over Grey's head, and shattered against the wall.

MINISTRY OF S.U.IT.S HANDBOOK

TOOTH FAIRY
CONTRACTUAL RIGHTS

Many people wonder where the Tooth Fairy obtains his contractual rights. The original contract forms part of a child's birth certificate. Parents register children when they are born and get a birth certificate. What most parents don't realize is that they are signing away a number of rights on behalf of their children—this is the real reason for the creation of a birth certificate. One of the pages of a birth certificate specifically says that any teeth placed below a pillow automatically become the property of the Tooth Fairy.

It is amazing that more people do not realize the purpose of a birth certificate. After all, what is the point in having a document to prove that you were born? You exist—therefore you must have been born at some stage. The logic is simple and inescapable, therefore the document must be for some other reason than to prove the obvious fact of birth.

A death certificate is much more important. Obviously. After all, people don't want to be dead. Often after they die they decide to ignore the fact and carry on living. When someone tries to do this, it is absolutely vital that you have the necessary paperwork to show them that they are in fact dead and should not try and drive a motorcar or operate heavy machinery.

An interesting connected fact is that 98 percent of zombie attacks are the result of poorly completed paperwork.

As any civil servant will tell you, well-completed paperwork is all that stands between us and a state of anarchy.

12

DINOSAURS AND HOUSEWORK

As they walked down the corridor Grey brushed fragments of glass paperweight out of his hair.

"How come I've never heard of the M-SUITs before?"

"Well, we're sort of semisecret. We call ourselves the Men in Suits."

"I've heard of men in suits before," said Jack.

"Yes, people generally refer to any officials as men in suits. But we are actually *the* Men in Suits."

"And you deal with dinosaurs and things?"

"We deal with anything that people don't believe in anymore. How do you think the dinosaurs died out?"

Jack felt smug—he knew the answer to this. "Well, it was a meteorite. It hit the Earth and . . ."

Grey laughed. "You really think that a single meteorite could have wiped out all the dinosaurs on Earth? How would that even work? What about dinosaurs on the other side of the Earth from where the meteorite struck?"

Jack shrugged. "I don't know, I think it threw up dust or something. Dust killed them . . . didn't it?"

Grey laughed even more. There was a distinct possibility that he was going to choke. "You think the dinosaurs went extinct because of dust. Because they didn't do their housework?"

Jack thought about it for a moment. If you could really become extinct from dust, then he risked death every time he checked under his bed for a lost pair of sneakers. "So you're saying that dinosaurs still exist?"

"Of course they do!" Grey managed to stop laughing. "Dinosaurs killed by dust? Next thing you'll be telling me you believe that pirates were all wiped out by an unsanitary bath plug, or that vampires all died out because they couldn't find a mop to rinse their coffins out with."

"So what happens when people stop believing?" asked Jack indignantly.

"When people get tired of something, or just don't want to believe in it anymore, the Ministry steps in to deal with it. We put the pirates in Piratoriums, we hide the dinosaurs. Of course they aren't forgotten entirely, so they're remembered as fairy tales, myths, or legends."

"And it's dangerous?"

Grey shrugged. "Well, yes, but aren't dangerous things always the most fun?[29] And, more importantly, we get to

[29] Please refer all the way back to footnote 5.

laugh at the 'normals.' All the stupid people who don't realize that the world is literally chock-full of danger and fun . . .
So do you want to join up?"

Jack thought about this. He wasn't naturally inclined to
danger, but the thought that there were things happening
in the world that he knew nothing about frustrated him. If
he refused the offer to join up, he would never find out about
thousands of other secrets. "Okay. Count me in. It seems
slightly clearer now," said Jack, thinking that slightly was
the most important word in that sentence.

Grey clapped his hands. "Wonderful! Then you'll be
wanting to meet your partner."

"Partner?" said Jack. "No one said anything to me about a
partner."

Grey looked at him quizzically. "Yes, I did. I just said it
there now."

"What I meant was . . ."

"Enough talking. Follow me!" Grey spun around on his
shiny, polished shoes and started striding down the corridor. Jack had to almost run to keep up with him.

The corridors were becoming more and more full of
people—and not just people, but also *things*. Jack noticed a
very odd one walking down the corridor dressed in what
looked like a dark blue monk's robe and carrying a large
accordion paper file. It was a strange humanoid creature
with enormous folded batlike wings on its back and a head
that looked like a squid. Its skin was gray and decaying, ooz-
ing with green pustules. It looked as though lumps of it
would come off if you touched it. Of course, you would never

have touched it, precisely for that reason. Jack blinked—he couldn't believe that creatures like that existed. It looked horrifyingly real in exactly the same way that cheap special effects don't. Jack shuffled over to hide behind Grey while trying not to look like he was hiding behind Grey.

"That is the ancient Cthulhu, an evil being with unimaginable power. It longs to watch the world burn and send all its people into madness and insanity," Grey said. He paused for a moment. "Cthulhu works in the filing branch."

"You have an evil being with unimaginable power working in the filing branch?" Jack thought that if he ever had to conduct a job interview one of the first questions he would ask would be "Are you an evil being with unimaginable power?" If they answered yes, he almost certainly wouldn't employ them. Unless of course they promised to bring doughnuts into the office on a Friday. Because everyone knows that jam-filled doughnuts cancel out evil.

"Well, apart from being impossibly evil he's also very efficient. Anyway, it suits everyone, really. We can keep an eye on him, and since he wants to drive the world mad, working in bureaucracy is pretty much his ideal job."

"This place is crazy!" said Jack.

Cthulhu stopped walking down the corridor and stared at Jack. He seemed to realize that they had been talking about him.

Jack was understandably nervous. "Umm, Grey, I think he may have heard us talking about him."

Grey nodded. "Yes, it seems that he did. He has very good hearing. I've noticed that before. It's especially strange because he has a squid head. And ordinary squids don't have ears."

Jack really didn't care about the problems that squids had because they lacked ears. He was rather more concerned that there was a creature starring at him who had recently been described as "impossibly evil."

Cthulhu made deep breathing noises and his batlike wings unfolded from his back. When opened, they blocked the corridor and made it impossible for Jack or Grey to walk past him. From inside the squid face, two green eyes lit up and a beam of light emitted from them. Unlike ordinary light it didn't travel in a straight line, but rather snaked out like translucent emerald lightning. The beams hit Jack and swirled around him. Jack could feel his body starting to glow. And for some reason he could sense it glowing the color green. Turning green wasn't a pleasant experience. Jack really wouldn't recommend it to anyone. He didn't understand how frogs lived with the feeling.

"Grey, this is making me feel very uncomfortable."

"Yes, I think this has gone quite far enough. Cthulhu, stop it at once!" Grey snapped.

Cthulhu turned his gaze away from Jack. The green beams ceased and Jack turned back to his more familiar pinkish color. Cthulhu spoke to Grey. However, it wasn't any language that Jack recognized. In fact, it wasn't even a sound that Jack recognized. The closest Jack could get to describing it was the sound of a fat man with a particularly bad head cold trying to eat raw oysters without chewing. As Cthulhu talked he grew animated and waved his hands around. Each finger seemed to have three or four knuckles that could move in different directions. At the end of each finger was a frighteningly sharp claw. Occasionally Cthulhu stretched and flapped his bat wings.

Grey just shook his head. "Yes, Cthulhu, we were being impolite talking about you. But how else is the boy meant to learn?"

Cthulhu made more oyster-slurping noises.

"I appreciate that, but you have to understand that it's also a breach of etiquette to use evil energy to make him go mad."

Cthulhu frothed some more, and a long tendril of saliva fell from his mouth.

"No! Banishing him to a dark dimension would be rude. Now, if you'll excuse us, we have work to do."

Cthulhu stared at Grey. After a few moments he folded his bat wings and let them carry on down the corridor. Jack could feel Cthulhu's green eyes piercing his back.

"Do I run the risk of being driven insane every time I come here?" he asked.

"Don't worry about Cthulhu; for a multidimensional manifestation of evil he's very sensitive. Mind you, so would you be if you had the face of a squid."

"I suppose so," said Jack.

"I sometimes wonder if he perhaps had a more pleasant face . . . well, then maybe he wouldn't want to destroy the world so badly."

"Perhaps," said Jack, who was beginning to wonder if he really wanted to be part of an organization where madness and banishment to strange dimensions were serious risks when you were trying to get paperwork filed. Maybe he could seek some counseling for his curiosity instead of join-ing the Ministry.

He felt slightly more reassured when he noticed a five-foot teddy bear walking along the corridor. It was a pleasant gold shade, and bits of its fur looked slightly worn, as if it had been well hugged over the years. "Maybe it would be better if Cthulhu looked like that," he said to Grey.

"The Bear?" Grey tilted his head to one side. "Perhaps. Of course the Bear is even more dangerous than Cthulhu."

"What? That huggable lump of fur?" asked Jack.

"He's the agent we send in when everyone else fails." Grey shook his head. "When persuading the bad guys doesn't work, when speaking to them nicely doesn't produce results, when we can't capture them . . . Well, then the Bear goes in to finish them off."

"You're telling me that that teddy bear is a killer?"

"You'd better believe it."

"Then why does he look like a teddy bear?"

"Because when you lean in for a hug with something that cute and adorable, the last thing you expect is that it's going to rip your face off."

The Bear was now alongside Jack and Grey. He looked up and smiled in an impossibly cute way.

Grey nodded at the Bear. "Everything going well, Bear?"

The Bear smiled. His head bobbed from side to side as he talked. His voice sounded like church bells ringing. "It's been an amazingly brilliant day. But then every day is an amazingly brilliant day, isn't it?"

Just after he'd finished talking he dropped something

that clattered to the floor. It made a metallic sound and Jack realized it was a dagger covered in blood. The Bear had also dropped something small and fleshy that looked like part of someone's vital organs.

Jack, Grey, and the Bear all looked at one another awkwardly for a moment.

"I've made an oopsie!" said the Bear, still in the cute singsong voice.

"Been taking care of business?" asked Grey.

"You betcha," said the Bear.

Jack bent down to pick up the dagger and hand it back to the Bear.

"Just leave it, kid," said the Bear, suddenly dropping the singsong. "You'll get blood all over your hands."

The Bear held up his golden paws and Jack noticed for the first time that they were covered in blood. "This stuff is impossible to shift. Especially when you're covered in fur." The Bear looked sad for a moment. "This is the worst part of my job."

"What?" asked Jack. "Killing people?"

"Not the killing, no," said the Bear. "It's getting clean afterward. Looks like I'll be spending the rest of the day in the hot water cycle of the washing machine. Anyway, you guys have a"—the Bear switched back into his cutesy voice—"lovely day."

The Bear bent down and picked up his dagger and the small piece of red flesh. The Bear thought for a moment and then popped the flesh into his mouth. Jack gasped.

"Sorry," the Bear said, swallowing, "I missed lunch."

Jack and Grey continued down the corridor.

Jack didn't know which he found harder to believe, that the Bear was a merciless killing machine, or that he got himself clean by getting into the hot water cycle of a washing machine.

Grey noticed how quiet Jack was being. "The Bear is only used as an absolute last resort, you understand. It's not how the Ministry normally works."

Just as Jack was thinking that he was glad all his stuffed animals were safely locked in the loft, Grey turned to him and smiled.

"We're here!" said Grey.

"Where?" asked Jack.

"Behind this door is your new partner. Prepare yourself."

Jack did his best to prepare himself. Would his partner be a cuddly toy? Or a mermaid? Or perhaps a clear blue beam of talking light? Jack wouldn't have been surprised by anything.

SQUIDS
LACK OF EARS

Squids don't have ears. Which is why you never see one on a mobile phone. Which is also why the EE network was ridiculously unsuccessful when it launched its special squid promotion a number of years ago. The idea was they would release a phone that would have three keypads instead of the conventional one. This would allow a squid with its many tentacles to dial more of its friends at once. Of course, without ears the squids couldn't actually hear what their friends were saying (although they do like texting).

Squids are therefore very selfish conversationalists. They only ever talk about themselves and rarely actually listen to what you are saying. It should also be noted that without ears squids find it difficult to wear glasses. The arms of the glasses have nothing to prop themselves against. This is why (a) you never see a squid in the local branch of Sunglass Hut and (b) they always look as if they are squinting slightly. Next time you see a squid, look closely at him and you will notice that he is squinting like a nearsighted human who has forgotten his glasses.

13

A TRULY SURPRISING PARTNER

Jack's partner looked like a perfectly ordinary girl sitting on the edge of an office desk. Her back was turned to them.

"Not a girl with the head of an otter, then? Or a being of monstrous power? Or a small plastic soldier with a real gun?" asked Jack.

Grey shook his head. "Not everything in this place is odd. Otherwise you wouldn't be here, would you?"

There was a sharp cough from across the room. The girl had stood up from where she had been perched on the edge of the desk and was looking at them. She had put her hands on her hips and cocked her head to one side. "It's rude to talk about someone as if they aren't there."

You would have thought that Jack would have learned that lesson after his recent brush with Cthulhu. However, he wasn't as worried about offending a perfectly ordinary girl as he was about offending a dark squid-being who could banish you to an alternate dimension.

And then Jack looked at the girl more closely and realized he had made two crucial mistakes. Firstly, this wasn't a perfectly ordinary girl. Secondly, if Cthulhu the squid-faced-one had wanted a few pointers in how to be truly, mind-numbingly terrifying, this girl could have shown him where he was going wrong.

"Moody Trudy!" exclaimed Jack.

"Moody Trudy?" Trudy Emerson snorted. "How dare you call me Moody Trudy!"

"Ermm, hello, Trudy," said Jack. He considered pointing out that by being so annoyed at being called Moody Trudy, she was kind of proving the fact that she had a tendency toward moodiness.

However, equally he felt that (a) this was not the time or place to make such a point and (b) any satisfaction he gained out of making such a point would almost certainly be canceled out by the reduction in satisfaction he would get from being punched in the mouth by Trudy.

"Moody Trudy?" asked Grey, who was slightly concerned that both Jack and Trudy had gone completely silent.

Jack looked as if he was worried that Trudy was going to punch him in the face. Trudy looked as if at any minute she was about to punch Jack in the face. So, essentially, Jack was quite right to look like what he looked like.

"Moody Trudy," Jack whispered to Grey. "It's her nickname in school."

Trudy winced. "It might be my nickname, but no one's ever brave enough to say it to my face."

Jack put up his hand, almost as if he was asking Trudy's permission to speak. "Just to clarify here, Trudy. I wasn't brave enough to say it to your face. On this occasion I was stupid and startled enough to say it to your face."

Trudy smiled at what he said. You could tell she didn't want to—she wanted her face to continue conveying anger and annoyance—but a smirk escaped from her lips nonetheless. "All right," said Trudy, "I suppose I can forgive you for being stupid."

"Great!" said Grey, clapping his hands. "We all forgive Jack for being stupid."

Jack wasn't altogether happy with this turn of events, but since it seemed to significantly lower the chances of him being battered by Trudy, he was willing to roll with it.

"So the two of you know each other?" asked Grey.

Jack nodded and explained they were in the same year at school together.

"Brilliant, you ought to make a perfect partnership, then."

Jack wasn't keen on Trudy being his partner. In school she had a reputation for being dangerous and punching people who irritated her. Jack was sure that if he teamed up with Trudy, a long future of detention awaited him.

Jack looked up and saw that Trudy and Grey were both staring at him. He realized that he had been thinking to himself when he should have been saying, *"Yeah, Trudy as my partner. That would be great."* For a moment he considered saying it; however, he suspected that it would only sound sarcastic at this stage.

"You don't want to be my partner, then?" asked Trudy.

"I never said that!" grumbled Jack.

"No. But you were thinking it."

Grey stepped in to defuse a conversation that was clearly about to metamorphose into an argument. "Look, we can talk about this."

"Talking's good," said Jack. He shot a meaningful look at Trudy. "Punching's bad."

Trudy smiled sweetly at him before she shot out a fist that connected hard with his shoulder, making the same noise a cabbage would make if you dropped it off the top of a three-story building.[30]

"Owww!"

"Punching isn't bad," said Trudy. "Punching is frequently fun."

"Trudy, no punching!" said Grey. "Violence never solved anything!"

"Didn't it?" asked Trudy. "What about World War One?"

Grey thought about this for a moment. "Well, yes, granted World War One was solved partially by violence."

"And World War Two."

"Okay, yes, and World War Two. I will agree that if there

---

[30] To clarify, we are only talking about the noise that the actual cabbage itself will make if you drop it into a street without people in it. If you drop a cabbage into a street *with* people in it, the noise it will make is a dull thud followed by, "Hey, who's dropping cabbages?"

hadn't been any violence in World War Two the Germans would still be in Poland, and Warsaw would therefore be frightfully crowded. But violence is not appropriate in this situation. All right, Trudy?"

Trudy sniffed haughtily. "I never said it was appropriate." She glared at Jack. "I just said it was fun."

Jack was about to speak, but he looked at Trudy and took a step backward before he said anything. He then took a second step backward just in case. "Look, Grey, obviously this isn't going to work. I can't work with Mo . . . with Trudy."

"Why not?"

"Well, apart from the fact that I can't always explain mysterious bruises to my parents as dodgeball accidents," said Jack as he rubbed his still-sore shoulder, "she clearly hates me! And she is definitely slightly mentally unbalanced."

Trudy made a fist and moved toward Jack. Grey threw out an arm to stop her from getting too close.

Jack put his hands up. "I said *slightly*!"

"Well, in that case," said Trudy, "I'm just going to *slightly* pulverize your face."

"Enough!" said Grey. "Look, the Minister himself put you together for a reason. He told me to make you partners. So it's happening. *If* you want to continue working for the Ministry, that is."

Trudy grumbled but Grey shushed her.

"Why did he put us together especially?" Jack asked. "Is it because he thinks that I can learn self-reliance and mental toughness from Trudy's uncompromising approach to the world? And perhaps she can learn something from my approach—like that you don't have to punch everything to get a positive result?"

"It might be that," agreed Grey. "Although it also might just be that you both go to the same school." Grey thought for a moment. "In fact, I'd almost be certain that it's just because you go to the same school."

"Oh," said Jack.

Trudy unclenched her fist and looked Jack straight in the eyes. "Jack," she said, "I've only been working for the Ministry for a few months now. But they've been the best months of my life. So if I've got to work with you in order to continue, then I'll do it."

"No more hitting?" asked Jack.

Trudy paused for a long time before she spoke. "Okay, no more hitting. But can you work with me?"

Jack thought about this. He decided that the only way forward was to be honest. If he didn't tell Trudy the truth now, they'd never work well together as partners.

"Trudy, I've got one question I'd like to ask. Why do you seem to hate everyone so much?" Jack asked. "I mean, did something happen? Some . . . tragedy?"

Trudy looked at Jack. There was a real sadness in her eyes, and for a second it looked as if she was about to cry. Then in a second her eyes went from glassy to steely.

"That's none of your business."

Jack knew it was none of his business. And that's what made it so very interesting. He knew that he'd have to stick around Trudy at least long enough to find out what made her so angry all the time.

"I think I can work with you, Trudy," said Jack.

Trudy looked bewildered; she obviously hadn't been expecting that.

Jack looked straight at Trudy. "I also should say that I'm really sorry, Trudy. I made judgments about you before I ever really got to know you . . . that whole Moody Trudy thing. That was unfair. I should have gotten to know you first."

"Thank you, Jack. That's the nicest . . ." Trudy launched herself at Jack. For a few moments Jack was terrified, but then he realized that she was only going to hug him. He was still a little bit scared but not quite as much. She wrapped her arms around him and squeezed him tight. "Thanks . . ."

After a few seconds Trudy realized she was hugging Jack. It clearly made her feel slightly uncomfortable, so she stepped backward and playfully hit Jack in the arm, almost immediately breaking her promise to stop hitting. Jack laughed and mimed as if he was in pain. Trudy turned to speak to Grey and then Jack stopped miming that he was in pain and got on with properly being in pain.

"We're both in," said Trudy.

"Wonderful," said Grey. "Jack, I think you'll find Trudy a very useful partner."

Jack decided that it would be a good idea to butter Trudy up; after all, if she liked him, maybe she'd punch his arm slightly less often. "I know Trudy will be a great partner. She can do all that cool gymnastics stuff, can't she? That's bound to come in handy."

Grey laughed. "You don't know the half of it, Jack. Trudy,

perhaps we should show your partner what you've been working on."

Grey and Trudy strode off down the corridor. Both clearly knew where they were going, and Jack had no choice but to follow. After a brief walk they arrived at a door marked "Practice Room—DANGER—DO NOT OPEN."

It was exactly the kind of sign that made you really, really want to open a door.

"Now stand behind me," Trudy said to Jack, "and try not to get hurt."

It was a ridiculous thing to say. Jack never *tried* to get hurt. He doubted if anyone ever did. Trudy swung open the door.

MINISTRY OF S.U.IT.S HANDBOOK

VIOLENCE NOT SOLVING ANYTHING
INVADING COUNTRIES AND CLOTHING CHOICES

Clothing choices are absolutely essential in life. If you wear all black, then you are probably a ninja (please see the section **Ninjas: Clothing Choices** for further detail). If you wear a football top, it tells people what team you support. If you wear a bow tie, it tells people that you are less interesting than you think you are.

Generally, when invading countries, armies tend to dress up in dark black and gray uniforms. Many uniforms make soldiers look like traffic wardens. This was certainly the case when the Germans arrived in Warsaw during the second world war. It was also a crucial mistake.

Warsaw is one of the most beautiful cities in the world. When it was invaded by thousands of people who resembled traffic wardens, naturally the world took notice and a considerable amount of fighting broke out.

However, every year Warsaw is invaded by hordes of tourists and no one says anything. The lesson in all this is simple. Armies don't need to wear camouflage to hide themselves. What they need is to adopt a uniform consisting of shorts and Hawaiian shirts.

And instead of shooting things with guns, they should shoot things with cameras. If only they did this, the world would be a much happier place.

* * *

What you wear is almost as important as what you hold in your hands. If you wish to learn more about this, please read the section **Power of Imagination: Efficacy of Clipboards.**

14

PORCUPODS

Jack looked inside the room and was shocked to find it full of . . . of . . . of . . .

Here was a problem. He didn't know what he was actually looking at.

There was a series of black shapes, each about the size of a large dog, but that was where their similarity to a canine ended. They had thick, wide bodies and their legs were only twelve inches long. Their bodies were covered in a series of quill-like spines, each as thick as a finger at the base but tapering to a pin-sharp point at the end. Their faces were like the snout of a badger and their mouths contained row upon row of razor-sharp teeth. Most bizarre of all was that just in front of their forelegs was a set of two black claws covered in rough, black, scarred armor plates.

The creatures ran round the room snorting, sniffing, and

nipping each other with their claws. Suddenly one of their snouts looked up and noticed the humans standing at the door. It hurled itself at them. Jack tried to take a step backward but stumbled and fell flat on the ground.

He was filled with fear and a certain amount of disappointment. He'd just started on an amazing adventure and now he was going to be killed by a . . . killed by a . . . That was disappointing as well. He didn't even know the name of the thing that was about to kill him.

Trudy and Grey hadn't moved. In fact, they didn't even look worried. Jack sat up and saw that the creature had smacked against a solid plate of glass that was in place across the doorway. Grey looked amused and reached out to rap the glass with his knuckle. "Safety glass," he said to Jack. "Keeps us safe from the Porcupods."

Jack stood up and touched the glass with his hand. It covered the entire door opening and was hinged on one side. Emboldened by the thick layer of safety glass, Jack gazed at the scurrying Porcupods. "So what is a Porcupod, then?"

"That," Grey said, pointing through the window. "That is a Porcupod. You really must start paying attention, Jack."

"Well . . . but . . . okay, another question. Why are they called Porcupods?"

"Because they look like Porcupods."

Jack watched them through the window. The creatures did indeed look like Porcupods. There was something "Porcupod-ish" about them.

"If you want a more detailed answer, it's because they look like a cross between a porcupine and a lobster. And lobsters are from the group of animals scientists call the Arthropoda."

Jack was still peering at the creatures, fascinated. "They also look like they have a bit of hedgehog in there as well."

Trudy nodded. "The snout is a bit hedgehog-ish."

Grey agreed that was true. "Yes, but it would have been stupid to call them Porcuhogs."

Jack shrugged. "You could always have called them Hedge-pines."

"Possibly," said Grey, "but then they would have sounded like they were an air freshener."

"Where do they come from?" asked Jack. "Are they some kind of experiment by a mad scientist?"

"Mad scientists don't make hybrid creatures, Jack," said Grey. "They try and invent bananas."

"But you don't need to invent bananas. They already exist."

"Well, yes, but what you have to remember about mad scientists is that they're mad, Jack. Mad! They do crazy things. Rational scientists invent things. The mad ones try and invent things that already exist. And occasionally they fling their poo at you."

Jack nodded. "Maybe I was thinking of evil scientists."

Grey continued. "Either way, the answer to your question is no. The Porcupod is a perfectly ordinary creature that just happened to evolve."

The Porcupod didn't look like a perfectly ordinary creature. Jack suspected that Grey was making fun of him.

"Think about this, Jack: If the conditions exist for a porcupine to evolve, and the conditions exist for a lobster to evolve, then it stands to reason that the conditions must exist for a Porcupod to evolve."

Jack couldn't fault Grey's logic. He wanted to. But he couldn't.

"How come I've never seen a Porcupod before?"

"They're one of the things that the Ministry keeps covered up. They're one of those odd animals, one of the animals that make people nervous. We round them up and keep them locked safely away from the rest of the human race. Generally people only stop believing in creatures if they're really unpleasant or evil and serve no useful purpose. Like the Porcupod or the unicorn."

"Unicorns are evil?" Jack had never really thought of unicorns as evil. He thought of them as sickeningly sweet and all too often pink.

"Of course they're evil!" said Grey. "What kind of nice animal would wander around with an enormous horn in the middle of its head?"

"Well, maybe they use it to hunt," said Trudy. "I mean, unicorns have to eat, don't they?"

"They do use it to hunt. They use it to skewer bunny rabbits. But don't forget, the horn is right in the middle of their foreheads. So they don't hunt to eat. You can't eat a dead bunny rabbit that's stuck to a horn in the middle of your forehead. Unicorns just like killing things. They can't even get the bunny rabbits off their foreheads. So they just leave them there to rot and decompose. That's another thing I hate about unicorns. The stench of dead bunny. Makes me want to retch just thinking about it."

Trudy shook her head. "Look, I've seen lots of pictures of unicorns and they *never* have dead bunnies impaled on their horns."

"Where have you seen these pictures?" asked Grey.

Trudy looked embarrassed; talking about unicorns clearly didn't fit with the hard-girl image she presented to the world. "...I have one on my duvet cover."[31]

"And you believe everything that you see on a duvet cover, do you, Trudy?"

"Well, no, but..."

"Because you're going to end up with a pretty strange worldview if you believe everything that you see on an eiderdown. Next thing you'll be telling me that you believe in Thomas the Tank Engine and superheroes."

Trudy fumed silently. Jack couldn't help enjoying this a little. It was nice to see it happening to someone else for a change.

"And tell me this, Trudy, is it just duvet covers you believe? Or is it any item of bedding, generally? I mean, is your pillow well-informed about the world? If a blanket told you that the world was flat, would you believe it?"

"Have you finished?" Trudy asked through pursed lips.

"Not quite," said Grey. "I also wanted to point out that the people who make duvet covers aren't in the business of being purveyors of truth. They're in the business of selling duvet covers. How many parents would buy their beautiful

---

[31] Duvet covers aren't inherently interesting. Although what is interesting is how they actually make the duvets that are inside them.

daughter a duvet cover that had a picture of a unicorn with a dozen dead bunnies impaled on its horn? With little bunny intestines falling out and bunny blood drip-drip-dripping on the ground?"

"So the Ministry keeps all the odd creatures here?" said Jack, deciding to try and change the subject as Trudy seemed to have had enough.

"Well, most of them, but occasionally we don't manage to round them all up."

"What happens then?"

"You'll see them running about. Odd creatures that really don't seem to fit in."

Jack racked his brains and a few examples sprang to mind. "Duck-billed platypus?"

"That's one."

"Kangaroo?" Jack suggested.

"Clever boy!" exclaimed Grey. "A lot of the strange creatures live in Australia because the Ministry didn't have an office there until 1973."

Trudy cleared her throat. "Perhaps we can get on with the reason we came here?"

Grey pointed at her. "Good idea. Are you ready, Trudy?"

Trudy took her blazer off and handed it to Grey. "Ready."

"Wait a minute," said Jack. "What's going on?"

"Ohh, not much. Trudy's just going to demonstrate to you what she's learned since she joined the Ministry."

Grey leaned out and pushed the glass door open with the palm of his hand. There was now no longer anything to protect them from the Porcupods.

KANGAROOS
Role in Duvet Manufacture

Many people have wondered why the Ministry of SUITs has not hidden kangaroos away from people in the same way they did with dinosaurs. The reason for this is simple. Kangaroos need to be allowed to roam free across the outback in order to manufacture duvets.

Have you ever noticed how over a few days your belly button will build up a small ball of fluff? A kangaroo's pouch is much larger than a belly button and therefore generates much more fluff than a belly button. Their constant jumping and leaping across the vast desert outback of Australia creates pouch friction and therefore speeds up the fluff-creating process immeasurably.

This fluff is then harvested and used to stuff duvets.

Next time you find some belly button fluff, roll it between your two fingers and feel the texture. You will realize that it feels almost identical to a very thin duvet.

15

"GO, TRUDY!"

Jack watched as the Porcupods realized the door was open and began to scuttle toward them. Trudy walked inside the room and Grey closed the glass door behind her.

"You can't do that!" cried Jack. "They'll rip her apart."

Grey leaned against the wall. "Just watch."

There were four Porcupods in the room but their rapid movement made it seem like many more. A Porcupod lunged, snapping at Trudy. But Trudy wasn't in the space where she had been a few seconds before. She had neatly somersaulted over the Porcupod and landed on one knee behind it.

Two other Porcupods dashed at Trudy from opposite directions. Their open mouths were filled with rows of tiny, sharp teeth glazed in a bubbling foam of saliva. Trudy's head rotated from side to side, her eyes seeing both attackers. The

Porcupods were almost on top of her as she took off running like a sprinter. She seemed to be moving impossibly fast, almost blurred.

The Porcupods were shocked by Trudy's speed and didn't have time to stop. They smashed into each other head-on, their muzzles making a satisfying *crack*.

"Go, Trudy!" Jack shouted. Then he noticed Grey was looking at him and shaking his head.

"Sorry," said Jack. "I got slightly overexcited."

Trudy sprinted across the room. The Porcupods had recovered from their cranial collision and were scuttling after her.

Trudy didn't seem to be slowing as she reached the corner of the room. She was sure to run smack into the wall, and with the two Porcupods behind her, that would be the end of Trudy.

Jack tensed up his face and got ready for a crunch. The crunch never came. To Jack's astonishment, when she got to the corner she started running straight up the wall.

Jack turned to Grey. "That's impossible."

"Is it?" asked Grey, laughing. "Well, if it is, we really should tell her so that she can stop doing it."

If Jack hadn't been ready for Trudy running up the wall, the two Porcupods pursuing her certainly weren't. Unable to stop in time, they clattered into both each other and the corner and collapsed, unconscious.

Trudy continued running up the wall and, just as she reached the top, she placed a foot on the ceiling and pushed herself off. This allowed her to perform a perfect backflip and land gently on the floor.

She turned around from the wall, and Jack noticed that she was barely out of breath. The two remaining Porcupods, having seen what had happened to their comrades, slowly approached Trudy. One moved toward her and lashed out with its lobsterlike claws. They cracked and snapped in the air around Trudy, but she dodged them easily, smiling as she did.

The other Porcupod shuffled backward a foot or two. At first it looked afraid, but then Jack realized that it was going to take a run up and then launch itself at Trudy. Jack wanted to shout out and warn her, but his breath caught in his throat.

Jack needn't have worried. Although Trudy was still dodging blows from the nearest Porcupod, she noticed the other scuttling rapidly toward her. It leapt in the air, clacking its claws together like an insane maraca player. As it reached the peak of its leap Trudy bent backward. The Porcupod looked as startled as a creature can look when it has an armored snout for a face. It sailed over Trudy as she snapped into a backflip. Just as the Porcupod was directly over Trudy's flipping body, she whirled her feet around and kicked it, forcefully propelling it into the wall and making its body crumple up like a concertina. Jack winced, almost feeling sorry for the animal.

There was only one Porcupod left in the room now. It stopped trying to attack Trudy and looked at its three friends, all of whom were lying unconscious and battered around the room. It snapped its claws once in a rather thoughtful manner. It looked at Trudy again and then scuttled backward into a corner of the room before lying down and making a strange rasping-breathing noise. If Jack hadn't known better, he would have thought that it was trying to whistle in an innocent manner.

Trudy brushed down her school uniform and walked toward the glass door. Grey opened it and bowed to her as she exited the room. Jack had a million questions he wanted to ask, but he couldn't seem to persuade them out of his mouth.

Before Jack could say anything Grey looked at his watch. "I'm afraid we don't have time for anything more tonight. If you two stay here any longer, your parents will be asking difficult questions. I'll get a Ministry car to take you home." Grey left to make the arrangements.

Trudy and Jack were left standing in the corridor by themselves. Jack's jaw was still hanging open in amazement. Trudy looked very pleased with herself, but Jack felt that that was understandable. She probably wasn't allowed to use her amazing skills in everyday life and it must have been a wonderful feeling to be allowed to show off. It would be like winning a gold medal at the Olympics and not being able to tell anyone about it.

Jack pulled himself together. "I've just got one question."

"Yeah?" said Trudy. "What's that?

"Well, with all the skills you have, why on earth would you want to be my partner? I mean, surely there are better people you could be working with. Like a ninja or something?"

Trudy sighed. "Not that many other people would agree to work with me. People tend to find me scary."

"I do find you scary," confessed Jack. "But I still want to work with you. You're . . . amazing."

Trudy smiled and stuck out her hand. Jack shook it. "I'm not sure I'm amazing," said Trudy. "But I'm certainly Strange and Unusual. Maybe a little bit Impossible too . . . sometimes."

Grey came back to find them shaking hands. It seemed to make him happy.

"I've got a Ministry car waiting for you outside."

Trudy's shoulders slumped. "Do we have to travel by Ministry car?"

"It's late already; your parents will be wondering where you are. You know a Ministry car will get you back home in half the time of a normal car."

"I know, but . . . ."

"But me no buts," insisted Grey as he hurried them down a corridor toward the exit.

Once outside, Jack was impressed by what was waiting for them. He couldn't understand why Trudy had been reluctant to travel by Ministry car. It was a long black limousine, polished to such a high shine that even in the twilight it seemed to shimmer.

"After you," said Trudy.

Jack didn't have to be asked twice. He heard Grey say good-bye as he scrambled into the back of the car. It wasn't quite what he had been expecting.

Inside, the car was disgusting. When he had opened the door, a cloud of noxious air had rolled out, the smell of which was almost unbearable.

Although the car was spacious with two wide leather seats facing each other, it was filled with . . . well, it was filled with deeply unpleasant things. Some organic unpleasant things. Some man-made unpleasant things. And several organic man-made unpleasant things.

It took Jack several minutes to find somewhere to sit down that wouldn't make a squelching noise.

Trudy climbed into the car and flopped down on the seat beside him. "The first time anyone travels in a Ministry car they always take a few minutes trying to locate the cleanest part of the seat to sit on. After you've been in one of these cars a few times you'll realize that it's all equally filthy."

Trudy waved good-bye to Grey as he slammed the door of the limousine shut.

Jack couldn't see the driver; they were separated from him by a smoked-glass screen. He could see the outline of a head with a black chauffeur's cap on it. The glass screen was never moved down, but Jack could hardly blame the driver. After all, the passenger compartment smelled awful. The driver would either have to keep the glass up to avoid the smell or would have to have his nose removed. And if the driver did have his nose removed, then his sunglasses would always be slipping down his face.[32]

"Is this really the best car that the Ministry can afford?" asked Jack.

---

[32] As well as not having ears, squids don't have noses either. Yet another reason they don't wear sunglasses. If you read much about squids, you will also come to realize they frequently live in deep underwater, dark, shady environments. This is because they don't want to have to spend all their life squinting, because their sunglasses have fallen off again.

"Not the best, it's just the fastest," said Trudy.

"I don't understand: Is it so fast that the cleaning staff can never catch it? I'm sure there has to be some kind of speedy valet service somewhere that could have it looking spick-and-span."

Trudy shook her head. "If it was cleaner, then it wouldn't be as fast."

Jack frowned. "Sorry? I think I may have misheard you. I thought you said that if this car was cleaner, then it wouldn't be as fast."

Trudy nodded. "That's exactly what I said. Simple physics."

Jack was willing to concede that it might be because of physics, but it certainly wasn't simple physics. Simple physics was about lights being powered by electricity or magnets attracting metal. Simple physics was gravity causing an apple to fall to the floor.[33]

Jack tried to make himself comfortable but failed. "Explain how physics makes this car travel faster."

---

[33] Actually, gravity is anything but simple physics. Try asking your physics teacher to explain why it works. She will tell you about objects attracting each other and that this is how gravity works. Then say to her that you didn't ask how it works, you asked *why* it works. Watch as her face crumples and she finds herself completely stumped. This will generally give you a pleasant feeling of smugness. It is a feeling that you will be able to enjoy at your leisure that afternoon when you find yourself in detention.

On some occasions this approach has caused high school science teachers to have mental breakdowns. In the event that this happens it's only fair if you occasionally go and visit them in whatever home they've been put into.

"Isn't it obvious?" asked Trudy.

It isn't, Jack thought. *It really isn't.*

NINJAS
CLOTHING CHOICES

People often wonder why ninjas wear black all the time. The most common explanation is that it helps them hide. Of course this is a ridiculous suggestion. If you are trying to stay hidden, black is the last color you should be wearing. Walk into almost any house anywhere in the world and check the color of the walls. They are almost always white, or apple white, or some type of fruit/vegetable white, or magnolia. Now, imagine a ninja standing against one of these walls. Now, some people may suggest that ninjas originated in feudal Japan and so they probably wouldn't have come up against magnolia-colored walls. And naturally this is true. However, in feudal Japan, although walls weren't generally painted magnolia, equally they weren't all painted black. To suggest that would be to suggest that

all Japanese in the Shogun era were Goths/
Emos. And they weren't. Evidence gathered
by prominent archaeologists, anthropologists,
and historians demonstrates that many parts
of Japan in the middle of the last millennium
wouldn't even have been aware of the work of
Marilyn Manson or the Sisters of Mercy, much
less would they have been able to tell you that
Robert Smith was the front man of The Cure.

So we have to accept that the Japanese weren't
Goths. In fact the walls in their homes were
frequently made of paper and were therefore
white or whitish. (This must have made it
very confusing for toddlers growing up in
Japan—"Hey, stop drawing on the wall with
your crayons ... use this paper instead ...
never mind.")

So the color that ninjas wear clearly wasn't for
concealment. And yet ninjas were considered to
be invisible. The reason for this is simple. The
power of the mind can bend much of what
people consider reality. Ninjas could sneak into
places because they *believed* they were invisible.
Those who taught ninjas picked only the very
fattest children to train. A key part of the
training was a crash diet. Previously fat children
were slimmed down to half their previous

size—and such a change made them feel that they were fading away to nothing. When they started believing this, they naturally believed that people would have difficulty seeing them. Merely having this belief made them harder to see.

But the question still remains, why do ninjas wear black? Well, you never quite forget it if you are ever overweight. Ninjas might have slimmed down, but they always remember that they used to carry a bit more heft. And so they still have a tendency to wear black. Not because black helps them remain hidden, but rather because they remember that wearing black is meant to make you look slimmer.

The moral of this story is that you should never bully the fat kids in school. They may well not be fat at all. They may just be ninjas in the early stages of training. You won't notice them when they come for their revenge. In fact, the first thing you'll know about it is a throwing star sticking out of the back of your head.

If you wish to learn more about the origins of karate, please read the section **Martial Arts/ Karate: Origins**.

16

TIME GOES PAST SO SLOWLY

Trudy explained the physics of the Ministry car as the chauffeur drove through the streets of the city.

"I refuse to believe that cars that smell bad move faster."

"Well, of course you don't believe that," said Trudy. "That would be ridiculous."

"Good, I'm glad we've established that," said Jack, unsure of where that left them.

"Have you ever noticed that when you're having a good time, days will pass in a flash? However, when you're having an awful time things seem to take forever."

"You mean the way that the summer holidays seem to pass in the blink of an eye? While the last math class on a Friday afternoon seems like it'll never end?"[34]

---

[34] Or how when you're doing well at an exam and have lots to say it

"That's it." Trudy nodded. "Or like how when you have to get a tooth drilled at the dentist it seems like it takes hours but when you walk outside and look at your watch you realize it only took five minutes. That happens because time actually *does* slow down when you're having a bad time. Simple as that," said Trudy smugly. "Negative emotions slow down time."

"Why?"

"No one knows precisely, but everyone experiences it. Everyone knows bad experiences last far too long."

"Supposing I believe you," said Jack. "What does this have to do with the car being filthy?"

"No one could enjoy a trip in this car, right?"

Jack nodded.

"So inside this car people are unhappy and their negative emotions make time move more slowly."

"But shouldn't that make the car move more slowly?"

"No, it actually makes the car move more quickly. The car creates a bubble of slow-moving time around us. But we continue to move at the normal rate inside this slow time. So to the world outside we move a lot more quickly. Does this make any sense to you?"

"No."

"That's good, because it makes no sense whatsoever. It also breaks most of the major laws of physics."

---

seems to be mere seconds before the teacher tells you to put down your pen. But if the exam is going badly, and you have nothing to write, it seems to drag on forever. Make your own list of these. I shouldn't have to do all your thinking for you.

"So how does it work, then?"

"Don't know," said Trudy with a shrug, "but it does."

"Is that how you were able to move so fast when you were fighting the Porcupods?"

Trudy nodded. "You think of the saddest thing you can possibly remember and then you can move at impossible speeds."

"That's amazing! I thought it was martial arts or something."

"Not martial arts, although the gymnastics helps."

"It feels like people are always explaining things to me at the moment," grumbled Jack.

"Don't worry about that," said Trudy.

"Because I'll eventually learn the ropes and then I'll know as much as they will?"

"Oh no," she said, laughing. "It's just that you'll eventually get used to the feeling."

The car dropped Jack off at his house first. He said goodbye to Trudy and walked inside. His parents were watching a wildlife documentary. His mother greeted him, smiling. "I've kept your tea in the oven."

"Did choir practice really take all this time?" his father asked.

Jack didn't want to lie to his parents, but he thought about trying to explain the Ministry with its evil squid creatures, homicidal teddy bears, and grotesque Porcupods. He decided that he'd tell them eventually. Just not tonight.

"Sorry, Dad, I got talking to a girl."

"A girl?" his father asked.

"Yeah, I got dropped home by her lift." At least that was the truth.

"All right. Just make sure you let us know how late you're going to be in the future," said his father. "I mean, it's a very strange world. Anything could happen."

He didn't realize quite how right he was.

MINISTRY OF S.U.IT.S HANDBOOK

DENTISTS
WHY THEY DRILL TEETH

Have you ever stopped to wonder why dentists drill holes in people's teeth? For many years dentists have claimed that if someone has a hole in a tooth, they will fix it by drilling a much bigger hole into it. This is plainly absurd. It would be like a builder repairing a crack in a wall by knocking it down or a doctor trying to fix a broken arm with a hammer.

You don't fix a hole in a tooth by making it bigger. So why are they drilling the hole?

The answer, of course, is simple. Dentists are in the pay of the Tooth Fairy. Naturally the more teeth that decay and crumble, the less money the Tooth Fairy can make. Therefore the Tooth

Fairy pays dentists to drill into decayed teeth and insert tiny monitoring and tracking devices.[35] That way he can keep tabs on people to ensure they are brushing their teeth appropriately and protecting his investment.

* * *

This is why the Ministry of SUITs issues all its operatives a toothbrush. Keeping your teeth clean isn't about decay. It's about trying to avoid being tracked by the Tooth Fairy.[36]

[35] It is interesting to see how as technology has improved, these tracking devices have become more effective and miniaturized. If you look at your parents' fillings, they are large, clunky metal things, whereas modern fillings are elegant and white. Personally I suspect the people who design the tracking devices these days are the same people who design Apple computers.

[36] Sadly, Jack already had two fillings before he joined the Ministry. The Tooth Fairy would always be able to find him.

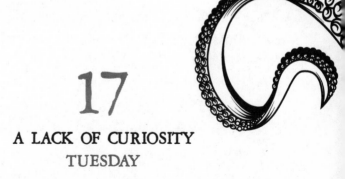

17

A LACK OF CURIOSITY
TUESDAY

The next morning Jack found himself in a strangely cheerful mood. "Good morning, parents!"

Jack's father's mustache did its trick of peering at him over the paper. "We're in good form this morning considering that we have to go to school, aren't we?"

Jack grabbed one of two bacon rolls off the table and wolfed it down as he dashed out the door. "Gotta rush. Don't want to be late."

Jack's father and mother looked at the empty space where Jack had been.

"There's something going on with that boy," Jack's mother said, shaking her head.

"Yes. There certainly is."

"Well, shouldn't we ask him what's going on?" she asked.

"Most certainly not. Then he might tell us what's going on and we'd have to do something about it."

Jack's mother thought about this for a while before she spoke. "Blissful ignorance?"

"Indeed," said Jack's father.

Jack's father's mustache silently agreed with them. Picking up the second bacon roll, Jack's father munched on it contentedly. His mustache enjoyed some of the crumbs.

———

Jack was disappointed when he got outside and realized that being early for the bus didn't actually make it arrive any sooner. For the first time in his life he was in a rush to get to school. More than anything else he wanted to get to see Trudy again and talk to her about the Ministry.

When the school bus came Jack bolted into it and was just about to sit down when he noticed David.

"Hi, Jack," said David. "So what happened last night?"

Jack had been so excited about seeing Trudy again that he had totally forgotten that this moment was coming. No one at the Ministry had told Jack that he couldn't talk about his work. But, on the other hand, it did feel as if he was part of a spy ring or something of that nature. And Grey had called it semisecret. After all, what was the point in the Ministry hiding things like Porcupods, unicorns, and dinosaurs if the minute that Jack got into school he blurted about them to all his friends?

"It was . . . interesting." Jack felt strange not telling David exactly what had happened. A major part of his reason for joining the Ministry had been to ensure that David wasn't one of the next odd kids to go missing.

"I can't help feeling that if it was really interesting you would have something more to say about it than that," said David.

Jack thought about it. Would telling David mean that he was betraying Trudy, Grey, and the Minister?

"I can't tell you . . . yet," said Jack.

"Okay," said David. "Did you see the documentary about tigers last night?"

"Aren't you the slightest bit curious?"

"Not really. I'm talking about tigers now. Tigers are probably more interesting than anything you got up to last night."

The only thing that was more annoying than someone badgering you to tell them a secret was when someone had no interest in your secret at all. David seemed to lack any curiosity. Jack thought that must have made his life very easy indeed. He would never have agreed to join the Ministry of SUITs. He would never even have gone to the museum to find Grey.

Jack and David walked in the school's front door to find Trudy sitting on the foyer reception desk. When Trudy saw Jack she pushed herself off it and bounded over to speak to him. Jack couldn't help himself from smiling.

"Trudy, great to see you! This is my friend David."

To David's credit, this time he hadn't curled himself up into a tortoiselike ball, but he did make a little high-pitched scream and throw his hands up in front of his face.

"I was only coming over to say hi," said Trudy.

"That seems unlikely," said David.

Trudy looked as if she was about to hit David. Jack felt he

had to say something. "Look, Trudy's my mate now, David. I was hanging out with her last night."

"What?" asked David. "Moody Trudy?"

There was silence for a minute.

David breathed out slowly. "I said that out loud, didn't I?"

Jack nodded gingerly. "But I'm sure Trudy won't mind."

"Won't she?" asked Trudy. Trudy was clearly fighting against every violent instinct she had. Both Jack and David noticed that her right hand was curling up into a fist.

"Of course not," Jack said pleadingly. "Because Trudy is my friend. And David is my friend. And friends don't hit friends."

Trudy cocked her head to one side and looked at Jack. "We're friends?"

"Yeah, course we are."

"Not just partners? Actual friends?" asked Trudy. "Really?"

"Really," said Jack.

"Really?" asked David.

"*Really*," said Jack more forcefully. Sometimes he wondered what was going on in David's head. Did he actually want to get beat up?

Trudy's fist slowly relaxed and became a hand once more. Jack was amazed that he'd managed to negotiate the situation without violence. Apart from anything else, David had a face that looked as though it wanted to be punched, in exactly the same way that a bouncy castle looks as though it wants to be jumped on.

"Anyway, Trudy, we need to speak. I've been thinking about the new uniforms that Mr. Teach from Chapeau Noir Enterprises gave us. There's something not right about them."

"Okay," agreed Trudy, "how about we meet at break time and discuss it?"

Jack nodded in agreement and Trudy ran off to registration.

"You're friends with Moody Trudy?" asked David. "Maybe last night *was* more interesting than tigers."

MINISTRY OF S.U.IT.S HANDBOOK

BOUNCY CASTLES
ORIGINS

Many people assume that bouncy castles are actually a modern invention and were made purely for children to play on. However, this is quite ridiculous when you consider the matter carefully. Every year hundreds of children are injured with twisted ankles or broken legs on bouncy castles. Why would anyone invent a plaything for children that is patently so very dangerous with the potential to break bones?

The truth, of course, makes much more sense. Originally, bouncy castles were much bigger and were invented to be actual castles. They had many advantages over traditional stone castles. Firstly, they could be moved from place to place, so they could be located wherever the enemy was attacking (it was rather pointless to spend a hundred years building a stone castle when your enemy could bypass it entirely by going a different route). Secondly, they were impervious to battering rams and catapults.[37] If someone fired an enormous boulder at your castle, it would rebound directly at them. Finally, if someone actually got inside your bouncy fortification, they found it very hard to fight with everyone bouncing around all over the place. Inevitably their army would find themselves forced to retreat with injuries ranging from sprained ankles to motion sickness.

Possibly the most famous bouncy castle ever was that of King Harlam II. King Harlam II was a tactical genius and came up with the brilliant idea of filling his bouncy castle with helium. This meant he could float around the country in his castle, dropping rocks on people until they surrendered.

However, ultimately no one really took King Harlam II seriously. Although he was a great warrior, his helium castle was slightly leaky, which meant that he always spoke in a rather peculiar, high-pitched voice.

[37] It should be admitted that they were rather vulnerable to bows and arrows, but as long as you had a team of loyal knights with a puncture repair kit and a set of pumps, this wasn't an enormous problem. It's much easier to reinflate part of your battlements than it is to actually rebuild them.

18

A BONA FIDE SUPERHERO

The morning session of classes seemed to drag by as Jack was keen to speak to Trudy. When the break-time bell rang, Jack leapt out of his seat and was the first out of the classroom door. He immediately fell flat on his face.

He expected to flatten his nose on the cold stone floor of the corridor. However, his first thought when he hit the ground wasn't "Ouch." Instead it was *That's unusual.*[38]

Instead of coming into contact with concrete Jack's nose was squashed against fluffy red carpet.

Of course the headmaster had said that Mr. Teach had agreed to spruce up the school, but Jack hadn't thought they would really put carpet in the corridors. It seemed madness

---

[38] He was not thinking how unusual it was to be loved by anyone. Mr. Tom Jones has been very clear about that point. That is not unusual at all.

to put carpet in a corridor where kids would continually be walking, running, and dropping sticky stuff. After a few weeks so much food and drink would have been dropped and trampled into the carpet that Heston Blumenthal would have been able to cut it into squares and serve it as the main course in one of his strange restaurants. Jack assumed that if Heston Blumenthal had served carpet as a main course, he would also serve an appetizer of rug and finish it off with a desert of fluffy hand towel.

Jack stood up and walked down the corridor where carpetfitters were finishing the final few sections. *Curious*, Jack thought to himself. *What was the rush?*

Trudy was waiting for Jack on a bench in the front playground. "So what's so odd about these new uniforms?" she asked.

"They're exactly the same as the old ones," said Jack.

"So?"

"Well, that's it. When someone gives you a new uniform they normally redesign it. Make it more dynamic. Add new colors. These new uniforms are exactly the same as the old ones. What's the point?"

Trudy looked down at the new uniform she was wearing. "Well, this one's made of polyester. It's machine washable."

"But why's that so important? Most of the kids here are growing so fast that by the time a uniform needs to be washed it doesn't fit anyway. Either that or they've fallen and torn the knee out of their trousers. Uniforms rarely last long enough to get properly dirty!" Jack shook his head, trying to figure the problem out. "Whatever way you look at it there's something fishy here. Why would a big business want us to have uniforms that are machine washable? It just doesn't make sense."

"It is strange," agreed Trudy.

"Are these the kind of mysteries that I should be thinking about if I'm in the Ministry?" Jack asked.

Trudy shrugged. "Yes and no. The Ministry deals with strange and unusual things."

"Hence the name," interrupted Jack.

"Hence the name," agreed Trudy. "And this doesn't seem that strange and unusual, but in my limited experience, this is the way the cases always start. Something small, something everybody else ignores. That's the first clue. And then behind a small clue you find there's an enormous case, something sinister, something awful."

Jack nodded. "I also think the uniforms might have something to do with the box of odds and ends we have in the P.E. stores."

Jack explained to her about the spare kit box in P.E. He also told her how he was especially worried as David was most definitely an "odd kid." Jack felt slightly guilty talking about David. David had been the main reason he'd sought out Grey, but it seemed as if Jack was continually getting sidetracked. As much as he was worried about what might happen to David, there were so many curious and interesting things to learn about in the Ministry. Jack's mother had said his curiosity would be the death of him. Jack was now more worried that it might be the reason that David would end up going missing.

Trudy told Jack that the girls had a similar box in their

changing room. ". . . But wouldn't someone report children if they went missing?" asked Trudy.

Jack shrugged. "Maybe the kind of parents who don't make sure you have a proper P.E. kit are the same kind of parents who'd just think you've run away from home. Or maybe they're the kind of parents that the police just don't take seriously."

"Maybe. I've certainly heard of stranger things."

Jack paused for a moment. "I've got something else to ask you, Trudy."

"What?"

"It's about David. Can I tell him about the Ministry?"

"What do you mean?"

"Well, the Ministry is kind of secret. I didn't know if we could tell our friends about it."

"I'm not sure," Trudy said. "It's not a problem I've ever really had. Up until I met you I never really had a friend close enough for me to worry about telling."

This was one of the saddest things Jack had ever heard.

"The Ministry is semisecret. But . . . you trust David, right?"

Jack nodded. "He can be a bit useless, but I do trust him."

"Then tell him."

"Really?"

"I don't think that the Ministry is really top secret. I think that we just don't talk about it because people wouldn't believe us."

This made sense; up until two days ago Jack wouldn't have believed in any of the things he now knew.

Trudy continued. "I mean, a Ministry to deal with

zombies and vampires, to cover up the Loch Ness Monster? It probably isn't the kind of thing you should mention to your next-door neighbor over tea. But I think you're safe enough in telling David. Who knows if he'll even believe you?"

"Thanks, Trudy." Jack felt better knowing that he could tell his best friend about what was happening.

They got up and walked into the entrance of the school. Jack was careful not to trip on the thick shag carpet.

In the middle of the entrance hall three older children were throwing a schoolbag through the air. It belonged to Edwyn Jones, a small, weedy kid from Jack's class.

"Guys, this isn't funny," squeaked Edwyn as the bag sailed over his head again, despite his best attempt to catch it.

The three bullies seemed to think it was very funny and continued throwing the bag. Edwyn got bored of the whole process and moved to the side of the corridor to lean against the wall. One of the bullies went over to Edwyn and made a fist right in his face. "Listen, you little squirt: You jump, you pretend you want your bag back, or I'll get my fun by pummeling you."

The argument was a persuasive one and Edwyn started jumping again as they threw the bag back and forth. However, his cries of "Give it back" and his leaps in the air seemed rather unenthusiastic.

Jack turned to Trudy. "We should do something about this. And when I say *we* should do something about this, I mean *you* should do something about this."

"What?" asked Trudy.

"Edwyn's in my class. He isn't a bad guy. I've seen you in

action, Trudy. If you can take out a room of Porcupods, those bullies shouldn't be a problem for you."

Trudy sized up the bullies. "They wouldn't be a problem. But that isn't what the Ministry does. We deal with people who are plotting against the country. Kidnappers, murderers, thieves..."

"Which are all just types of bullies. Look, what's the point of being able to do what you can do, if you walk away from situations like this?"

"Jack, if I start destroying bullies in the middle of the corridor, then it won't be long before everyone knows about the Ministry. Telling David is one thing, but the whole school finding out? That's different."

Jack knew that Trudy was right. "I just wish we could do something. I hate bullies."

Trudy let out a long sigh before speaking. "I've hit bullies before, but without using any of the Ministry skills."

Jack shook his head. "Without the Ministry skills you'd never be able to take out three bullies. And they all look like they're from fourth year."

One of the bullies had grabbed Edwyn by the collar and pushed him up against the wall.

"We have to do something," Jack sighed. "Maybe together both of us could..."

Before Jack finished his sentence something happened that surprised him. Considering everything that had happened the other night at the Ministry, Jack thought that he was pretty much surprise-proof at this stage. He was wrong. Quite badly wrong.

Just as one of the bullies looked as though he was going to punch Edwyn in the face a figure appeared out of nowhere.

"Stop and desist your nefarious activities, bullies!"

Standing on the window ledge, with bright light streaming in from behind him, was what looked like a superhero. A bona fide superhero.

MINISTRY OF S.U.IT.S HANDBOOK

VAMPIRES
CLOTHING CHOICES

Many people wonder why Vampires wear black all the time. They wonder if it is a question of style.

The real reason, of course, is simply that wearing black is a good tactical decision to make if you spend your life drinking blood from someone's neck. Black doesn't show the bloodstains. Additionally, since vampires don't have reflections, it's very hard for them to put together a really cool modern outfit. This is why in movies you see them wearing dinner suits so frequently. It's a classic look that anyone can pull off.

19
STATIC

Jack squinted at the light shining in through the window and realized that it wasn't really that much of a superhero at all. In fact, it was Dawkins from his class, standing on a window ledge, wearing two new school uniforms. The first he wore in a conventional way, blazer on his back, tie around his neck, both arms in the armholes of his shirt. But the second he had fashioned into a superhero costume. A very bad superhero costume, but a superhero costume nonetheless.

A second white shirt was tied around his neck to give the impression of a cape. He'd also cut eye-holes in a second tie and tied it around his head like a mask to protect his secret identity. Like almost all superheroes ever, the mask did nothing to protect his identity whatsoever. He just looked like himself, but wearing a very small mask.

The bullies stood amazed for a few moments before they

spoke. Dawkins waited silently, posed heroically on the window ledge, hands on his hips.

Eventually one of the bullies broke the silence. "What are you doing, you mentalist?"

"Mentalist?" sneered Dawkins from his windowsill. "Supermentalist, you mean. No—wait a minute, not supermentalist. Superhero! Look upon me, bullies, and quake, for I am STATIC!"

"He is very static—do you think he's just going to stand posing on that windowsill all day?" Trudy whispered to Jack.

Jack had no idea what Dawkins was going to do. At this stage Jack had very little idea what anyone was going to do anymore. It was as if the world had got up this morning and decided to go insane without telling anyone.

The bully who had pinned Edwyn up against the wall decided that it would be more fun to bully the strangely dressed Dawkins. He pushed Edwyn to the ground. "We'll be back to bully you some more later," he told Edwyn. "So just stay there, but in the meantime we're going to have some fun with the nutcase."

The three bullies closed in on the windowsill where Dawkins stood. Jack thought that now would be an ideal time for Dawkins to run, but he just stood there looking majestic. Or at least as majestic as you can look with a white shirt tied around your neck and looking out from behind a school tie with two ragged holes in it.

Jack felt sorry for Dawkins. Apart from his slightly unusual dress sense he really wasn't a bad guy.

"We are going to kick you to bits," one of the bullies said as they closed in.

"HA!" yelled Dawkins. "Static laughs at bullies."

The bullies stopped. "Who is Static?"

"I am Static," yelled Dawkins.

Jack whispered to Trudy, "Apparently Dawkins thinks he's called Static now."

Trudy whispered back to Jack, "Yes, I also picked that up."

Static/Dawkins suddenly leapt from the windowsill. Jack thought he had probably meant to land heroically on the ground, but unfortunately Dawkins wasn't the most agile of kids. He gave out a slight "Ouch" as he hit the carpet, stumbled, and then stood up.

Static/Dawkins limped toward the bullies, still trying to look heroic. "This is your last chance, bullies. Cease your evildoing and run. Or face the wrath of Static."

The lead bully sneered. "Go on, then, let's see your wrath."

Dawkins seemed to do a dance, shuffling his feet back and forth on the carpet. "You are going to regret this," he said.

The lead bully just laughed.

Dawkins/Static finished his strange feet-shuffling dance and reached out with a hand. The bully watched Dawkins's hand, thinking that it wasn't moving fast enough to do any damage.

Dawkins's outstretched finger lined up with the bully's nose. Unexpectedly a blue-electric flash jumped from Dawkins's finger and cracked the bully on the nose. The bully jumped back with pain and let out a frightened yelp.

"Feel the power of Static!" yelled Dawkins/Static. He was shuffling his feet back and forth again.

"What was that?" yelped the bully.

"Had enough?" asked Dawkins, his feet still moving.

One of the bullies went to grab Dawkins by the front of his shirt. There was another small blue crack as he touched Dawkins. The bully fell backward, clutching his hand.

Dawkins's feet were still shuffling. "That's the beauty of Static's powers. I touch you and it hurts you. You touch me? It still hurts you. I am invulnerable!"

"You're insane!" said the third bully.

Dawkins held out a hand. "Shake my hand and say that!"

The bully recoiled from Dawkins's outstretched hand in fear. Dawkins's feet were still shuffling and scuffling on the carpet.

"I have ten shocking fingers here," Dawkins said, stretching them out toward the bullies. "Who wishes to feel my power first?"

The bullies looked at Dawkins for a second. "Let's leave him be. It's not worth it."

Jack and Trudy turned to look at each other, both of their mouths hanging open in astonishment. Realizing how stupid they must have looked, they clamped their jaws shut and turned back to Dawkins.

"More enemies vanquished by the power of Static!" Dawkins/Static yelled triumphantly, punching the air as the bullies slunk away down the corridor.

Dawkins held out his hand to help Edwyn up. When Edwyn touched it he flinched back in pain.

"Whoops. Sorry about that, must still have a bit of a charge left over. It'll wear off eventually."

Trudy and Jack walked over to Dawkins. Jack could tell that Trudy felt a bit put out. She'd finally decided to use her skills to help someone, and at the last moment had been upstaged by a nerd with a tie wrapped around his head.

"What are you doing, you nutcase?" she asked.

"Vanquishing evil. For I am the superhero Static."

Jack shook his head. "You are not the superhero Static. You're Dawkins. Putting a tie around your eyes and using a shirt for a cape isn't going to fool anyone."

"Oh. Well, yes, by day I am the mild-mannered Dawkins, popular classroom clown. . . ."

"You aren't that popular," interjected Jack, but Dawkins ignored him and continued.

". . . But when I see injustice I transform into STATIC! The superhero with the power to control static electricity."

"Is that really all that was?" asked Trudy. "Static electricity?"

Dawkins/Static nodded enthusiastically. "Yeah, it's amazing. There's something about these new uniforms. I mean I know polyester creates a static charge, but this stuff seems to create a huge static charge. And the carpet seems to be made of polyester as well." Dawkins rubbed his feet furiously on the carpet. "So it's really easy to build up a painful charge."

Dawkins demonstrated by putting a finger next to a door handle. A tiny blue electrical spark jumped from the tip of Dawkins's finger.

"The brilliant thing about it is that bullies can't touch me even if they want to."

"Well they can't touch you directly," said Trudy, "but they could use wooden sticks to beat you. Wood doesn't conduct electricity."

Dawkins clearly hadn't thought of this. He looked worried, but after a few seconds he put on his best superhero face. "Static will still be triumphant. Watch for me in the *skies*."

"Are you claiming that you can fly now?" asked Jack.

"Well, no . . . Okay then, watch for me in the *corridors*."

Jack and Trudy watched Dawkins limp down the corridor, his leg sore from when he had jumped off the windowsill. "Where are you going, Dawkins?"

"Gym lockers," said Dawkins. "I'm going to hide the cricket bats."

Dawkins walked out the door and at the moment he did so, the lights flickered briefly.

Trudy looked astonished. "Now, if Dawkins did that, he is impressive!"

Edwyn had recovered from his unfortunate shock. "Who was that masked man?" he asked.

"Weren't you listening? That was Dawkins. He's a nutcase."

"He's a hero!" exclaimed Edwyn. "He saved my life."

"At no stage was your life in danger. He is not a hero. Please don't start going around and telling everyone that . . ."

Edwyn cut Trudy off. "I'm going to tell everyone in the school that I was saved by Static. People will sing songs and write poems about him."

Edwyn ran off.

"I really hope no one starts singing songs about this," said Trudy.

SUPERHERO COSTUMES
SECRET IDENTITIES

Many superheroes protect their identities by wearing costumes under their everyday clothes. That means if they need to burst into action and save a life they have only to shed their regular clothes to be ready.

However, this means that in the height of summer they will be forced to swelter with a layer of Lycra under their regular clothes. Therefore, if you're sitting next to someone on the bus and they smell really, really sweaty there's a fairly good chance they're a superhero.

If supervillains realized this, they would be able to track down their superhero enemies by hanging round the toiletries section of supermarkets and watching to see who bought the most antiperspirant.

20

BEAKER OF FOAM

Between break time and lunch Jack had double science. Some days it was interesting when you got to do experiments and create beakers full of foam. Some days it was dull, like when you had to write up notes and draw diagrams about experiments that had created beakers full of foam.

It was rarely practical. Jack couldn't imagine a situation in real life where it would be necessary to create a beaker full of foam except, of course, working in a coffeehouse. He was also slightly suspicious of scientists. Anytime they turned up in movies they were always putting together a device that would be used to destroy the world. Normally because they'd been bullied at school or picked on by work colleagues. As a member of the Ministry, Jack imagined this was exactly the sort of thing that he had to watch out for.

Jack's science teacher was an oldish man called

Dr. Holmes. He had twinkling blue eyes and a dramatic thatch of blond hair. He looked more eccentric than evil. Jack decided that as he was now a Ministry Agent he should check that Dr. Holmes was not, in fact, an evil genius with a taste for world destruction.

"Umm, sir?" Jack sidled up to Dr. Holmes.

"Yes, boy, what is it?"

"I don't suppose you've ever suffered humiliating treatment at the hands of a bully that has made you hate the world?"

Dr. Holmes considered this question for a minute. "I don't think so. I'm sure if I had been humiliated in such a way I would have remembered."

"Umm, what about . . . have you ever had your heart broken so cruelly that it has left you dead inside? Left your insides burning with an ice that makes you insensible to the suffering of others? A suffering that could only be ended by the destruction of the world?"[39]

Again Dr. Holmes carefully considered the question before answering. "I've certainly had my heart broken, but not that badly. It was broken by a girl when I was six years old. But later that day I was given a pedal car for my birthday and the heartache seemed to disappear."

Jack wondered how many of the world's great villains could have been morally turned around if only someone had given them a pedal car at the right time. Would Hitler

---

[39] If you haven't guessed already, Jack read a lot of comics and graphic novels.

have still felt the need to invade Poland if only someone had given him a scooter? Would Osama bin Laden have turned out as bad if he had been presented with a red hula hoop?

"So generally you haven't been scarred by life?"

"No," said Dr. Holmes. "Not so badly. Life's been pretty pleasant, I would say."

"Good," said Jack, reasonably happy that Dr. Holmes would not turn out to be an evil scientist.

Dr. Holmes turned away from Jack and let him get on with making his beaker of foam. "I don't know," Dr. Holmes mused to himself. "You pupils ask the funniest questions." As he walked away he laughed in an almost maniacal way.

"Maniacal laughter," muttered Jack to himself. "Maybe he is an evil scientist after all." Jack decided he would later check with Grey to see if there was a standard test for insanity in scientists.

"What were you asking those questions for?" David had wandered over to Jack to see how he was getting on with the beaker of foam. David was always Jack's lab partner. However, it was generally agreed that, considering David's clumsiness, he should always be kept far away from experiments involving volatile chemicals or flames.

Jack decided that now was the time to tell David about the Ministry.

"Sit down, David. I have something to tell you."

And so, while his classmates were completing their experiments, Jack explained to David about the secret elevator at the museum, the stone guardians, the insane Minister, the Porcupods, Trudy's amazing skills, the squid-headed lord-of-filing Cthulhu, and all the other bizarre events that had taken place on Monday.

For a few moments David just stared blankly at Jack. Then he spoke. "So what you're telling me is that you have an after-school job?"

Jack couldn't believe how calmly David had taken it. "Haven't you been listening to what I was saying? I'm working for the Ministry of Strange, Unusual, and Impossible Things."

"Yes," David agreed. "You have an after-school job."

"But isn't it amazing that all this strange stuff is going on in the world?"

David shook his head. "I always kind of expected it. I mean, think about it. All the mad things that we're meant to accept. Computers that can think a million thoughts at once, people on the bottom of the Earth that don't fall off, huge metal tubes that can fly through the air. It's all mad."

"But that's just science."

"Explain how metal planes can fly. Or how metal boats can float."

Jack shook his head. "I don't know...."

"You see," said David triumphantly. "If you pay attention, everything in the world is very odd indeed."

"I ... I suppose you're right."

"Look, if you ever need any help with the Ministry stuff, I'm always here to lend a hand."

Jack smiled. "I could always ask them if you could join up."

"No, thanks!" David said. "I'll help out if you need a hand, but I've already got an after-school job in my folks' corner store. I don't need two jobs. Especially when I could get killed in one of them."

"I understand," said Jack solemnly.

"I don't think you do." David shook his head. "Corner stores are dangerous. My Uncle Cecil was once almost crushed to death by a delivery of the Sunday papers."

EVIL SCIENTISTS
CAREER PATH

If you want to be an evil scientist, it's worthwhile consulting your school's career adviser or guidance counselor. You will need to study all the sciences and achieve good grades in them.

The only other qualification that you need is the ability to look sinister and evil while stroking a white Persian cat that is wearing a diamond collar.

* * *

Sadly the careers of many evil scientists have been ruined before they even properly got started due to a cat-hair allergy.

21

BACK DOOR AND
BLACK DOOR

At the end of the day Trudy was standing outside the front gates waiting. Jack had just called his parents to tell them he was going to Trudy's for tea and would be home late.

"What are we doing tonight, then?" asked Jack.

"Training." Trudy smiled. "Tonight I take you to the Misery."

"The Misery? I don't really like the sound of that."

Jack had a suspicion that training was going to be hard. But he hadn't expected it to be miserable.

"Look, I'm sure training's important and everything, but the reason I joined up with the Ministry was to try and find out if the box of spares is caused by odd kids going missing. I just want to make sure that David doesn't end up . . . missing."

"Okay, well, we could go out and try and find out if someone is kidnapping the missing kids."

"Great!"

"Of course, then we'd have to stop them somehow. Do you feel strong enough to fight a gang of sinister kidnappers?"

Jack admitted that he wasn't exactly ready for that eventuality.

"And that's why tonight you're going to get trained," Trudy said, ramming her point home.

The Ministry car had pulled up outside the school. Jack held his breath and clambered into the back of the smelly car.

When they reached the museum Jack headed for the elevator. Trudy caught his arm. "Not that way."

"But I thought this was the way in? I mean, the stone giants and . . ."

Trudy shook her head. "Kevin and Barry are all right, but it's a lot quicker to sneak in the back entrance."

Trudy led Jack up a flight of stairs and into the mummy exhibit.

Jack had visited this room before on a school trip. It held the remains of the Lady Takabuti, an ancient blackened mummy. Her skin was dark, withered, and leathery. But that was understandable considering she was more than two and a half thousand years old and had been born in an era before moisturizer. She lay beside her intricate sarchophagus, which was covered in tiny hieroglyphics.

"She gives me the creeps," said Jack, leaning over the glass case and looking into the empty eye sockets of the ancient, bandaged corpse.

Trudy shot a disapproving look at Jack. "Don't say that, Jack. She might hear you."

Jack looked startled. "What, you mean she's alive?"

Trudy laughed at Jack. "Don't be ridiculous. She's been dead for more than two thousand years."

"I knew that," Jack said, pretending to be considerably braver than he felt.

"But she still might hear you."

Jack stood quietly. "She can still hear even if she's dead?"

"Yeah, mummies. You've seen the movies. Part alive, mostly dead, wander around attacking people."

Jack thought that was all make-believe, but from his recent experience with the Ministry he knew that was not the right thing to say.

"Don't worry about her now, though; generally she's asleep during the day. She only gets up when the museum's closed. She's kind of like the night-watch-woman."

Jack didn't want to think about that. "So you were going to show me a back door?"

Trudy looked around and confirmed that they were the only visitors in the mummy display. She reached over to a gray stone object—an enormous sculpture of a hand, which presumably had broken off of a much larger statue. She pressed three of the fingernails[40] in a rapid sequence. There was a brief sliding noise and the glass case that had surrounded Takabuti and her sarcophagus lifted upward.

---

[40] The stone hand was enormous. Jack imagined that if he had heard fingernails this large being pulled down a huge chalkboard his head would have exploded.

Jack silently prayed that he wasn't going to have to move the blackened corpse to get to the back door.

"Follow me," commanded Trudy as she walked over to the display. She reached out a hand, and for a minute Jack thought she was going to touch the mummy. Instead she had grabbed ahold of the front of the sarcophagus. It was sitting beside the actual mummy, looking much friendlier with a pleasant, painted face.[41] Trudy moved the lid and Jack was shocked to see that it was secured to the display by hinges. Trudy jumped up on the display. She started walking down stairs and into a hole that had been hidden underneath the lid of the smiling sarcophagus.

"Hurry up!" insisted Trudy. "The whole setup is on a timer switch. In about thirty seconds the sarcophagus lid snaps shut and the glass display pops back up."

Jack followed her quickly.

"It doesn't pay to dawdle when you're using the back entrance. One time I was slow and got trapped underneath the glass display. No one came and got me out for thirty minutes. Let me tell you, it isn't fun having school trips of primary school children pointing at you and saying that you don't look particularly Egyptian."

After the first fifteen or twenty meters the stairs started curving to the right and spiraling downward.

Trudy and Jack walked along one of the Ministry's

---

[41] Jack noticed that the face painted on the lid of the sarcophagus had large black lines painted around its eyes. He wondered if the ancient Egyptians had been big fans of pandas or were just Goths.

corridors until they came to a door made of rotten timber. At one stage it had been painted black, but the paint had clearly grown tired and was starting to flake off.

Trudy knocked on the door. Instead of hearing a rap, there was a dull echo. "I'd say try and enjoy yourself, but it really won't be possible."

"What's going to make the training so miserable?"

"What makes it so miserable is the Misery," said Trudy. Jack opened the door.

MINISTRY OF S.U.I.T.S HANDBOOK

MUMMIES
THE WEARING OF BANDAGES

Over the years many people have wondered why the ancient Egyptians covered their dead in bandages. Given even a minute's thought, the answer is obvious. When people were unwell in Ancient Egypt they would go to the doctor. Ancient Egyptian doctors had no penicillin, they had no X-ray machines, and they had no vaccines or antibiotics.

What they did have was a lot of bandages.

Therefore, when you went to the doctor in Egypt you generally got covered in bandages.

Many people who did get sick went on to die. They were then buried in the bandages they already had on . . . because . . . who wants to use a bandage that has been used on a corpse?

It is also interesting to note that many archaeologists now believe that the number-one cause of death in Ancient Egypt was "Accidental Smothering Due to Excessive Bandages." The number-two cause was crocodile bite.[42]

[42] There is also evidence to show that 86 percent of people who were bitten by crocodiles in Ancient Egypt were bitten only because they could not run away, as their legs were overly covered in bandages.

22

THE MISERY

Jack looked inside the room and saw a slouched figure wearing a pair of black jeans and a large, black, baggy, handknitted sweater with the letter *M* in white on the front. Initially he couldn't see the figure's face at all because its head was facing toward the floor. All that was visible was a mop of black, greasy, tangled hair.

"Jack Pearse, meet the Misery," said Trudy.

The head of the Misery snapped up as it heard its name. It was a he. He looked to be about fourteen, but it was hard to tell in the gloom. The Misery looked at Trudy and Jack in the same way you would look at dog poo that you had just stepped in. He sighed.

Jack held out a hand to be shaken. The Misery stared at Jack's hand as if he had never seen one before. Jack put his hand back down by his side.

"We're here for training, Misery."

The Misery sighed. "I was just getting myself ready to go out." The Misery sighed again. "And now . . . this?"

"Afraid so," said Trudy.

". . . I suppose we'd better begin."

Jack wasn't actually sure how large the Misery's room was, because all he could see was an infinity of darkness. Walls could have been just out of view, or they might not have existed at all. The Misery slouched off into the gloom and returned with six glass bottles filled with water. He put them at Jack's feet.

"These are bottles." The Misery pointed at the bottles.

"Bottles," agreed Jack. So far the training was turning out to be easier than he thought it would be.

The Misery picked up one of the bottles and walked ten paces away from Jack. Jack looked over his shoulder—Trudy was smiling. That made Jack nervous.

Still slouching, the Misery stretched one arm out. "Now, Jack Pearse, catch the bottle."

The Misery let go of the bottle. It fell to the ground and shattered before Jack could take a single step.

The Misery sighed and shook his head in despair. "Too slow. You moron. You absolute moron."

"How on earth was I meant to . . . ?" But before he could complete his sentence the Misery had pressed his face right into Jack's. The Misery had moved the ten paces in a fraction of a second.

"Jack Pearse doesn't get to talk until he catches a bottle. Jack Pearse is a moron. Jack Pearse has no friends."

"Now, wait a minute . . . ," said Jack.

"I could wait a minute; I could wait an hour. But it doesn't really matter, does it? Jack Pearse isn't going to get any smarter, or faster, or better-looking."

Before Jack could complain further, the Misery picked up another bottle and walked ten paces away. He held the bottle out in front of himself. "Catch the bottle, Jack Pearse."

The Misery dropped the bottle. Jack almost managed half a step before the bottle shattered on the floor.

The Misery stared at Trudy. "Couldn't you have brought me a monkey instead of Jack Pearse? You can train monkeys. I can't train"—the Misery looked at Jack with disdain—"I can't train whatever this is."

"I didn't come here to be insulted," said Jack.

Once more the Misery had moved fast and was leering directly into Jack's face. "No? Where do you normally go to be insulted? I hope you don't pay them too much to insult you. It's very easy to do. I have rarely seen a creature more ugly than you."

Jack balled up a fist and swung it at the Misery's head, but the Misery ducked under it as if it was moving in slow motion. Before Jack could react, the Misery was standing behind him. As Jack turned around to meet him, the Misery shouted at the top of his voice, "What makes you think you could ever hit me!" Little pieces of saliva flew out of the Misery's mouth as he bellowed.

The Misery picked up another bottle and walked across the room, talking as he went. "You are such a dull person. A slow person. A boring person. A person who can't even *catch a bottle!*"

The Misery dropped the bottle. Jack didn't even manage a half step this time. The bottle shattered and the Misery sighed.

"I'm never going to be able to catch the bottles!" Jack shouted. "So let's get this over with." He picked up the three remaining bottles that were left at his feet and threw them across the room in different directions. He smiled at the Misery. "Game over."

The Misery shook his head and then blurred into action. He moved faster than anything Jack had ever seen in his life. He ran toward the bottle that Jack had thrown first and jumped into the air, spinning. A hand snapped out of the black rotating mass and grabbed the bottle. Then, quick as a flash, the Misery landed in a crouching position and sprinted toward the second bottle Jack had thrown. The second bottle was closer to the ground but the Misery caught it with two feet to spare.

There was one bottle left, but it was too close to the ground for the Misery to catch. *Wasn't it?* The Misery launched himself so quickly it looked like he was flying horizontally along the ground. Before he got to the bottle he tucked his head and went into a forward roll. One of the Misery's pale, bony hands shot out and caught the bottle. As the bottle had been falling it had turned on its side and several droplets of water had fallen out. The Misery's hand moved the bottle so expertly and quickly that all the drops of water fell back into the bottle instead of hitting the ground.

Holding all three bottles, the Misery walked back, moving at an ordinary pace. He set two of the bottles down in front of Jack. The third he took ten paces away.

Jack gulped. "Okay, we'll do these last three bottles. You can shout at me all you want. But after we've done three bottles that's it, right?"

For the first time there was a hint of a smile playing around the Misery's lips. The smile lingered briefly before it realized that there had to be a better place for it to be. "Trudy?"

"Yes, Misery?"

"There's another crate of bottles in the back there." He jerked a thumb over his shoulder, indicating a direction in the darkness. "Go and fetch it for me."

Trudy wandered off into the darkness. Although he couldn't see her, Jack heard her huffing and straining with effort as she picked something up that rattled annoyingly.

The Misery's hand snapped out. The single word "catch" escaped his lips and another bottle dropped to the ground.

Jack felt like crying. Was he going to be stuck in a dark room with this maniac forever?

MINISTRY OF S.U.IT.S HANDBOOK

THE MISERY
What Makes Him So Miserable

SECTION DELETED BY NERVOUS EDITOR[43]

[43] Because even the editor of the Ministry Handbook is terrified of the Misery.

23
CATCHING A BOTTLE

Time passed. The Misery had gone through an entire milk crate's worth of bottles, and Jack had yet to take more than a single step before the bottle hit the ground and shattered. The Misery had started on a second crate. Each time Jack failed the impossible task the Misery shouted at him and called him horrible names. The names fell into one of three categories. There were (i) names that were unfair, (ii) names that might have been unfair as Jack had not known what they meant, and (iii) names that Jack was fairly sure were medically incorrect and used out of context.

Jack had pleaded to be allowed to leave the room. He'd said he would give up working for the Ministry. He'd said that he wouldn't mention any of this to anyone. And yet the Misery ignored everything he said and kept dropping bottles.

"I hate this. I hate you," said Jack. "This is the worst day of my life."

The minute he said those words the Misery looked at him with his head tilted to one side. "Let's see just how bad," he sneered. As usual, the Misery's hand snapped out and he dropped a bottle. Jack couldn't have felt worse. He took a step toward the bottle. Then another step. He'd taken two steps and yet he hadn't heard the bottle shatter. Jack took a third step, then a fourth. He looked up. The bottle seemed to be hanging in midair, moving down perhaps, but incredibly slowly. Jack sprinted the final six steps and managed to catch the bottle before it hit the ground. He had stopped it a *bare inch* before it hit the ground. But he had caught it.

"I caught the bottle!" Jack yelled.

Trudy clapped her hands together with excitement.

For an instant there was a smile on the Misery's face, but it was quickly replaced with a scowl. "Big deal."

Jack realized what had been happening. The Misery had made him so unhappy that time seemed to drag, which in turn allowed him to move faster than lightning.

"So I can do what Trudy can do now?" Jack asked.

The Misery snorted with laughter. "Not yet—not even close. You need to practice."

"Practice what?"

"Well, every time you need The Speed, you can't rely on me being there to make you miserable. You need to be able to conjure up that feeling of unhappiness instantly."

"And how do I do that?"

The Misery shrugged. "Think of something sad. Something that makes you unhappy."

"And..."

"And I've had enough stupid questions for one night," the Misery said, putting up a hand to silence Jack. "Now get out of here; I've got a lot of sweeping up to do."

"But..." Before Jack could say anything more Trudy put a finger to her lips to keep him silent. As she was leading Jack out of the room he looked back and saw the Misery reach into the darkness and grab a broom.

***

Jack and Trudy stood outside the Misery's room. "Well, that was intense."

"Yeah, the first training session's always like that," said Trudy. "It gets easier from here on in."

"Well, it couldn't get any harder, could it? I don't imagine the Misery has many friends."

"He doesn't have any. He's kind of tragic, really. I feel sorry for him."

Jack found it difficult to feel sorry for someone who had spent so many hours making him feel deeply unhappy. "I'd better be getting home now. We were in there for ages. My parents will be..." Jack looked at his watch and was shocked to see that only half an hour had passed. He looked at Trudy. "We were only in there thirty minutes! How is that possible?"

"How many times do I have to explain? You were unhappy. When you're unhappy time slows down."

"The Misery called it 'The Speed.'"

"Yeah, I don't think there's actually a proper name for it. But that's what the Misery calls it. And no one wants to argue with him."

"Shouldn't we tell people about The Speed? I mean, think how useful it would be to businesses. Think about how productive they could be."

Trudy laughed. "You think businesses don't know about this?"

"They do?"

"Of course they do. But no one ever talks about it because it's immoral to make people miserable to get more work out of them. Think about it, Jack. Think of restaurants. Which ones serve food the fastest?"

Jack wondered if this was a trick question. "The fast-food ones?"

"Exactly. How do you think the food gets served so much more quickly in fast-food restaurants? In an ordinary restaurant it can take twenty minutes to get a burger. Yet in fast-food places it'll be there in two minutes. How do you think they do that?"

"I'd always just assumed it was because they were really well organized and used some kind of assembly line."

"Jack, they're building a burger, not a laptop. How much of an assembly line would you need? Burger-bun bottom. Meat patty, throw some salad at it. Mayonnaise. Burger-bun top. That's it. How would an assembly line speed that up?"

"So how do they do it?"

"The Speed, Jack. *The Speed*. The staff they employ are high schoolers. You know that all high schoolers are desperate to be cool. So the fast-food restaurants make them dress up in ridiculous costumes, often with cardboard hats, they put them in garish-looking plastic restaurants, and then they make them look after groups of screaming six-year-olds. The high schoolers who work in those places are miserable. So time around them slows down to the extent that when they're making a burger it takes two minutes instead of twenty to cook it."

"Should we do something about it?"

"Meh," said Trudy. "I don't really like sixth formers."

"Me neither . . . So if I make myself unhappy now, I could run really fast like you. Could I do the backflips and things?"

"I've been training for longer than you, Jack, and the gymnastics helps a lot. But if you keep practicing it is possible to outrun gravity. Have you ever noticed that when you knock something off a table it seems to hang in the air for a few seconds before it falls? That's just gravity taking a second to catch up. So if you run really, really, really fast you can defy gravity."

Jack had an idea. He started focusing on his time with the Misery and how unhappy he had been. He could feel himself becoming sadder. And as that happened the world around him started to slow down. He started running down the corridor at an incredible rate. Then he put one foot followed by a second on the wall. He was running sideways along the wall, moving slowly toward the ceiling. Instead of stepping onto the ceiling he made a leap and landed with both feet on the ceiling at the same time. His legs were frantically pumping as he ran along the ceiling. It felt like nothing he had ever experienced before. He let out a yell of happiness and exhilaration. A huge smile spread across his face.

And that was when he fell off the ceiling and landed on the floor.

Jack had learned an important lesson. No matter how happy you felt about running on the ceiling, it still hurt a lot when you fell off the ceiling and landed on the floor.

He was a crumpled mess and in quite a lot of pain. He started untangling himself and noticed that Trudy was standing above him.

"Did you hurt yourself?"

"I fell off the ceiling. Of course I hurt myself." Jack had never thought that this was the kind of sentence that he would ever find himself saying. "What went wrong?"

"What do you think? You have to keep the unhappy frame of mind to move faster than normal. You got excited about being able to run on the ceiling and forgot to keep the unhappy feelings in the front of your mind. You became happy and time started moving at the proper speed. And that was when gravity caught up with you and beat you down."

Jack rubbed an elbow and thought about how mean gravity was. "That's an important lesson."

Trudy held out a hand and helped Jack up. "Don't worry about it. We all do it the first time. Now I'll see if I can get the Ministry car to give us a lift home."

THE SPEED
Use in Schools

Of course, it should be noted that The Speed is used in all sorts of situations without people noticing. Teachers have known about The Speed for many years and use it to try and get children to study for longer. This is why they insist on ties being tied up tight and all shirts being tucked in. Why would a teacher care how neat pupils' uniforms are?

The answer is, of course, that teachers do not care about clothes at all—just look at the way they dress. But they do know that a tight tie and a restricting collar button will make a pupil slightly uncomfortable. And a slightly uncomfortable pupil will be slightly unhappy. And that unhappiness, however slight, will cause time to slow down *a little bit*. And so the pupil will have longer to study. This effect can be observed in real life by the fact that children whose parents make them do their homework *before* getting changed out of their school uniform always get better marks. It is also the reason the very best private schools have the most ridiculous uniforms (generally anything with a straw boater, gown, or a bow tie) and therefore get the best results.

24
EVERYTHING CHANGES
WEDNESDAY

The next day on the school bus Jack could tell that David had something he wanted to say. Rather ironically, Jack knew that David wanted to say something because he wasn't saying anything. He sat with his arms folded and his mouth pressed tightly shut.

"Anything you want to say, David?"

David shook his head.

"Sure?"

David said absolutely nothing. Jack sighed and looked out the window.

After a few minutes David spoke. "Okay, okay, if you aren't going to stop badgering me about it, I'll tell you..."

"What?"

"It's about Trudy."

"What about her?"

"Is she going to be your new best friend?"

Jack laughed out loud. "What do you mean?"

"You know exactly what I mean."

"I really don't."

"We all know the way it works. A slightly popular kid always has a slightly strange kid as their best friend. You're slightly popular, I mean, people like you."

"David. People like you too."

David shook his head. "No, they don't."

Jack was about to argue, but David held up a finger to silence him and then turned around to speak to the two kids behind them on the bus.

"Guys, do you like me?"

They were both kids from their class, Alex and James.

James spoke first. "Not really. I mean, I don't hate you, but . . . well, I probably just dislike you. You can be irritating."

Jack leapt to his friend's defense. "He isn't irritating!"

David silenced Jack again. "James has a point—I am irritating. I've just asked two boys in our class if they like me and it isn't even nine o'clock yet. I mean, that's very irritating."

"Exactly," James said, nodding. "I mean, that'd be an irritating question to ask someone even if they actually liked you. And as we discussed . . . I don't really like you."

"Thank you for your honesty," said David. "What about you, Alex?"

Alex took a deep breath. "I don't really have strong feelings one way or the other. I mean, we hardly ever talk. So it's kind of hard for me to say whether I like you or not. But going on a gut instinct I'm willing to dislike you at this stage. Because if I start disliking you now I think it'll proba-bly save me time later on."

"Thanks, guys. That was very helpful." David sat back down in his seat. "You see, Jack, people don't like me."

"They might like you slightly better if you didn't ask them stupid questions on the school bus."

"They might, Jack. They might, but even them liking me slightly better isn't going to make me popular. Every loser needs a more popular friend."

Jack shook his head. "I'm not that popular."

"Ask Alex and James if they like you."

Jack laughed. "No!"

"And it's precisely because you don't do stupid things like that, that you're so popular!"

Jack sighed.

"And now you've got another loser kid as a friend."

"Trudy isn't a loser," snapped Jack.

James from the seat behind poked his head through the gap in the seats. "Moody Trudy? She is too a loser! She doesn't have any friends."

Jack put his hand on James's forehead and pushed him back into his own seat. "Yes, thank you for your contribu-tion, James. You aren't helping."

"But he's right," agreed David. "Jack, I know you like Trudy. That's fine, but she's clearly a loser. You like losers."

"How do you figure that one out?"

"Who's your best friend?"

"Well, you are."

"Exactly! And I'm a loser! Proof positive!"

Jack realized it was hard to argue with David on this one. He decided to take a different approach. "So what? I like Trudy and I'm going to be friends with her. But I'll still be friends with you."

Now it was David's turn to laugh. "Be friends with me and Trudy? Two losers? Jack, you're popular, but you aren't popular enough to have two loser friends!"

Although Jack was slightly hurt by this, he decided to ignore the insult. "David, we will always be friends. And you know what—maybe I'm not popular enough to have two loser friends."

David shook his head sadly.

"But that's okay, because if I'm not popular enough to have two loser friends, then by definition I'll become a loser too. And we can be three losers together."

David's eyes widened for a second as he looked at Jack. "Jack . . . Jack, that's the nicest thing anyone has ever said to me."

Jack and David smiled at each other for a minute. They both realized what good friends they actually were. It would have been a beautiful moment if it hadn't been spoiled by James pushing his head between the seats and pointing out that maybe that wouldn't have been the nicest thing that anyone had ever said to David if he'd been a bit more popular.

Jack gestured at James. "You. You really aren't helping."

Jack's lecture on how unhelpful James was being was cut short by a series of gasps from around them. All the kids had rushed over to the windows on one side of the bus.

"What's going on?" Jack and David pushed their way through the crowd and squashed their faces against the windows. "I really hope it isn't another bear."

A series of enormous trucks were outside the school unloading mobile classrooms. There were six classrooms in all. They looked like oversized mushroom-cream-colored house bricks, and one by one they were being lifted by a crane and put into the back playground. The trucks had the words *Chapeau Noir Enterprises* plastered over the sides in green lettering.

"Now Mr. Teach is giving us mobile classrooms? Did we really need any more classrooms?" asked Jack, but no one was listening to him. Mostly the children were praying that the crane would drop one of the mobile classrooms on the teacher's parking lot.

Jack had barely exited the school bus when Trudy caught him by the arm. "I need to speak to you."

Jack felt nervous. Given the conversation that he'd just had with David he was worried that Trudy's sudden appearance might make him jealous.

However, as usual, David was being mercurial and unreliable. "Trudy!" David smiled so broadly at her, Jack thought his face was in danger of cracking open. "We're all going to be losers together!" Then, incredibly, he leaned forward and hugged Trudy. "I expect you guys have some Ministry business to chat about. I'll catch up with you at roll call, Jack!"

Trudy looked stunned and took several seconds before she could express what she was thinking. "I don't think anyone has ever hugged me who wasn't a member of my family."

Jack chuckled. "You really are a loser!"

Trudy punched Jack hard in the shoulder. Jack had made the critical error of forgetting that Trudy was a loser with a pretty mean right hook. "Why am I a loser?" Trudy asked.

"I'm not sure I could explain it even if I wanted to," lamented Jack. "I think the outcome of it was that David is happy we're friends as long as we're all losers together."

"I don't understand."

"It's 'David thinking,'" said Jack. "No one really understands it except David. Forget about it. You wanted to speak to me?"

"I did! It's about kids going missing. You were right. There's something very sinister going on."

MINISTRY OF S.U.IT.S HANDBOOK

POPULARITY
THE IMPORTANCE OF BEING TRUE TO YOURSELF

The world is full of movies, books, and songs that will tell you that it isn't important to be liked or popular. It is more important to be true to yourself and to be an individual.

This, of course, is simply not true. The reason for the books, movies, and songs saying otherwise, is that all writers are losers. Popular kids don't have time to write novels or films. They're out going to parties, spending time with their friends, and going on dates.

The people who write books and other things are generally sad loners who spend hours sitting in front of a computer screen wearing a *Star Wars* dressing gown, surrounded by piles of books.[44] Their best friends are generally fictional ones from books they have read. And that really is stretching the definition of "friend." After all, the chances of getting a tweet from Bertie Wooster inviting you out to a party on a Friday night are fairly minimal.[45]

[44] This would be less tragic if I weren't currently sitting in front of a computer, surrounded by piles of books, and wearing a *Star Wars* dressing gown.

[45] And even if I did get that tweet I wouldn't be able to go. I don't have anything to wear, and I'm pretty sure that a Sith dressing gown doesn't count as "black tie."

25

THE MISSING KIDS

"I think you're right about the box of spares," said Trudy.

When Jack had first mentioned the idea that the spare kit might be a sign that kids were going missing, he had believed it. However, when someone else said it, it sounded . . . well . . . kind of stupid.

"It doesn't sound very likely," he found himself saying.

"And that's how we know that it's probably true!"

"What?"

"Think about it—do you believe in gravity?"

Jack looked down and was reassured to see his feet were still sticking to the ground. "Well, yeah. I mean the whole gravity thing seems to be still working fairly effectively to me."[46]

---

[46] Jack was annoyed to have to admit that gravity was still working effectively. He was still rather irritated about how mean gravity could

"But think about gravity! The idea that the Earth is round but you won't fall off if you're on the bottom—then why doesn't your foot stick to a ball when you kick it? Or what about the sun! It's a big ball of gas that's on fire. But when you set fire to gas it just explodes! So why hasn't the sun exploded? I mean, do any of those things sound likely to you? *So—things that don't sound likely are normally true.*"

When Jack thought about it, a lot of things he took as facts seemed to be peculiar. "Okay, so tell me why you're convinced about the kids going missing?"

Trudy set down her backpack and took several packages of paper out of it. "I did some research last night." She handed Jack sheet after sheet, pointing out figures to him. "I went on the Internet and found stories about kids that have gone missing in the last thirty years."

"And? Was there a pattern?"

"Well, yes. I was mostly working from online newspaper reports about kids going missing. The stories rarely mentioned what the kids' gym kits were like. But I did find these photos."

Trudy showed Jack a series of black-and-white photos of kids who had gone missing decades ago. In a few of them the children were outside playing in sports clothes. Jack grimaced at the P.E. kits they were wearing. "That is the worst P.E. kit I have ever seen."

"I know, that's what makes me think you're right. These kids were picked because they had bad gym kits. Because they were oddballs in school who would be less likely to be missed."

---

be after what it had done to him in chapter twenty-three.

"And are there any other common links?"

"All the schools where children went missing were sponsored by Chapeau Noir Enterprises."

"So Mr. Teach is . . . ?"

"We don't know what Mr. Teach is or what he's doing, but he's definitely involved somehow. There's something sinister about his company Chapeau Noir."

"And I bet there's something fishy about the mobile classrooms."

"In what way?"

"Have you ever noticed how there are always empty seats in class?"

"So?"

"So clearly we don't need any more classrooms."

"What are you suggesting?"

"I think we need to go and look at the mobile classrooms."

Before they were halfway to the back playground the bell rang, signaling that it was time to go to class.

Jack realized he'd missed roll call. "Trudy . . . we need to get to class."

"Jack, someone's been kidnapping kids. What's more important?"

Jack knew that Trudy was right, but he still muttered underneath his breath that while saving lives was generally a good idea, he didn't see why he had to end up in detention because of it. His muttering cost him another punch on the shoulder.

The corridors were full of pupils going to their first class of the day. Jack noticed David heading in the opposite direction.

David was going to geography—which was where Jack should have been. Trudy was still pulling Jack by the hand and he barely had time to yell, "Missing class—saving lives—cover for me!" before Trudy had dragged him out the door into the back playground. Jack looked over his shoulder at David before the door shut. David was smiling and gave Jack a thumbs-up.

<hr />

"This is very strange." Outside the school Jack and Trudy were surprised to find how eerily quiet the back playground was. No pupils, no teachers, not even a caretaker in sight. Whatever the mobile classrooms were being used for, it wasn't lessons.

"So, what do we do?" asked Trudy.

"I don't know," said Jack. "You've been doing all the thinking up until now. I thought I was just here to be the muscle."

Trudy bunched her fist. Even before she struck, Jack winced slightly. "Do you mind hitting me on the left shoulder this time? I'd like to give the bruises on the right one some time to heal."

Trudy laughed and didn't hit him. Jack wasn't sure exactly what he'd done, but if he could figure it out, it might well save him a considerable amount of pain in the future.

The mobiles were large, rectangular, mushroom-colored boxes. Their windows were covered on the inside with brown paper.

Trudy walked around to the other side of the mobile, circling it in case one side was more suspicious than the other. "Didn't find anything," she said.

"If there's something in there that we're not meant to see,

I want to see it." Jack always felt that way about things. It was one of the reasons his parents had such strong filters and access controls on their Internet.

"Let's try the door," agreed Trudy.

The door was a large, dark brown slab of wood with a small window set in its center. As with the other windows, this was covered with brown paper, preventing Jack from looking inside. Trudy turned the handle and shoved the door with her shoulder. It didn't move an inch.

"Stand back," said Jack. "I've got this." Jack decided to use The Speed. He focused his mind on the training session with the Misery and how unhappy he had been. Then, just to make himself slightly sadder, he thought about all the times at Christmas when he had been given jigsaws, socks, and pants instead of proper presents. When his mind was sufficiently focused on unhappiness he threw a hundred punches into the door in a matter of seconds.

As a result of this, Jack hurt his hands a hundred times in a matter of seconds. After he had finished, the door looked both distinctly unimpressed and completely unharmed. His flurry of punches hadn't even dented the surface.

Jack massaged his hands. "How come that didn't work?"

"The Speed makes you faster. It doesn't make you any stronger."

"Right," said Jack. "Important lesson there. Could have done with being told it about five minutes ago, but important to learn nonetheless. I don't suppose the Ministry has supplied you with a set of skeleton keys?"

Trudy shook her head. "You don't get any standard

equipment. If you want something, you have to go and requisition it from the quartermaster. And apparently that isn't a good idea."[47]

"Why not?"

"Not sure, just what Grey told me one time I asked for equipment. Anyway, I think I can probably make a skeleton key."

Initially Jack was impressed that Trudy was such a skilled locksmith. However, it soon became apparent that Trudy's definition of what constituted a skeleton key was profoundly different from Jack's. She looked around the playground until she found half a brick and then used it to smash the small window in the door. Trudy carefully reached through the hole in the glass and turned the lock from the inside.

It turned out that the mobile wasn't a classroom at all—instead it was a storeroom, filled with digging supplies—spades, shovels, and picks. There were also medical supplies—crutches, surgical scalpels, bone saws, and bandages, among other things.

"This isn't school equipment, is it?" Jack asked.

---

[47] Jack would find out himself why it was a bad idea to go to the quartermaster for equipment. But not until chapter thirty-eight. I wouldn't hold your breath until you get there if I were you. Unless you are either a phenomenally fast reader, or alternatively able to hold your breath for a very, very long time because you are a whale or some other kind of aquatic mammal. If you are a whale and are reading this, how are you keeping the pages dry? I assume you can achieve it by laminating each page individually. However, that seems very labor-intensive.

"No, it looks more like...I don't know...Is the school going to landscape the playing fields? Maybe plant some flowers?"

"But, then, what would the crutches be for?" Jack wondered.

"Why would anyone want to dig at a school?" asked Trudy.

"And kidnap children?"

"And why did Chapeau Noir give us school uniforms, carpets, and a wind turbine?"

Jack and Trudy stood still for a while and felt confused.

MINISTRY OF S.U.IT.S HANDBOOK

AQUATIC MAMMALS
READING HABITS

Generally speaking, aquatic mammals, because they live in the sea, don't get much reading done. And because they don't read a lot, they generally aren't that smart. Which is why there has never been a world leader who was a whale. You may have heard that dolphins are the smartest of all aquatic mammals, and this is true. The reason is simple and you will be aware of it if you have ever visited a sea park. Dolphins can perform the most amazing jumps out of the water. Therefore, while they are out of the water they can get little bits and pieces of reading done (without the need for enormous amounts of arduous lamination). Whales can't jump as high out of the water and therefore have less time to read.

Because dolphins get their reading done during shortish jumps out of the water, they tend to prefer books with short chapters. Which is why *The Da Vinci Code* topped the "Undersea Mammals Fiction Chart" on Amazon for three years. Dolphins also love conspiracy theories.

Because of their water-based lives, dolphins rarely if ever use a Kindle. Because (a) electronic devices are dangerous in their environment *and* (b) salt water invalidates the warranty.

26

SUSPICIOUSLY UNSUSPICIOUS

It wasn't even lunchtime, but Jack and Trudy decided to go to the Ministry to talk to Grey. Jack persuaded Trudy to get the bus to the museum rather than calling for one of the unpleasant-smelling Ministry cars.

Jack paid their fares and Trudy got them seats right at the back of the bus. She was fidgeting when Jack sat down next to her.

"What's wrong with you?"

"Can't you feel it? Someone's watching us."

Jack panicked just a little. "A teacher? Are we going to get caught for playing truant?"

"It's not that . . ."

"Just to clarify something, Trudy, if we do get caught, you do realize that I'm not going to be like one of those tight-lipped gangsters in the movies. You know, the ones who they question for hours and they never break. The minute they start asking me whose idea it was to skip school I'm going to say that it was all down to you, that you made me do it, and I might also tell them that you are plotting to take over the world."

Trudy gave Jack a withering stare. "I sort of assumed that's what you'd do."

"So, is it a teacher?"[48]

"I'm . . . just not sure. But it's, like . . ."

And then Jack felt it. It was like a tiny insect creeping along the back of his spine. Jack looked around the bus. "I feel it now too. What do we do?"

"We need to keep an eye out for someone acting suspicious," said Trudy.

Jack shook his head. "No, that's the exact opposite of what we need to do."

Trudy looked at Jack as if he was crazy. When people look at you as if you are crazy, most of the time it is an indication

---

[48] If a teacher had been watching them, they would have had no idea that it was happening. Teachers spend years in college learning to watch people without their realizing it.

Some people believe that teachers learn about the subject they teach while at college. However, if teachers really knew about their subject, schools wouldn't need textbooks. Textbooks are only necessary when someone doesn't know what they're talking about. With a textbook a teacher just needs to ensure that they have *read one chapter ahead* of the kids they are teaching.

If you wish to test this, read an entire textbook on your first day of class and watch how nervous it makes your teacher when you tell them.

that you have said one of the sanest things you will have ever said in your life. This time was no exception to that rule.

Jack explained his thinking. "Someone has been sent to follow us. Or at least that's what we think. And they haven't said hello, have they?"

"Well, of course they haven't. They don't want us to realize we're being followed."

"Precisely!" said Jack. "They don't want us to know that they're following us. And because of that they won't act or look suspicious. In fact, they'll go out of their way to look deliberately unsuspicious . . . if that's a word."[49]

Although Trudy was clearly disappointed that Jack was right, she couldn't fault his logic. Whoever was watching them wouldn't want to be noticed and so would behave, act, and dress in as unsuspicious a manner as possible.

They looked around the bus. There was a man with a Mohawk wearing a long leather trench coat who seemed to be hiding something underneath it. It could have been a gun or a knife or something even more sinister. He was acting very suspicious indeed. So they knew it couldn't be him.

Farther along the bus there was an older man who was wearing a tracksuit and a hooded top. The hood covered his eyes and so you couldn't be sure who he really was. Again, this was suspicious and so Jack and Trudy ruled him out of their consideration.

---

[49] It is. It sounds like it shouldn't be, but it is.

There was a young mother who was sitting with a pram. Inside the pram was a smiling baby. The mother was leaning over him and dangling keys in front of his face. The baby was trying to reach for them, and both mother and baby were making goo-goo gah-gah noises at each other.

Trudy nudged Jack. "What about them?"

Jack considered for a moment: They certainly looked less suspicious than the others, but he felt that they were suspicious enough. "I don't think so; they're still slightly suspicious."

"In what way?"

"Well, the baby keeps trying to grab the car keys. Why would a baby want car keys? It's clearly too young to drive and it's certainly too small for its feet to reach the pedals. Also, that goo-goo stuff always worries me. It could be a code. I mean, parents are meant to teach their children to speak. So why would they say goo-goo gah-gah? That isn't going to help them learn to say anything worthwhile."

The elimination of the baby and the woman left only one other person on the bus.

At the front of the bus sat a sweet, little old woman. She had short, silver-gray hair and wore a pair of glasses that were fastened around her neck by a long gold chain. Beside her was a tartan shopping bag filled with Mr Kipling Battenberg cakes and Angel Slices.

If you had asked an artist to draw you a picture of a typical innocent-looking grandmother, they would have drawn the woman with the tartan bag.

"Bingo," said Jack.

"That's probably where she's headed to, all right," agreed Trudy.

"No—I mean *bingo* in the sense of that's the person who's following us. I mean . . ." Jack tailed off as he realized that Trudy knew exactly what he meant and was just making fun of him.

"Anyway, she's definitely the least-suspicious-looking person on the bus, so she's almost certainly the person who is following us."

"So . . . what next?"

"Well, our stop is coming up. We get off and see if she follows us."

Jack and Trudy walked down the aisle of the bus nervously. The old lady didn't turn or acknowledge them in any way.

They jumped off the bus and headed toward the museum. It was only a hundred yards away. They turned right at the metal railings that stood outside the park in which the museum was located.

"Do we turn around and check yet?" asked Jack.

"Let's wait until we're a little closer to the museum," said Trudy. They walked until they got onto the first of the stone steps that led up to the museum's front door.

"I think we turn and look now."

The old woman was standing there, watching them. Initially she had a smile on her face that reminded Jack of Christmas holidays—it was sweet, pleasant, and it made you feel warm inside. It was a smile that felt like a hug from a six-foot bunny rabbit.[50] But then her face changed as she realized her cover had been blown. There was no need to look unsuspicious anymore. Her face stopped looking like that of a kindly and sweet granny and started to look like that of a sinister and evil granny. The kind of granny who would bake you an apple pie filled with razor blades for Halloween and give you a real egg for Easter.

Jack and Trudy stood transfixed for a moment.

"She's definitely following us," Jack whispered to Trudy.

"I know," Trudy whispered back.

"And she knows we know."

"I know she knows we know."

"So what do we do?"

Trudy paused. "I don't know."

"Let's go inside the museum. We'll be safe in there … probably."

"I don't like the sound of *probably*," said Trudy. "She's an old woman. I could use The Speed to beat her up."

"You want to beat up an old woman?"

"She's clearly evil."

"Might be hard to prove that if the police turned up."

---

[50] Actually, this may not be a good metaphor. A hug from a six-foot bunny rabbit would most likely be terrifying. Apart from anything else you'd be asking yourself questions like "What evil scientist has made a six-foot bunny rabbit? And while the scientist was making it larger did he change its dietary preferences from raw carrots to raw human flesh?" Please feel free to scribble out this metaphor and write in a more appropriate one of your own devising.

Trudy acknowledged Jack's point. They both turned and started walking up the steps toward the museum. Jack could feel the old woman's eyes burning into their backs. It felt like at any moment she would attack and beat them to death with her Battenberg-cake-filled tartan bag.

It was a relief when they walked through the door and into the large entrance hall. "We're safe!"

They turned around to see that the old woman had followed them inside.

"So what do we do now?" asked Jack.

Without a better plan, Jack and Trudy walked through the museum. They went neither to the elevator nor to Takabuti's mummy case as they didn't want to lead the old woman inside the Ministry itself. They climbed a central flight of stairs, went through the Spanish Armada exhibition, passed an exhibition on fossils, and finally found themselves in a long art gallery.

A metallic voice came over the loudspeaker. "*The Museum will be closing in fifteen minutes. Could all visitors please make their way to the front exit. Thank you.*" The other visitors in the art gallery made their way to the door at the far end. Trudy and Jack turned around to see the old woman walk into the gallery.

She was practically snarling at them now.

Jack spoke to Trudy out of the side of his mouth, hoping that the old woman couldn't hear. "Is this going to be one of those moments when the old lady turns out to be some kind of horrific monster with enormous teeth and claws?"

"Possibly."

"Oh, good."

All three stood looking at one another.

The old woman broke the silence first. "Now that we're alone I don't suppose there's any point in pretending anymore."

"You were following us."

"Yes."

"Why?"

"I work for Chapeau Noir. All I was supposed to do was follow you, keep an eye on you. But you figured out that I was following you. And if you figured that out, my orders are to eliminate you."

"Oh, good," said Jack. "So you're going to kill us because I figured out you weren't acting suspiciously. This is exactly what my mother meant when she said that I was too smart for my own good."

Trudy turned to Jack. "Did your mother really say that to you?"

"No, but it would have been appropriate if she had. Don't you think?"

"Well, not . . ."

"Shut up!" yelled the old woman, becoming impatient. "Get ready to die."

"Okay," said Jack. "If you want me to get ready to die, I'm going to need to make a will. So I'll probably need a lawyer. And obviously an undertaker for the funeral and everything." Jack found it hard to take threats from a little old lady seriously.

"Is this really the time for jokes, Jack?" asked Trudy.

"Yes!" laughed Jack. "She's an old woman—what's she going to do, throw a Battenberg cake at us?"

The old woman set her tartan shopping bag on the ground and reached into it. Jack felt less confident than he had. Maybe there were more than Battenberg cakes in the bag. Maybe she had a knife, or even worse, a gun. Or maybe Battenberg cakes were heavier and more aerodynamic than he thought. Were Battenburg cakes explosive under the right circumstances?

BEING FOLLOWED
PEOPLE LOOKING SUSPICIOUS

People who are up to no good will go out of their way to look innocent.

Often the police investigating a crime will ask, "Have you seen anything suspicious going on?" Which is clearly the wrong question. Thieves, not wanting to get caught, do everything in their power to avoid attention. As a result they act in a very unsuspicious manner.

Detectives in whodunit novels often claim they are suspicious of an individual and therefore they investigate them further. What they should really say is, "That bloke Simon is acting in a very suspicious manner; therefore I know he can't be the murderer."

If the detectives on television were smart enough to show up on the scene of a crime and arrest the person who seemed to be acting in the most unsuspicious way, there would never be the need for *Midsomer Murders* or *Columbo* to last a full hour.

BATTENBERG CAKES
POTENTIAL LETHALITY

Theoretically it is possible to kill someone by throwing a Battenberg cake at them. But only if they have a nut allergy. Because the yellow slices in the cake have almond in them. But the individual you are trying to kill has to be very, very, very, very allergic to nuts indeed. And you'd have to throw the cake at them, very, very, very hard. I'm not saying that it's impossible to do, just very unlikely. To put this in context, assassins and secret agents often carry guns, knives, blowpipes, throwing stars, and Tasers, but they rarely carry any Mr Kipling products. Not even the Angel Slices. And they are delicious.

27

JUST WHISTLE

The old woman's wrinkled hand slowly emerged from her tartan shopping bag holding a silver whistle. She put it to her lips and blew as hard as she could.

Nothing happened. The gallery was silent.

Trudy looked around. Jack just laughed. "That's it? That's how you're going to kill us? With a whistle that doesn't even work?"

Jack noticed that Trudy was scanning the room around them. If Trudy was worried, something had to be wrong. "What is it?"

"Jack, some creatures hear at a higher pitch than us. Think about it: It could have been a dog whistle... or worse."

"Oh."

At that moment there was a brief scrabbling and the

doors to the gallery burst open. Galloping through them were two creatures that looked as if they were half-man, half-dog. They had hairy legs and arms and ran on all fours with their hands touching the ground and propelling them through the air. Their eyes looked human but their noses and mouths were swollen and puggish.

"Not good," said Jack. And although Jack's analysis of the situation was reasonable, it was not entirely accurate, as not only was it not good . . . it was about to get worse.

The man-dogs were the first creatures to enter the building, but they were followed by others. Another three creatures entered that were a hideous mishmash of human and bluebottle flies. They walked in a crouched fashion and had two pairs of buzzing, silvery wings affixed to their backs. It didn't seem as if they could fly, but as they walked they occasionally took a gigantic hop powered by two or three buzzing flaps from their wings. Instead of hands their arms finished in two long, black, serrated pincers. Their eyes were a honeycomb pattern of silver mirrors and below that there was a small black tube, which must have served them for both a mouth and a nose.

The last creature into the gallery was possibly the most disturbing of all. Although it looked the most humanoid, it had been crossed with a lizard or a snake. Walking upright with two arms and two legs, its body was covered in dark green scales that seemed to ooze some kind of oily black fluid, but that wasn't what made it look so disturbing. It was the eyes, the human eyes in the flat, featureless face. Its head was smooth with no ears or nose. Instead of a nose it had two small black nostrils and its mouth was a horizontal, lipless slash.

Jack gulped. He literally gulped. He'd read about people gulping when afraid but it had never actually happened to him. *So that gulping-when-terrified thing does actually happen, then,* he thought. That's an interesting fact to find out. Although its level of interestingness[51] didn't really outweigh the fact that in order to learn this he had to be put in a horrific and life-threatening situation.

The six man-beasts lined up beside the old woman. "You see, I really am nothing more than an old woman. But I am an old woman who works for Chapeau Noir Enterprises. And Mr. Teach has a lot of people and . . . creatures who work for him. You'd be surprised how many strange creatures you can get an evil scientist[52] to make for you when you have a few chests full of gold to throw at him."

Jack turned to Trudy. "Have you ever come across this situation before?"

"Jack, I've only been a Ministry agent for a few months longer than you have."

"Right, so you haven't come up against weird man-

---

[51] Like *unsuspicious*, *interestingness* sounds as if it shouldn't be a real word either. But it is. Believe me. The way they sound, I imagine that the two words are probably good friends. They probably collect stamps and play MMORPGs together.

[52] Jack quietly wished that Mr. Teach had employed one of the mad scientists who tried to invent bananas rather than one of the evil ones. (See chapter fourteen.)

creatures that want to kill you. Nice to know that this is a first for both of us. So what do we do?"

"Fight."

Secretly Jack had been hoping that Trudy would say "run away." But if she was ready to fight, he wasn't going to leave her by herself. "Succinct and to the point, Trudy. I like it. I suppose now is the time to use The Speed."

Trudy nodded. "Yeah, if you don't use it now, you'll probably never get the opportunity to use it again."

"Thanks for the inspiration."

Trudy bunched her fists and moved toward the man-beasts. The two man-dogs leapt toward her. Trudy blurred into action, skidding feet-first under the man-dogs. She lashed out a hand, grabbed one by the tail, and swung it into the other. They smashed together and fell crumpled to the ground. Trudy jumped up and ran toward the snake creature.

The bluebottles started moving toward Trudy. Jack had to stop them. He felt a brief flash of guilt for not having gotten involved more quickly. What would have happened if Trudy had gotten hurt or even killed? The thought made him feel like a concrete block had been dropped through the bottom of his stomach. It was exactly the kind of negative emotion he needed for The Speed to kick in.

Jack ran over and stood between Trudy and the bluebottles. He felt as though he should say something clever and intimidating like an action hero in the movies.

"I am going to give you such a slap."

It wasn't a great line. Jack thought that action heroes

probably prepared lines beforehand for this kind of situation. He decided to work on some later, assuming he wasn't dead, of course.

A bluebottle whipped out a black pincer at him, and he dodged, bending backward. The second bluebottle dived at his legs. Using The Speed, Jack jumped and put a foot square on the bluebottle's back. He launched himself into the air and kicked the third bluebottle in the face. The third bluebottle went tumbling to the ground as Jack landed awkwardly beside it. The Speed made him faster, but not any more agile.

The second bluebottle tried to grab Jack with its pincers. Jack dodged under the pincer, grabbed the creature's wrist, and spun it in a circle. He put a foot against the wall and kicked himself into an attempted backward somersault. He had planned to land elegantly on his feet, but underestimated the distance and instead smashed awkwardly down on top of a bluebottle, causing it to stumble sideways.

Jack scrambled to his feet and glanced over to see how Trudy was doing. The man-dogs and snake-creature kept trying to grab her, but every time they looked as though they would get ahold of her she cracked two or three punches into their bodies before dodging out of the way.

"Everything going well?" he called over to her.

"Brilliant! How about you?"

"Better than average, I'd say."

Two of the bluebottles were moving toward Jack. He held up his fists and pretended to be brave. In reality he was savoring the momentary respite. Unfortunately, the two bluebottles weren't really trying to attack Jack. They were just distracting him from what the third bluebottle was doing. Jack felt a slamming impact in the center of his back. The bluebottle had run at him at full speed and then leapt, using its wings for momentum. The impact carried Jack into the air for ten feet, and the bluebottle who had hit him was along for the ride, clinging and scratching his body.

For a few seconds Jack felt as if he would be flying through the air forever. Feeling like flying wasn't entirely unpleasant and was certainly a lot better than the feeling that replaced it—the feeling of crashing into the double doors.

Jack felt like he had broken a few bones and the door was partly off its hinges. The bluebottle leapt up, grabbed a vase from a nearby plinth, and threw it at Jack's head. It exploded on the wall, showering Jack with pottery fragments.

Jack scrambled to his feet and ran out the doorway. He was now standing on a balcony overlooking the entrance hall. There was a sheer drop of thirty feet to the ground.

The bluebottle dived at Jack, trying to knock him over the balcony. Just as the bluebottle was about to hit him, Jack used The Speed and grabbed both of the bluebottle's wrists. Jack rolled onto his back, pulling the bluebottle's hands with him. A final kick propelled the creature over the balcony.

The museum had been hosting a dinosaur exhibition recently, and the bluebottle crashed into a large fiberglass model pterodactyl hanging from the ceiling. The bluebottle got caught in the metal wires that attached the model to the ceiling. The more the bluebottle struggled, the more it became entangled. Suddenly its thrashing caused the wires to snap. The ruined model, the bluebottle, and some plaster from the ceiling dropped to the floor and smashed to smithereens. Jack looked over the balcony. The bluebottle twitched a few times and then lay still. "That's one down."

Jack ran back through the doorway back into the gallery. Trudy was lying on the floor unconscious and the old lady was fastening her wrists with plastic ties. One of the man-dogs was slumped against the wall and the other lay spread-eagled and motionless in the middle of the floor. Trudy must have knocked them out before she was captured.

Whatever confidence Jack had felt after beating the bluebottle left his body. If Trudy hadn't been able to handle the remaining creatures, how would he? She was ten times more skilled and experienced than he was.

"Come back for more?" the old lady sneered at him.

Jack couldn't leave Trudy, but at the same time it wouldn't do her any good if he got himself caught.

Then he had an idea. The museum had lots of old stuff in it, including medieval weaponry. Maybe he couldn't defeat these creatures with his bare hands. But if he could find a sword or an ax . . . With that kind of weapon and The Speed he would be unstoppable.

"Back in a minute," said Jack as he ran back out the double doors.

SNAKES
Hearing Difficulties

Snakes don't have ears and therefore can't hear. They can sense vibrations, but that isn't really the same thing. Some scientists claim that it is, but it's about as similar as sitting on a washing machine during the spin cycle would be to listening to a world-class philharmonic orchestra.

People often claim that rattlesnakes use their rattle to scare people off. However, the fact that snakes can't hear clearly means that they have no idea that they're even doing it.

This was proven by a Ministry scientist years ago, who managed to use a thought-transference device to speak to a rattlesnake. Although the snake could not actually use words, computer software interpreted its thoughts so that they could be relayed through a computer screen:

Scientist: SO WHEN YOU RATTLE YOUR TAIL, YOU'RE TRYING TO SCARE PEOPLE OFF?

Snake: WHAT?

Scientist: IF YOU SEE A HUMAN OR SOMETHING, YOU GET AGGRESSIVE AND RATTLE YOUR TAIL TO THREATEN THEM.

Snake: MY TAIL RATTLES? I NEVER KNEW THAT. THAT'S A BIT ODD. I WONDER WHY IT DOES THAT?

Scientist: BUT THEN WHY DO YOU SHAKE IT WHEN A HUMAN FINDS YOU?

Snake: I DON'T DO IT DELIBERATELY. I'M JUST SCARED OF HUMANS. SO WHEN I SEE ONE I START TO SHIVER AND TREMBLE. THAT'S PROBABLY WHAT CAUSES THE RATTLING SOUND. IT'S ALL BEEN A BIT OF A MISUNDERSTANDING.

Scientist: YES. JUST OUT OF INTEREST, WHY ARE YOU SO SCARED OF HUMANS?

Snake: BECAUSE THEY KILLED ALL THE REST OF MY FAMILY AND TURNED THEM INTO SHOES AND HANDBAGS.

Scientist: ACTUALLY, NOW THAT YOU SAY THAT, I COULD DO WITH A NEW PAIR OF LOAFERS.

The scientist who invented the system for interpreting animals' thoughts as words was clearly a genius. Although it is interesting to note that although he had an IQ of over 200, he still hadn't figured out how to switch off the caps lock function on his keyboard.

Unfortunately the technology to speak to animals no longer exists. This is made worse by the fact that the scientist who created it is no longer around to reinvent it. Shortly after finishing the above conversation he died of sixteen snakebites to the face.

28

RUN!

Jack sprinted out onto the balcony, which led to more doors and more corridors. He was hoping to find the historical weapons section. He wasn't too worried about the creatures following him. They were quick, but not quick enough to catch him as long as he was using The Speed.

Running through the first door he reached, Jack found himself standing in a room that was full of rocks, fossils, and stones. It was enormously disappointing. Apart from anything else he thought that rocks and stones were stupid things to have in a museum. The cards underneath the pieces of stone claimed they were very old stone. But of course they were! All stone was very old, as old as the earth itself. It made sense—after all, no one was making new rocks or stones.[53] So, therefore, they were all the same age as the Earth was when it was made.

Jack thought back to Monday, when he had been in the museum. He knew that while wandering around he had seen a collection of swords and daggers. But where had they been? The problem with museums was that they were incredibly confusing places. Normally when you were thinking of directions there were street names and buildings to help you. It was much harder orienting yourself when you were surrounded by dozens of strange and exotic objects from a variety of time periods.

He knew that to get to the weapons he had to first go past the silver shrine of St. Patrick's hand—but then did he turn right or left at the Fairy Fountain?

Jack wished he'd paid more attention during previous school visits to the museum instead of spending almost all his time in the museum store trying to figure out which plastic dinosaur he would buy.[54] If only he'd paid more

---

[53] People who study stones are called geologists. It's strange that they can't think of anything better to do with their time. Stones never move or do anything interesting. Being a geologist must be even more boring than being a urologist ursinologist.

[54] Jack is the only person ever to wish this. The purchase of a plastic dinosaur is an important transaction and significant lifestyle choice. It is essential to take your time and think about what kind of plastic dinosaur would make you happiest. There's a natural instinct that suggests you just go straight for the *Tyrannosaurus rex*. But the beauty and

attention he would have known where the weapons were kept in the museum.

Jack ran onward to a door marked "Living World." But, yet again, he found no weapons. Just stuffed animals.

For a minute he considered the damage he could do to the snake-creature if he hit it with a stuffed weasel. He thought that although it would be funny, it was unlikely to knock the snake unconscious.

Jack looked around for the next door and his heart sank when he realized that this room was a dead end. He turned toward the door he had come in, but it was too late. The creatures had just entered.

Jack raised his fists and took up a fighting stance. The creatures fanned out from the door. They were taking no chances this time. One bluebottle approached him from the right, one from the left, and the snake-creature came straight ahead.

Jack blurred into action, his foot connecting with the snake-creature's groin, and at the same time he smacked one of the bluebottles with a fist.

The remaining bluebottle cracked a pincer into his face, making him stumble backward and fall. The blow had caught him just above the eye and Jack could feel it stinging. Blood streamed down his face, blurring his vision.

The three creatures crowded around him. One kicked his

---

understated grace of a *Dyoplosaurus* has a lot to recommend it. In terms of color, it's hard to go wrong with purple.

leg and Jack twisted in pain. He scrabbled backward on his hands and feet until he bumped into something. He turned his head to see that his escape was blocked by an enormous stuffed polar bear. The bluebottles and the snake-creature advanced on Jack. They stretched out their arms, ready to tear him apart.

Jack was without hope. But seconds before the creatures laid their claws on him, he had an idea. Potentially the best idea he had ever had.

FOSSILS
EFFECT ON LASAGNA

Fossils are created when many layers of rocks are placed over objects. If enough layers of rock press down on an object, it will eventually turn into a fossil fuel.

Applying this geological knowledge to the realm of culinary arts, this explains why you should never make a lasagna with more than six layers of pasta. If you do, there is a grave risk that the bottom layer of beef will spontaneously transmute into coal.

29

KILLING WITH HIS BEAR HANDS

Jack remembered that the polar bear behind him wasn't stuffed at all. All the animals in the museum were actually live animals who had been told they were playing musical statues. That was why there was no background music in museums.

He looked above him and saw the massive polar bear. Then he looked in front of him and saw three horrible, hybrid creatures closing in on him. The snake-creature hissed and a forked tongue flicked out of its mouth.

Jack had one chance, but it involved him doing something he really didn't like doing: singing in public.

Jack actually had quite a nice voice, but that was what made it worse. At every opportunity his mother would tell people what a great singer Jack was. She would then proceed to nag, poke, and prod him until he agreed to sing a few verses for whoever happened to be in the vicinity. It was excruciatingly embarrassing, and Jack had sworn to himself that if he ever found he had any other talents, he would carefully conceal them from his mother in case she started making him juggle or stilt-walk every time they went to the supermarket.

Jack started singing. He chose one of the songs that his father used to play at Christmas. He started patting the floor to get a rhythm going for himself.

"I ain't got nobody..."

The creatures stopped. They were curious as to why Jack would start singing. Didn't he realize how much danger he was in?

Of course Jack realized exactly how much danger he was in—that's why he was singing. *"And nobody cares for me..."*

At that moment Jack felt a large globule of drool fall onto the top of his head. Because the polar bear could hear music, it stopped playing musical statues and started moving. It had been standing still all day, so it reared up to stretch its back muscles. Jack rolled backward through the bear's legs and curled himself up behind it. There was now a nine-hundred-pound polar bear between him and the three creatures. The obstacle of the bear made Jack feel safe. It was like when he had been younger and he had worried there had been monsters in his bedroom. He had felt safer by pulling the covers over his head. For some reason he had always felt that even if there had been a werewolf attacking him, it would have never managed to claw its way through a warm, snuggly duvet.[55]

A polar bear makes a very effective duvet. Potentially it would have a tog rating of over fifteen.

Jack was still singing, hoping he could remember all the words. The bear had stopped stretching and was looking around the room. The three hybrid creatures stood in front of it. Although the creatures were grotesque and violent, they weren't desperately bright. They were still going to try and attack Jack. That meant they would have to attack the polar bear first. Given that the bear was nearly ten feet tall when standing on its back legs Jack really didn't fancy their chances.

One of the bluebottles advanced first, and it was met with the swipe of an enormous, shaggy paw. The blow contacted the side of the creature's head, but had an effect on its entire body. The bluebottle lifted off the ground, flew sideways through the air, and crashed into a wall where it crumpled and fell to the ground.

Jack watched with satisfaction and continued singing.

That's why I'm so sad and lonely, baby,
Won't somebody take a chance with me.

Jack knew that he had to keep singing so that the polar bear did not go back to playing musical statues. And so he moved seamlessly from verse to chorus.

---

[55] One made from especially tough kangaroo pouch fluff.

In the next two minutes Jack found it hard to continue singing. Even though the hybrid creatures had been trying to kill him, it was difficult not to feel sympathy for anything that was being so comprehensively mauled by a polar bear. Occasionally when the bear did something particularly unpleasant Jack found himself wincing and hitting the wrong note.

At the same time, it was marvelous to feel safe and watch his enemies being destroyed. Jack managed to find enough joy in this to cause him to waltz around the fight between the polar bear and the creatures.

'Cause I sing sweet love songs
all the time,
Won't you come and be,
my sweet baby-mine.

The remaining bluebottle and its reptilian friend were stomped, clawed, bitten, and generally thrown around the room until they were piles of bruised and battered flesh.

Jack suspected that the polar bear had merely been playing with the creatures and could have finished them off in a few seconds. Instead it had wasted time picking them up in its maw and shaking them like a dog with a chew toy.

The creatures now lay motionless on the ground and the polar bear turned toward Jack. It took Jack a second to realize that he should now be terrified. Up until this moment Jack had looked upon the polar bear as a comrade, an ally. Now he realized that the polar bear had merely been doing what came naturally to it. It had attacked creatures that it saw as a threat.

Previously Jack had been endangered because he was being attacked by three hybrid creatures. Now he was in trouble because he was about to be attacked by a polar bear. His situation hadn't been substantially improved. In fact, if anything, it had gotten slightly worse.

The bear stalked toward Jack and raised an enormous bloodied paw in the air. Every muscle in Jack's body tensed, his eyes closed, and his teeth clamped shut as he waited for the impact to come.

And he waited. And waited.

Nothing happened.

Jack opened his eyes and looked at the polar bear above him. Its paw was still in the air poised to strike, but it wasn't moving. Then it struck Jack.[56] Of course, the polar bear had stopped moving. When he had tensed his body for the impact he had stopped singing! And once he stopped singing the polar bear returned to the game of musical statues.

Jack was so happy he felt like singing. Which he didn't do. Because that would have made the polar bear start moving again. And it would have hit him. And then he wouldn't have felt like singing anymore.

Jack stood still for a moment, wondering what he should do next, then—"Trudy!"

Jack raced back toward the art gallery. He hoped that the old lady hadn't done anything to his friend. But before he made

[56] "It" being a thought, rather than a polar bear paw. For those of you who like to know all the little details, the name of the polar bear was Peter.

it as far as the door, Grey appeared. He was helping a limping Trudy walk.

"We saw the attack on security cameras down in the Ministry," explained Grey. "I ran up here as quickly as I could, but the old lady had already gone."

"Is everything okay?" asked Jack, looking at Trudy for signs of a serious injury.

"Well, there are a few broken bones," said Grey.

Jack gasped.

"But they're mainly in the dinosaur display, so we won't worry too much about that."

"I meant, how is *she*?" asked Jack.

"*She* . . ." said Trudy testily, ". . . has a name. And *she* is fine."

Jack was so happy that he felt like hugging Trudy. However, he refrained from taking this course of action as he was quite badly bruised and didn't want to have to suffer an additional punched shoulder.

"What happened with the old lady?"

"I think she panicked when the other creatures didn't return. One of the dog creatures revived and went with her. For some reason they stole a number of dinosaur bones when they were escaping, but we have no idea why."

"Well, at least they didn't get us," said Jack brightly.

Trudy stepped away from Grey and wandered over to the mangled hybrid creatures that had attacked Jack.

"Ewwww," Trudy said. "I can't believe you did this, Jack. You could have shown some self-restraint."

"I didn't do that. The polar bear did," said Jack.

Trudy looked as if she didn't believe him. "A stuffed polar bear?"

"I'll explain later."

Trudy nudged the body with her feet. "You know the snake-creature has actually been torn into two separate parts, don't you?"

Jack looked slightly squeamish. Trudy was right—the creature had been ripped apart. "Well, don't worry: If it's in two parts, they'll both grow into new snakes, won't they?"

"That isn't snakes you're thinking of," said Trudy. "That's earthworms."

"Oh, right . . . In that case it's almost certainly quite dead."

"I would have thought so," agreed Trudy.

"Enough talk about corpses; let's get you two down to the Ministry and bandaged up." Grey led them away.

The three companions wandered through the museum. Much of it was wrecked. "They'll have to close the museum for a few days," said Jack. "And people will ask questions about what happened."

"Nonsense," said Grey. "We have protocols for dealing with this kind of event."

Grey walked over to a blue, Chinese-style vase that had been knocked off its pedestal and broken. He picked up the pieces and replaced them on the pedestal. Then he took a sleek black fountain pen out of his jacket pocket and started writing on the information card that was beside the exhibit.

Jack walked over to see what Grey had written. At the bottom of the information card he had added one simple sentence: *Vase damaged during excavation.*

"Will that really fool people?" asked Jack skeptically.

"Think about it, Jack. Museums all over the world are filled with broken objects. The reason for this is simple. They're all Ministry buildings and they all get attacked occasionally."

Jack laughed, then realized that Grey was serious.

"Think, Jack! How come they only show partial dinosaur skeletons? If you find a dinosaur skeleton, it should all be in one place. After the dinosaur died it will have fallen over and the flesh will have rotted away. So all the bones should be in one place, unless of course a giant dog came and stole a few . . . but most of the time all the bones should be in one place. And yet museums hardly ever have complete skeletons. Why? Because when enemies attack Ministry buildings the bones get stolen or destroyed."

Almost all museums Jack had ever visited had broken or damaged exhibits. On a school trip to France when they had gone to see the Venus de Milo in the Louvre museum it had been missing its arms. At the time Jack had assumed that archaeologists hadn't found the arms, but on reflection he realized how ridiculous this was. Why would someone remove the arms from a statue and put them in a different place? The only explanation was that the arms had been damaged in an attack!

". . . So the Venus de Milo . . ."

"Now you understand!" said Grey with a smile. "The Venus de Milo was damaged when a rogue group of golems attacked the Louvre, which houses the French Ministry."

"Up until now I'd always thought that she got overenthusiastic about biting her nails."

"No. That wasn't the case, Jack. That would be crazy."

"I was just jok—"

Grey cut Jack off. "Anyway, we need to get downstairs. The cleaners will take care of all this."

Even as Grey was speaking, a number of men and women in white overalls were scurrying around the museum, putting exhibits back in their place and adjusting the cards describing the artifacts.

Jack hurt all over and was keen to get down to the Ministry. He was sure that they would have some kind of amazing way to help heal his bruised flesh and aching bones.

ATTACKS ON MINISTRY SITES
The Venus de Milo and the *Mona Lisa*

Many people think that the Venus de Milo is the most famous example of an artifact damaged in an attack on Ministry premises. But it isn't. The most famous example is a painting called the *Mona Lisa*. The *Mona Lisa* was attacked by a group of radical anarchists who stormed the French Ministry headquarters (called "Le Ministre," unsurprisingly). Ironically they all got away because they were so well organized, which in some ways undermines their status as anarchists.

Obviously the group did not manage to steal the *Mona Lisa*. However, they did manage to steal her eyebrows. Many people think that the *Mona Lisa* has an enigmatic smile. That was not the original intention of the painting. It was meant to be of a woman who was surprised. But without the eyebrows it's impossible to tell.

The *Mona Lisa* was very surprised that her eyebrows were stolen, but without her eyebrows she had no way to express this.

30

BANDAGES ON MY LEGS AND ARMS

Although there wasn't a mirror in the Ministry's medical room Jack was sure he looked like an absolute idiot. He was sure of this because Trudy looked like an absolute idiot and they had both been patched up by the same nurse.

Bandages were loosely wound around their arms and legs, not because they necessarily needed bandages on their arms and legs, but simply because limbs were the easiest part of the body to bandage.[57] Their faces were covered in a variety of Band-Aids. Several of Jack's Band-Aids ran across his eyebrows and he was not looking forward to trying to take them off later.

"I was sort of expecting you to have some kind of

---

[57] Jack secretly hoped to himself that they hadn't got any of the bandages from the Ancient Egypt section of the museum.

wonderful medical procedure that would allow us to recover in an instant."

Grey looked slightly offended at this suggestion. "Do you think if we had a magical medical cure we wouldn't share it with the rest of the world? We'd just keep it to ourselves so that we'd be okay while the rest of the world suffered? What kind of people would that make us?"

Jack frowned. "I hadn't thought about it that way. If you did that, it would have made you fairly awful people. Sorry."

"Mmmm. I should think so."

Trudy and Jack were sitting on two metal-framed beds. Originally Jack had tried lying down on his bed, but there was a sign placed on the ceiling above it. The sign read IF YOU CAN READ THIS, YOU PROBABLY AREN'T DEAD. In some ways it was quite an encouraging thought, but the fact it said "probably" had unnerved Jack and he felt more comfortable sitting up.

The nurse that was looking after them seemed kind, but Jack had begun to doubt her ability after she had applied the third bandage to his wrist. There was something odd about her, although Jack was struggling to figure out what it was. A badge on her lapel read *Nurse Nufty*.

"That's you all fixed up, my lovelies. You'll be right as rain in three or four weeks." Nurse Nufty smiled at them. "If you'll excuse me, I need to be getting on. Apparently Mr. Cthulhu has given himself a paper cut again, and you know what a big baby he is about things like that."

Nurse Nufty bustled out of the room, leaving Grey, Trudy,

and Jack alone. As she was leaving Jack figured out what was unusual about her.

"She has a foot on one of her arms!"

Grey shook his head. "No, she doesn't."

"She does! I saw it."

"I think you'll find that both her feet were on the ends of her legs. It's just that one of her legs is where one of her arms should be."

Jack thought about this for a moment. "I'm not sure that makes a substantial difference. How did it happen?"

"Well, let me put it like this: If you think our nurses are incompetent, you should see our surgeons."

Jack's eyes widened. "Right, so that's the Ministry health-care. I don't suppose there's any way I could opt out and get private medical insurance."

"Maybe one day, Jack. But in the meantime I'd suggest that if you lose any limbs in a fight, it's vitally important to remember to label them *before* the ambulance collects you."

"Helpful hint. Thanks."

Trudy sighed. "If you two have quite finished with your nonsense, maybe we can discuss something more important."

"Like?" asked Grey.

"What were those creatures that attacked us in the museum?"

"Good question," said Grey. "The old lady said they were made by an evil scientist, but I suspect they were something altogether more innocent."

"Like martial artists in fancy dress?"

"Of course not, Jack. I think whoever is behind this has hired some werecreatures. A lot of evil people do. Werecreatures are nonunionized and so they work for minimum wage."

"Werecreatures—like werewolves?"

"Exactly. The ones that looked like dogs, well, they were werewolves. The bluebottles were werebluebottles and the snake was a ..."

"Weresnake?" guessed Trudy.

"So you did know what they were, then?" Grey said, clearly impressed.

"I didn't realize you could get all different kinds of were-animals," Jack said, raising his eyebrows in a manner that would have made the *Mona Lisa* jealous.

"Oh yes. All animals can have a 'were' version."

"So how do they get created, then?"

"It's a genetic disease thing. Don't ask me to explain it. It involves the gravitational pull of the moon and some kind of viral infection, I think. You have to be bitten on the first day of the new moon, though. Even then it doesn't always work."

"I always thought that if all it took to become a werewolf was to get bitten by a wolf, there should be a lot more of them about," said Trudy.

"Well, few people ever get the chance to wait for the next full moon to turn into a werewolf. After all, normally when you start getting bitten by a wolf, you finish off being eaten by a wolf. But there are lots of other werecreatures—weredogs, werehamsters, werebeetles, wereants ... The list is endless. Wolves just tend to be the most frequently sighted. Also, some animals tend to bite people less often, so there are fewer werehamsters about, for instance. And the average werehamster is a lot less frightening than the average werewolf."

"Why's that?"

"Well, a werewolf is half man, half wolf. It has the cunning and the intelligence of a man along with the strength, the speed, and the hunger for blood that possesses a wolf. Therefore a werewolf may well try and kill people. Werehamsters, however, have the characteristics of a hamster, so they tend not to crave the flesh of humans. A classic werewolf will wake up in the morning covered in blood and with no idea why. The classic werehamster wakes up to find his cheeks stuffed with nuts and kernels and wondering why his head is stuck in a toilet roll tube. The werewolf's life is one of horror, misery, and loneliness; a werehamster's is one of confusion. Of course they spend a lot of money on paper towels and toilet paper that they don't use properly."

"I wish that we'd been attacked by werehamsters," said Jack.

"That would have been easier," agreed Grey. "They're especially easy to deal with during the winter months."

"Why's that?" asked Trudy.

"Normally they hibernate. So that means on the new moon in winter the only way to recognize a werehamster is that they'll turn up slightly late for work."

Jack laughed. "How come I've never seen a film about a werehamster?"

Grey turned to Jack. "If someone made a film called *Revenge of the Werehamster*, would you pay to see it?" [58]

"Probably not."

"Well, that's probably why the movie has never been made."

"The werehamster seems like the dullest type of animal possible," said Trudy.

"Maybe. Of course I did know a werebook once."

"A werebook?" Trudy laughed.

"A werebook. A librarian was staying late, updating the microfiche during the new moon. He accidently gave himself a paper cut from a Delia Smith book. Ever since then he wakes up after the new moon with all sorts of practical and delicious recipe ideas. Anyway, enough about werecreatures. The Minister wants to see you both, so we'd better get a move on."

"Great," said Jack. "Now that we know Chapeau Noir Enterprises are up to something I'm sure the Minister will want to stop them."

[58] If someone made a film called *Revenge of the Werehamster*, I, for one, would definitely go and see it.

BAND-AIDS
THE BEST WAY TO REMOVE THEM

You will probably already have figured this out, but Band-Aids were clearly invented by an evil scientist.

No one but an evil scientist would invent something that goes over a cut, but then actually causes more pain when it is removed than the cut caused in the first place.

The easiest way to remove a Band-Aid is to go to a public swimming pool. For some reason the minute you jump into a swimming pool, the Band-Aid will come right off and spend the next few weeks floating around and freaking out everyone else who uses the pool.

* * *

There is only one totally painless way to remove a Band-Aid. Take it off someone else's skin.

31

A DEAL STRUCK

Grey left Jack and Trudy outside the Minister's office.

"Aren't you coming in with us?"

Grey shook his head. "We used a lot of bandages. I've got to go and fill out the paperwork."

"Paperwork?"

"Ninety percent of Ministry work is paperwork. Nine percent is avoiding trying to do the paperwork."

"And the remaining one percent?"

"Mostly trying to avoid getting killed."

Jack knocked at the Minister's door.

"Come in!"

Jack and Trudy walked into the room to find that the Minister already had a guest. It was the strangest-looking guest that Trudy or Jack had ever seen.

"Ahh, Jack ... Trudy. If you just want to sit down for a

few minutes, I'll finish my conversation with this...
gentleman."

The "gentleman" to which the Minister was referring stood in front of the desk. He was a large, bulky man. Jack's father was six feet tall, but this man was considerably bigger than that. He was also very muscular, indeed, but not in the way that models in fashion magazines were muscular. A model's muscles are clearly defined and rippled. This man's muscles didn't ripple at all. Instead they bulged. He looked like a man who went to the gym to get stronger rather than to look good. He had a full head of hair and a rough brown beard. A long scar ran down one side of his face.

All of this would have been relatively unremarkable if it hadn't been for the fact that the man was wearing a pink tutu. It wasn't a flattering look. The tutu bulged and strained to try and keep the man's considerable bulk in check.

"So we have ourselves a deal, then, Minister?"

The Minister stared at the man with more than a hint of annoyance. "I suppose so. But I hardly think it's fair."

"Fair's got nothing to do with it," snarled the man. "I got the paperwork and you know it."

"I'll see you tomorrow then, Mr. Fairy."

"Yeah, yeah, you will." The man in the pink tutu turned to leave the room. On his way out he looked down at Jack and Trudy. He grinned at them in a very unsettling way. "Always brush your teeth, kids."

The door closed behind the large man and Jack felt he could breathe again. "Who on earth was that?"

The Minister lifted a decanter off his desk. It was filled

with a clear, brown liquid. He poured himself a glass from it and took a sip before he even spoke. "That, Jack, was the Tooth Fairy."

"The Tooth Fairy?" echoed Trudy.

"Remember I told you he took my teeth after I fell asleep with my head under the pillow? Well, we struck a deal for me to buy them back."

"Ah!" said Jack. "And then you can go to the Ministry healthcare staff and they'll reinsert them."

The Minister pointed at the bandages covering Jack's and Trudy's arms. "You've met the Ministry healthcare staff, so you'll understand why I'll be going to a private dentist."

"The Tooth Fairy looks a bit scary."

"The man is a *monster*!" The Minister was clearly quite passionate about this subject. "But never, never cross him. He has the strength of seven or eight men, and he never, never stops if he believes your teeth belong to him."

"I'll remember that," said Jack, thinking that this information would never be of any use. As usual, Jack was badly mistaken.

"Anyway, enough of my dental negotiations. What have you two learned?"

Jack and Trudy looked at each other before they began speaking. Then they both took a deep breath and began their story.

Jack was amazed at how easily the story tumbled out of them. They told the Minister of the theory of the children missing from gym class, the wind farms owned by Chapeau Noir Enterprises and Mr. Teach, the new uniforms and their ability to collect static electricity, and the werecreatures attacking the museum. Jack felt an enormous sense of relief. Once the Minister had heard the story he would make sure Mr. Teach was stopped and David would be safe.

As they talked the Minister nodded his head and looked as though he was thinking intently.

After they had both finished the Minister poured himself another glass of the clear, brown liquid and stroked his chin before he began speaking. "I know what this is," he said.

Jack leaned forward in his chair, excited to hear the Minister's explanation.

"What this is, is a mystery," said the Minister.

"That isn't very helpful," said Trudy.

Jack felt that he had wasted his effort leaning forward and so he slumped back in his chair. "Is that all you can tell us?"

"If I could tell you more it wouldn't be a mystery, would it?" asked the Minister.

"So, what next?" asked Trudy.

"Next you have to figure out exactly what's going on and stop it."

"Can't we just call the police?" asked Jack. He felt they had to do something. David's status as an odd kid was putting him at risk.

The Minister looked at Jack. "We are the police for things like this."

Jack felt his stomach turn. "Look, I have to admit that I'm a little scared. If I get killed, my parents will be most put out.

Apart from anything else they've just bought me a new schoolbag that they expect will last for at least a year."[59]

The Minister chuckled, then walked around from the other side of his desk to put a hand on Jack's shoulder. "Jack, it's good that you're scared. People who aren't scared tend to bravely walk straight into the lion's den, and you know what happens to them?"

"They get eaten by the lions?"

"Precisely. The Ministry doesn't want heroes. It wants people who stay alive long enough to find out what's wrong and fix the problem. Heroes aren't very useful. Not even lions like heroes, because with all that running about they do, heroes tend to taste rather tough and stringy. Or so I'm informed."

Although Jack was frightened, he wasn't sure that he enjoyed being told that he wasn't a hero. "But aren't heroes good in wars and things like that?"

"Goodness, no," said the Minister. "The problem with heroes is that they dive on top of grenades to save their friends."

"Isn't that a positive thing?"

"No! You just end up with one dead hero and an enormous laundry bill. Cowards are more sensible—they kick the grenade away. So, with a bit of luck and a good right foot, *everyone* survives."

Jack turned to look at Trudy. The Minister's speech seemed

---

[59] Jack's parents were very clear on this. A schoolbag was expected to last for at least a year, or until one of the other kids in his class had written a rude word on it. Whichever came first.

to have made sense to her. She was nodding quietly to herself.

"Since you seem to be up against some pretty tough competition, I'm going to suggest that you go and see the Misery. A little more combat training might be a sensible precaution at this stage."

Jack sighed inwardly. *Oh great*, he thought. *More time with the Misery.* He thought about refusing, but if he was going to have to fight to save David, he wanted to be ready. Their experience at the museum had proved to him he wasn't ready . . . yet.

TOOTH FAIRY
INTEREST IN DENTAL HYGIENE

The reason the Tooth Fairy tells people to brush their teeth is because he needs to be able to collect teeth in good, sparkling white condition in order to continue his business making white keys for pianos.

People often believe that the Tooth Fairy only collects teeth from the very young. Baby teeth are the whitest in color and therefore of the most use for making white piano keys. The Tooth Fairy rarely collects adult teeth, as over the years they become stained and yellowish through the continual drinking of red wine and coffee and from smoking.

Of course, the Tooth Fairy does sometimes collect the teeth of the very old (hence the reason that old people often have gaps in their teeth) to use for the black keys on the piano. But as the black keys on a piano are both smaller and fewer in number, the Tooth Fairy does not need to collect as many of these.

32

A TOTAL PLANK

Jack really wasn't looking forward to visiting the Misery. Previously he had been unsure about facing death, but if it came down to a choice of facing death or spending some time with the Misery, he was quite happy to call up the restaurant and make reservations for a dinner date with the Grim Reaper.

Trudy, on the other hand, was quite looking forward to it. "I love training," she said as they walked along the corridor together.

"You are a very, very strange girl," said Jack. "The Misery is appalling. He's going to be horrible to us for an hour and then tell us we haven't done a very good job."

"That's what I like about him."

"What? The abuse?"

"You don't understand, Jack. People *like* you."

Jack wondered why everyone thought this. "David said that to me as well. But people don't really like me that much, do they?"

"Well not *that* much," admitted Trudy. "But enough. They chat to you, talk to you."

"Maybe people would chat to you too if you didn't punch them in the shoulder so much...Owwww," said Jack as Trudy punched him in the shoulder.

"That doesn't make any sense. I punch you in the shoulder and you still talk to me. So, obviously, that doesn't make a difference."

"People are scared of you."

"They don't like me because I'm different. I don't know anything about pop stars, I don't care about makeup, I don't know which boy is the hottest, or what clothes are 'in.' And because of that they're horrible to me."

Jack couldn't say anything to this. He knew it was true. It was easy to make fun of someone who was different in the hope that people wouldn't notice that you were different too.

"I still don't understand why that would make you like the Misery."

"It's simple," Trudy explained. "I see everyone in school getting on, making friends, and generally having a laugh, right? Everyone is really nice to each other. But they're horrible to me. And that's why I like the Misery."

"But the Misery is horrible to you!"

"And that's why I like him. I know everyone else *can be nice* if they try. I see them being nice to each other. But they're *horrible to me*. The Misery is horrible to everyone. At least he treats everyone the same."

It did seem to make a little sense to Jack. Although not a lot.

"Being annoyed with the Misery for being miserable would be like being annoyed at a hedgehog for liking acupuncture. Or being annoyed at a giraffe for needing a really long scarf. They can't help it; it's what they are. But people in school being horrible to me ... that's something different. They have a choice."

When they got to the Misery's room the door was standing slightly ajar with a sign hung on it.

OUT FOR HALF AN HOUR—PLEASE COME INSIDE AND WAIT (or go away ... as if I care ...)

"We could just go away," suggested Jack.

Trudy scowled at him and walked into the training room.

Jack wanted to walk around the room to see what was beyond the gloom that pervaded the edges, but he wasn't brave enough. Who knew what horrible things the Misery kept under the bleak darkness that made the room seem infinitely big?

"Hey, look at this," said Trudy.

Unlike on their last visit, the room was not completely empty. A small pile of planks was set in the center.

"I wonder what these are for?"

Jack scoffed at her. "It's obvious what these are for. Haven't you ever seen any martial arts movies?"

Trudy said that she hadn't really seen many martial arts movies. Jack found this difficult to believe. He was sure that when she punched him in the arm she was imitating Chuck Norris, Jet Li, or some other legendary hard man.

"This is where we're trained for fighting, right? And martial arts training always ends with being able to break wooden planks with your bare hands."

Trudy looked at Jack, then at the planks. "Aren't these planks a little long for that?"

Jack studied the planks. Normally when you saw people breaking wood they were sections one or two feet long. These planks were considerably longer ... perhaps ten feet long? But surely there was no other reason that the Misery would have rough planks in his room.

Then Jack had a horrible thought. "He's going to expect us to break these with our hands." Jack punched one of the planks. The effect was predictable. His hand turned red and hurt. The plank was stoically unperplexed and completely unharmed.

Jack had an idea. He took one of the planks and set it on top of a pile of the other planks so it was suspended a few feet above the ground.

"Are you going to try and break that with your hand again?" Trudy asked. "You remember that The Speed doesn't make you any stronger, don't you? Just faster."

"Yeah," said Jack. Instead of hitting the plank with his hand he jumped into the air and landed with all his weight on its center. This time the plank was less silent; it creaked and bent. Jack continued jumping until with a sudden snap the plank split in two. Jack crashed to the ground.

"Why did you do that?" asked Trudy.

"Do you remember what happened with the bottles?" Jack pointed to the planks. "The Misery is going to keep us here shouting at us and insulting us until we've broken every single one of those planks with our bare hands. I can't do that; I'd go crazy."

"So . . ."

"So we jump on them and break them before he gets here. Then we tell him that we broke them with our hands."

Trudy was reluctant. "I don't know, Jack . . . I like training."

"Please, Trudy," Jack pleaded. "I know you like the Misery . . . but we're partners. And you know how horrible it was for me the last time. Do you really want to watch me being that miserable again?"

Trudy looked at Jack. Then, without saying a word, she put a plank on top of some others and jumped on it.

Jack had just finished jumping on the last plank at the very moment the Misery walked in. He jumped to his feet. "Look what we did with our fists of fury!" said Jack, pointing to the broken planks.

"Look what you did," said the Misery. He was aghast. He brushed his floppy, black hair out of his eyes and stared at them both. "Look—what—you—did!"

Jack had no idea what was going on.

The Misery's eyes widened with astonishment. "Why would you do this? I've always been nice to you." From the Misery's point of view this statement was entirely true. He thought he had been nice to Trudy and Jack. This is only because the kind of things that the Misery did to his enemies were truly horrific, outrageous, and not for the squeamish to hear about.

"We just broke the training planks," said Jack, unsure why the Misery was so upset. "Should we have waited for you first?"

"Waited for me first? These aren't training planks, you idiot."

"But they look like—"

"They look like scaffolding,"[60] the Misery interjected. "And the reason they look like scaffolding is because they are, in fact, scaffolding."

"Why do you need scaffolding?" asked Jack.

"Because I was going to decorate." The Misery held his arms out straight in front of him. For the first time Jack noticed that he was holding two tins of magnolia paint and a roller. "I was going to brighten the place up a bit. All this gloom was beginning to depress me."

The Misery looked sadly at the broken planks. "But now that you've broken the scaffolding I'll never be able to paint the walls in this place." He threw the paint pots and roller across the room. They clattered into the darkness.

Jack felt slightly guilty, but tried to justify his actions. "...Maybe you should have labeled the planks as scaffolding..."

"What?" The Misery gaped at him. "Who labels scaffolding?"

---

[60] It should be pointed out that the planks no longer looked like scaffolding. Now that Trudy and Jack had finished with them, what they looked like was the floor of a very bad woodwork class.

"I mean, just when they're in the training room. It was an easy mistake to make."

"No," the Misery disagreed. "It was not an easy mistake to make. A lot of people have been in this room before and never made that mistake. You must have been trying very hard to make such a ridiculous and stupid mistake."

"Be fair," said Trudy. "They did look like they were for training."

The Misery looked at Trudy, surprised that she had interjected on Jack's behalf. He shook his head and went to start a sentence, but found himself shocked into silence. Jack was pleased by this state of affairs, but then disappointed as the stunned silence lasted only thirty seconds.

"If you want to justify what he did, then you're both equally responsible."

"But the planks looked like . . ."

"Never mind what the planks looked like," snapped the Misery. "What are you here to do? Why am I teaching you how to use The Speed?"

"So we can defend ourselves?" Trudy offered.

"Genius," the Misery said. "I *am* here to teach you how to defend yourselves. Now, what kind of creatures might you end up fighting?"

"Uhh, werecreatures, Porcupods, bears? Potentially a businessman called Mr. Teach," said Jack.

Trudy nodded. "Pirates, zombies, evil beings from another dimension."

"Very good," said the Misery, smiling in the same way a shark would—all teeth with dead eyes. Jack knew that the smile was a clear signal that the killer question was about to arrive. "And do you think you will ever be attacked by a wooden plank? Or a house brick?"

And there it was. The killer question.

"I wouldn't think so." Jack winced.

"So, if you aren't going to be attacked by a plank or a house brick, why on earth would I teach you how to break one in half with your bare hands?"

Jack couldn't answer the question. Suddenly years of watching karate movies on television seemed rather pointless. Why did karate masters spend all their time attacking DIY materials? Why did they break planks in two, rather than practicing punching people in the face, which was clearly what they were best at?

"I'm really, really sorry," said Jack. "I didn't realize."

The Misery wasn't listening to him anymore. He sat down cross-legged on the ground.

"Would it help if I . . . ?"

Before Jack could finish his sentence Trudy had put a hand on his shoulder. She shook her head, indicating that there was no point in trying to cheer up the Misery.

Trudy nodded toward the door and they both left, leaving the Misery to his misery.

"Thanks for that," said Jack when they got outside.

"Thanks for what?" asked Trudy.

"You stuck up for me in there. You didn't need to try and defend me from the Misery, but you did."

"Didn't do much good, though." Trudy laughed.

"Well, no. But you tried and that's the main thing." Jack

smiled and decided to do something different. He punched Trudy in the shoulder in a friendly manner. Jack was slightly confused when it hurt his hand. He thought that either Trudy had very hard shoulders or he had very soft hands.

As a matter of fact, it was a combination of the two.

MINISTRY OF S.U.I.T.S HANDBOOK

MARTIAL ARTS/KARATE
ORIGINS

Many people wonder why karate masters attack bricks and planks with their hands. Interestingly enough, the answer to this question is rather straightforward. The original karate masters were Japanese builders. However, as they lived in a time before power saws and pneumatic drills they had to learn other ways of quickly cutting a plank in half or breaking a brick so it would fit at the end of a row. Years of practice taught them to cut and break planks and bricks with their bare hands.

Of course, as already noted, many houses in Japan were built of paper. So there wasn't a need for many builders. If you really wanted a lovely house put together in the latest fashion, a stationer was of more use than a builder. Either that or an origami master who could fold your walls into interesting shapes.

And so the master builders of Japan soon got called by the nickname "karate," which means "empty hand" because at the end of the week they generally hadn't gotten paid for any building work and so could never buy a round of drinks in the pub. Their hands were literally empty of money.

As you can imagine, the builders got a bit annoyed with everyone making fun of them having no money. One night, one of the builders got so annoyed at being called "karate" (empty hand) in the pub that he attacked the man who called him by the shameful name. The builder hit the man with the blow that he normally used on house bricks and was pleasantly surprised to find that a blow that would crack a house brick into two neat pieces also had a very similar effect on a man's arm.

After that, the Japanese builders who had previously had no work found that they could charge people to teach them how to fight. Over several hundred years the term *karate* changed from being a term of derision into a term of pride.

33

A MISSING FRIEND
THURSDAY

When Jack got on the bus the next morning David wasn't there. The thing that had been worrying Jack all this time had finally happened—his odd-kid friend had disappeared. With another friend Jack would have put it down to illness, but that would never be the case with David.

For all his lack of physical prowess and coordination, David was never ill. Jack and his classmates had several theories as to why this was true. Someone had suggested that as the outside of David's body was so hopelessly disorganized, he was probably equally hopelessly disorganized on the inside. Therefore once a germ or a virus got inside him, it would take a wrong turn, get lost, lose all sense of hope, and die of starvation before it got to the particular organ it was meant to attack. Another suggestion was that germs were house-proud little creatures and none of them would want to live inside someone like David. Possibly the most likely explanation was that David fell down so often that any germs that managed to find their way inside his system were subsequently shaken like maracas and were therefore too bruised to make anyone seriously sick.

As Jack was David's best friend, he felt these explanations were nasty and mean . . . even if they were very likely to be true.

Jack was desperate to find Trudy. He hoped she would know what to do, but the school bus seemed to be taking forever. Jack realized that he was inadvertently slowing it down with his negative emotions. Once at the school he dashed in the front entrance and found Trudy standing in front of the notice board.

"Look at this." Trudy was pointing at a poster on the school notice board. "Apparently they're taking the school boiler away because thanks to Chapeau Noir Enterprises we're getting solar panels."

"Trudy, I've got something important . . ."

Trudy kept on talking. "Why would they take the boiler away? It's too old to be of use to anyone."

"TRUDY!" Jack shouted.

Trudy looked at Jack and her eyes widened. She wasn't used to being shouted at by anyone, let alone her new friend. However, for once Jack wasn't worried about being hit. He had something more important on his mind. "David's missing."

"What do you mean 'missing'?"

Jack explained to Trudy that David hadn't been on the

bus that morning. Even after Jack explained that David was never ill she didn't seem worried. Jack had to convince her that this was serious. "Remember yesterday you stuck up for me because we were partners?"

"Yeah."

"Well this is a partner thing again, Trudy," Jack said as he stared into her eyes in deadly earnest. "I need you to trust me on this."

Trudy didn't hesitate. "What do you want me to do?"

Jack hadn't thought that far ahead. They still had no idea if the missing children were being taken somewhere. Their clues seemed odd: wind turbines, new carpet, missing children, stolen dinosaur bones . . . and now a school boiler being taken.

In fact, these things didn't seem like clues at all. When he watched Agatha Christie mysteries with his mother, these were not the kinds of clues that turned up. Miss Marple never solved a mystery due to shag pile carpet and alternative energy sources. Her mysteries always involved foreign dukes with obscure pasts and untraceable poisons made out of Amazonian frogs.[61]

"I don't know what we can do." Jack sighed, fidgeting with his hands. He was full of nervous energy but he had nowhere to direct it. His heart was thumping in his chest

---

[61] In the old days untraceable poisons would be made from Amazonian frogs. These days you could probably buy untraceable poisons from Amazon. Just goes to show you, the world likes balance and everything in life is circular (especially circles).

and his breath was coming faster and faster. What should he be doing? "If we go to the Minister, he'll just tell us it's a mystery and that we should solve it. The police would never believe any story we could tell them."

"Maybe there'll be a clue at David's house. We should go and speak to David's parents, at any rate."

Jack nodded and tried to get his breathing under control. "We can cut across the rugby pitches. There's a hole in the fence and it'll get us to David's house faster."

Trudy swung her bag over her shoulder and they set off at a fast trot. Within a few minutes they were halfway across the muddy pitches.

Jack was lost in thoughts of what would happen next. "What if it's my fault that someone kidnapped David? What if I hadn't joined the Ministry—would David have been . . ." Jack hadn't time to complete his thought because suddenly he was too busy falling ten feet straight down.

It took Jack a few minutes to orient himself and realize what had happened. Generally you didn't expect that kind of thing to happen when you were walking across the school rugby pitches. Some grass had gotten into his mouth and he spluttered, spitting it out.

At first he had thought that he must have fallen down something like an old abandoned well or a mineshaft, but as soon as he started looking around him he realized that wasn't the case at all.

He was in the center of a large bowl-like indentation in the ground. It wasn't that the ground had suddenly split open and swallowed him. It was more like a giant had suddenly reached down with his thumb and pressed it into the earth.

Trudy was standing at the edge of the bowl shape, looking down at him. She had been quick enough to leap back when the ground had collapsed. "Are you all right?" she called down.

"Yeah, fine," said Jack as he spat out more grass. "Although I really don't know how cows eat this stuff. It's disgusting."

He stood up and scrambled up the slope toward Trudy. "So what on earth do you think this is? It looks like a meteor's struck the ground."

"Mmmm," said Trudy. "Although clearly that didn't happen, because we would have noticed it."[62]

"I wasn't suggesting it had," said Jack. "But thank you for your sarcasm."

"I think this is another clue," said Trudy.

"Maybe it is. But it doesn't matter. At the moment we've got to focus on trying to find out where David is."

"We're looking for clues, Jack. If David is really missing, it's bound to be connected to whatever's going on at the school. I think if David's anywhere, he's under there." Trudy pointed to the indentation in grass.

Jack's jaw dropped. "You mean he's buried? Dead?"

"No!" Trudy said, trying to calm Jack. "In a tunnel."

---

[62] And obviously it would also have squashed Jack quite badly. It would almost certainly have resulted in a fatal squashing. Fatal squashings do occur occasionally. However, a friend of mine who is a coroner has reassured me that they are thankfully rare.

"A tunnel?"

"Think about it. The only reason the rugby pitches would have collapsed like this is if someone's been digging under them. And those mobile classrooms were full of digging equipment. Exactly what you'd expect if someone was tunneling underground. And if there is a tunnel, that would be the ideal place to hide missing children."

Jack looked at the ground. He wasn't entirely convinced by Trudy's explanation, but it was the best lead they had. "So what do we do? Get a spade and start digging?"

"No. We look for an entrance," said Trudy. "If they're kidnapping kids on their way to or from school, there has to be an entrance around here somewhere."

"So we look for the entrance. But where would they put it?"

"Well, it has to be hidden. So they'll put it somewhere that you would never go."

"The girls' toilets!" suggested Jack.

"Jack, you might not go to the girls' toilets, but lots of girls do. We're talking about a place that is useless for everyone."

"All right, then. We go back to the school and we search."

Jack and Trudy rushed back to the school and did their best to search anywhere they thought a tunnel entrance might be hidden. It wasn't an easy task as they spent half their time hiding around the corner from teachers rather than having to explain why they weren't in class.

They searched under the stage in the assembly hall; they sneaked into the back playground and peeked through the staff room windows; they even searched behind the bike sheds.

The problem was that the places where people said they never went were actually the places they went all the time. The teachers were always in the staff room marking homework, the sixth formers were always behind the bike sheds kissing each other, and the caretakers were always under the stage in the assembly hall watching a portable television.

"Somewhere totally useless. Think!" Trudy stamped her foot.

And then it occurred to Jack. "The P.E. teacher's office!" he yelled. "At the end of the changing rooms there's a P.E. teacher's office. But P.E. teachers never mark homework, or prepare lesson plans, or set tests . . ."

"And so . . . ?"

"Well, what is a P.E. teacher's office actually for? It doesn't make any sense. So it's a pointless room. Unless of course . . ."

Trudy finished his thought for him. ". . . unless of course that's where the entrance to an underground tunnel is."

"Precisely," said Jack, feeling slightly smug.

His smugness lasted about ten seconds and then Trudy spoke. "And that would make even more sense as that's where the odds and ends of the missing kids' P.E. kits are found. In the box of spares."

"I would have figured that out if you'd given me time," Jack grumbled.

It was halfway through the last class when Jack stuck his head around the door of the P.E. changing rooms. "It's empty," he let Trudy know.

"What is that smell?" asked Trudy as she walked into the changing rooms.

Jack barely even noticed the changing-room smell anymore. "Yeah, it's a bit of an acquired taste, isn't it? And it always seems to be here. No matter how many times the place is washed, cleaned, or has deodorant sprayed around it, that smell remains."

"That doesn't make any sense."

"No, it doesn't. Dawkins says that he thinks that it's a ghost fart. You know, a fart that died years ago. And now it lingers in the air forever like a ghostly presence."

"That doesn't make any sense."

"A lot of what Dawkins says doesn't make any sense."[63]

Trudy and Jack crept through the changing rooms until they reached the P.E. teacher's office at the back. The door had a pane of clouded glass in it. Jack reached out and pushed the door gently, leaping backward when it squeaked open. There was no one inside the office. Jack assumed Mr. Rackham was outside somewhere tormenting some boys who weren't any good at playing cricket by scratching his fingernails down his blackboard every time a batsman missed a ball.

The office was hardly an office at all, perhaps nine or ten feet square. There was no natural light and no windows, so it smelled musty and felt claustrophobic. Hundreds of leaflets were piled up on the floor in stacks. They offered advice

---

[63] For further evidence of this please see chapters eighteen and nineteen.

on how to avoid diseases like gout, leprosy, and polio. Jack was convinced that many of these diseases were out of date and didn't exist; however, the school rarely spent money on new pamphlets to try and improve pupils' health.

Jack had a theory that the school was never that keen on P.E. or anything that helped pupils become healthier. They wanted pupils to be unhealthy. The teachers' favorite pupils were generally pale, weedy, and slightly anemic looking. Jack thought the reason for this was that unhealthy pupils were less likely to run around the place causing trouble. An unhealthy, unfit pupil could be put in a chair at the start of a lesson and you could rely on them being lazy enough to still be there at the end of the class. Healthy children got into all sorts of trouble, and therefore health was discouraged. Jack knew this to be true as it was impossible to stay fit while eating the kinds of lunches they served in the school canteen.

Each of the piles of pamphlets had an object on top of it, pinning it down like a paperweight. Of course, none of the paperweights were actually paperweights. Rather, it seemed as if Mr. Rackham had used whatever object had been nearest at hand. One pile was pinned down with a hockey stick, another was pinned down with an old globe, and yet another was kept in place with a set of dumbbells.

In one corner there was a small desk, an old rickety chair that none of the proper teachers had wanted, and a series of posters of sports stars of the 1950s.

"What's stickball?" asked Trudy, looking at one of the posters.

"I'm not sure," said Jack. "I imagine it's a game where you hit a ball with a stick ... or perhaps a game where you hit a stick with a ball. Either way I'm fairly sure that both a stick and a ball are involved."

Jack recoiled with a shudder when he saw the box of spare P.E. kits. He pointed it out to Trudy. "Maybe something of David's will be in there." Jack moved toward the box, mentally steeling himself to rummage around in the cardboard cube of despair.

"I wouldn't bother," said Trudy. "Those clothes are only going to be from kids who went missing in gym class. As far as we know David went missing after school at some stage."

There was no obvious tunnel in the room and the only door was the one they had used to come in. Trudy looked around the tiny room. "There's a passage here somewhere."

"Why are you so sure?"

Trudy lifted up a hockey stick from on top of the pile of leaflets. "This is a small room. There are no windows. So why are all these leaflets weighted down with random objects?"

Jack didn't quite get Trudy's meaning. "To keep them in place?"

"Yes, but why do they need to be kept in place? Only one door and no windows. That means there can't be any drafts. No air blowing through the room. Unless, of course, there's another door that we can't see."

Jack and Trudy examined the walls, moved leaflets, and even turned the desk upside down. They found nothing. Jack tried kicking at the floor in the corner, hoping a trapdoor would reveal itself, but he only managed to scuff his shoe.

"What we need to find is something that is out of place. Something you wouldn't expect a P.E. teacher to ..." Before Trudy had finished speaking Jack had grabbed the globe off a pile of leaflets. "The globe! Why would a P.E. teacher have a globe?"

Trudy grabbed the globe from Jack. "Great! Even geography teachers don't have globes these days."

It was an old-style globe with vast blue oceans and small green continents. They spun it around and looked at it intently. The oceans on the globe were marked with pictures of small sailing ships with billowing sails.

"Umm, is there a country called *Button*?" asked Trudy.

"I don't think so."

Trudy showed Jack what she was looking at. In the middle of the Atlantic Ocean, there was a small roundish, green country that had been labeled *Button*.

"Worth a try," said Trudy as she pressed the island labeled *Button*.

For a few seconds there was silence; then a sound of grinding metal filled the air as if an enormous set of gears was moving into action.

"I think that may have done the trick," said Jack.

UNDERGROUND PASSAGES
How to Locate Them

Frequently in the course of an adventure a Ministry operative will need to locate a hidden passage. When thinking about where to hide these passages, villains always think, *Let's hide it in the last place anyone would look.*

Therefore, the quickest way to locate such a passage is to make a list of all the places you are going to search. Then skip all of the list except the very last item on it.[64]

* * *

One day villains will figure out that they should hide their underground passages in places where no one *will ever* look. When that happens we will all be in trouble.

[64] Alternatively, make up your mind to just look in one place. This will then be "the last place you would look."

34

THE TUNNEL

The floor under Trudy's and Jack's feet started slowly moving and sloping down. At the same time the wall at the far end of the office lifted up slightly, and they found themselves standing at the entrance to a long tunnel. Jack wasn't sure whether to be excited or terrified. He was sure the tunnel would lead them to finding David. However, he was equally sure it would lead them into some kind of horrible danger.

The walls of the tunnel were dusty, gray concrete. Large luminous electric lights hung at shoulder height on either side of the passageway. Apart from Trudy and Jack there was nothing in the passageway to cast a shadow, and yet for some reason it felt sinister. It looked like a medical laboratory where ghastly experiments would be carried out. And for all Jack knew, maybe that was exactly what was going on.

"So what do we do now?"

"David's down there," said Jack. "We go and get him."

Trudy nodded. "You're ready for whatever might be down there?"

In the past few days Jack had been attacked by a bear, fought werecreatures in a museum, and met a squid-headed being of almost unbelievable evil power. "You know, I'm almost certainly not ready for this. But I'm still going to do it anyway."

A smile almost split Trudy's face in two. "That's exactly how I feel."

Jack and Trudy marched down the tunnel side by side.

After the first fifty feet the concrete walls of the tunnel gave way to a soil passageway. The sides were braced at intervals with black metal beams.

"Do you think this is safe?" asked Jack.

"Almost certainly not. Remember the collapsed rugby pitch?"

"Mmm. Any thoughts on what we should do if we're crushed to death?"

Trudy shrugged. "If we're crushed to death, we won't really have to try and do anything much. Just lie still and try to look unappetizing to worms."

Jack looked up at the ceiling. Once they had moved on from the concrete tunnel, the regularly spaced lights had ceased. Now, there were a series of bulbs that flickered and sputtered. It felt more like candlelight than electric bulbs. Whatever was powering them seemed to be rather weak and worked only intermittently.

Although the bright white light had seemed frightening and sinister, the flickering light was infinitely worse. Occasionally the lights would pop out entirely for a few seconds. When this happened Jack found himself turning around so that he was looking over his shoulder when the lights came on. If horror movies had taught him anything, it was that when a light flickered out for a few seconds, it was only so that a large man could appear suddenly behind you, holding a large hooklike device normally seen only in a slaughterhouse.

Luckily this didn't seem to happen in real life. Jack swore if he survived the tunnel he would never watch another scary movie as long as he lived. Of course it was a promise he broke. He watched many horror movies in the future, but after going through everything he had, they just didn't seem that scary anymore.

"Look at that!" cried Trudy, pointing at one of the flickering bulbs.

"It's a lightbulb," said Jack. "They're very common. If we get out of this, I'll buy you one of your own."

Trudy ignored Jack. "Look at what it's connected to."

The lightbulb was connected to a strip of carpet that seemed to be hanging down from the ceiling.

"What on earth? Is that the same carpet that Chapeau Noir put down in the school?"

"Exactly."

"But what does that mean?" asked Jack.

Trudy had figured out that the reason the light was flickering was because the supply wasn't steady. The school was above them and strips of the carpet were hanging down from the carpeted corridors. The kids had been given new polyester uniforms because they helped hold a static electricity charge. Which was why Dawkins had been able to pretend to be the hero Static.

"So they're using the polyester carpet and uniforms to generate power to run these lights?"

"Precisely," said Trudy. "That's why the strips of carpet come through the ceiling and the static charges light the bulbs. Carpets in a school wouldn't make sense otherwise."

"But..." Jack hesitated. "That doesn't really make sense. If they're using kids to generate static electricity, why do they need the wind turbines?"

"That's the point. The carpet is used to generate power because the wind turbines aren't going to be used for that purpose at all. They're going to be used for something more sinister."

"Like what?"

Trudy took a deep breath. "I don't know...yet. But I've got a feeling that when we figure that out we'll know what Chapeau Noir Enterprises and Mr. Teach are up to. Think about it. They replaced the boiler with solar panels. Why would they do that if the wind turbines really worked?"

Jack had a feeling that they were very close to the solution to all the mysteries. He was just about to say this to Trudy; however, his breath was taken away when they turned the corner.

The floor dropped away in front of Jack and Trudy. If Jack had taken another step, he would have plunged fifty feet straight down. They had walked into a giant cavern that seemed to be endless.

Across the floor of the cavern were hundreds of tiny figures—digging, operating machinery, slowly enlarging the cavern.

Hundreds of figures, some of them young, some of them older. All of them in ragged school uniforms and looking slightly hopeless. Many of them seemed to be wearing chains around their necks or their ankles. They were being supervised in their work by a group of rough-looking men. There was something unusual about the men. They all had crutches, eye patches . . . some even had prosthetic arms. Digging must be dangerous work.

"I think we've found the missing schoolchildren," whispered Trudy.

"At least they're still alive."

"I know, but look at them. Some of them must have been here for thirty years."

"And what are they digging all this for? Why dig a huge hole under Northern Ireland?"

"Only one way to find out."

Trudy stood at the edge of the fifty-foot drop.

"How are you planning to get down?" asked Jack.

Trudy's eyes seem to go slightly moist and Jack realized she was conjuring up sad thoughts in her head. Jack wondered what sad thoughts Trudy used to conjure up the negative emotions necessary to use The Speed. He got the impression that her thoughts were considerably sadder than the ones he used. She was certainly faster than he was.

"See you at the bottom," Trudy said as she stepped off the edge of the fifty-foot drop. Instead of falling she reached out with a super-fast foot and was soon running down a sheer wall—straight at the ground. Her timing would have to be perfect. She was moving so fast that a split-second error would see her running straight into the ground.

Of course Trudy's timing was perfect, as always. She was six feet from the ground when she leapt away from the wall, performed a double tucked somersault, and landed like a cat.

Jack decided that next time he saw the Misery he would firstly try not to destroy any of his DIY supplies and secondly ask for extra Speed lessons. He was going to have to try very hard if he ever wanted to reach Trudy's level of perfection.

"Right, just remember to leap off the wall when you get close to the bottom. Easy," he reassured himself.

He thought about the time three years ago when his parents had told him they were going on a very special holiday. He'd assumed it was Disneyland, but it had turned out to be Paris. Jack would never understand the Parisians: Why would you use hundreds of metal girders to build a tower that just stood still when you could have used them to make a pretty amazing roller coaster instead? The memory made him sad and he felt the negative emotions flowing over him along with the familiar feeling of The Speed.

"Okay, Trudy, here I come." Jack launched himself over the edge and was running vertically down the wall. It was an amazing feeling, running down a wall, almost falling and yet being in total control.

Perhaps not total control. Jack was running faster than planned. He wouldn't have time to jump off the wall—he was going to hit the ground at full speed!

He felt a jolt and everything went black.

MINISTRY OF S.U.IT.S HANDBOOK

EARTHWORMS
STRANGE ABILITIES

You may have heard it said that if you cut an earthworm in two that both parts will grow into new worms. This is not true. You will probably just kill the earthworm. And then the earthworm police will hunt you down.

However, you may well get away with the crime. Earthworm forensic technology is quite limited and is mostly concerned with how nice soil is.

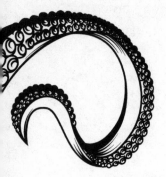

35

ANGEL ETIQUETTE

You know how sore you feel when you fall on the ground? Well, it is considerably more painful when you run into it at full speed.

Jack found himself floating in a black space. Everything was very quiet, but he had a strange feeling that someone was watching him. Then something slapped his face. His eyes snapped open and he saw two faces looking down from above.

"Are you angels?" asked Jack.

A hand reached down and slapped his face again. Jack didn't think that angels would be that violent.

"Trudy?" he guessed.

"Yeah. You were unconscious so I slapped you. And then I thought you were delirious... so I slapped you again."

Jack hauled himself up onto his elbows. "I'm not really

sure that's a great thing to do to someone who has just suffered severe head trauma.[65] What happened?"

Another voice spoke. "You didn't leap off the wall soon enough. But you managed to turn enough to avoid the worst of the impact."

Jack recognized the voice. He leapt up and threw his arms around his best friend. "David! You're alive."

"Yes. I knew that."

"We've come to rescue you."

"Oh, good, because it's been very impressive so far." Jack stopped hugging David. It was very hard to hug someone effectively when they were being that sarcastic.

"We can't stand by this wall for too long. The guards know that no one would be able to climb back up it, but they still come over here now and again just to check. There's an alcove over here where we can talk." David led them over to a small gouge in the wall that was out of sight from most of the rest of the cavern. Trudy, David, and Jack squeezed themselves into it.

"So what's this all about? Are you digging for oil? Coal? Diamonds?"

David shook his head. "I don't think so. They never told us. . . ."

---

[65] Slapping someone in the face is *exactly* the kind of thing that *you shouldn't do* to someone who has suffered from severe head trauma, but it shouldn't surprise anyone to know that it was also exactly the kind of thing that they taught you to do as part of the Ministry First Aid course. The Ministry's medical care *really* wasn't good.

"So you're just digging?" interrupted Trudy. "But that doesn't make any kind of sense. I mean, maybe they're looking for buried treasure. Or a doomsday weapon that was buried by the ancient kings of Ireland."

Why were they digging? Jack hated not knowing the answer. He wasn't good at waiting and mysteries. At Christmastime he hated having to wait to open his presents. And this was a much, much worse feeling. Because when you were waiting to open your Christmas presents at least you weren't worried that one of them might kill you.[66]

"So how did you get down here, anyway?" asked Trudy.

"Well, I got off the bus and was cutting across the park to get to my house . . . it was awful."

"What was awful?"

"Something burst out of the ground and pulled me under."

"What was it?" asked Jack. It seemed to Jack that everything in the world was trying to be deliberately suspenseful. Jack found it quite infuriating.

It was precisely at that moment that something burst through the alcove beside them. Soil and rock were sent flying.

Jack turned and looked. It was something that he would have previously greeted with surprise, but now he was kind of used to this sort of thing happening.

"Really?" he sighed with resignation.

---

[66] Unless you had really, really bad parents.

PIRATES
Buried Treasure

If you ever find buried treasure, it is reasonable to make the assumption that it was buried by a pirate. Pirates are slaves to tradition and therefore almost always bury their money rather than making use of more convenient online banking.

On the rare occasions that pirates do use banks, they tend to get irritated when, after making a deposit, they are given a cash card rather than a treasure map. Bizarrely enough, however, they do like putting their PIN numbers into cash machines. On cash machines the number comes up onscreen as XXXX. This gives pirates a feeling of inner contentment as four Xs literally mark the spot.

36

WE SUSPECT A MOLE

An enormous mole exploded through the dirt wall. It was unlike any kind of mole that Jack had seen before. For a start it was almost six feet from tail to snout, and that alone made it quite unusual. It had thick gray fur covering its plump body and its two long front paws each ended in five bony spikes.

The strangest thing about the mole was its nose. Rather than the little pink snout moles normally have, this one had two nostrils that were surrounded by a dozen little tentacles. They writhed in the air as if they were tasting it. Underneath the disturbing nose was a small mouth with a line of needlelike teeth.

David gulped. "Yeah, that's what dragged me under the ground."

Jack backed away from the star-nosed mole. "It looks

nasty. Do you think it'd like to go boating on the river? Or perhaps enjoy a pleasant picnic."

Trudy let out a short laugh. "I think we might find that this mole is quite different from the ones they had in *The Wind in the Willows*."

"Really, I can't believe that Kenneth Grahame would have lied to us." Jack was quite impressed with himself that he had remembered the name of the author who had written *The Wind in the Willows*.

"All books lie,"[67] said Trudy. "In fact, I'm fairly sure that toads can't even legitimately get a driving license. Even if they could, the insurance premiums they would have to pay would be crippling."

"So Kenneth Grahame[68] is a liar? Absolute shame," said Jack.

The mole swiped at Trudy with one enormous claw. Trudy hadn't had time to use The Speed, and the blow tore her shoulder open. She let out a gasp and fell to the ground.

Jack leapt forward, standing between his friends and the mole.

David's eyes widened. "Jack, what are you doing? That thing will kill you. You saw what it did to Trudy."

"Trudy wasn't ready," Jack snarled. "But I am. It hurt my

---

[67] Except this one. Obviously. This is all true. Totally.

[68] It should be pointed out that even though Kenneth Grahame wrote *The Wind in the Willows* (an absolute masterpiece of literature) he also worked in a bank. So not only did he lie to children, but he probably lied to just about everyone.

friend and that makes me sad. And thinking about people trapped in this hole for thirty years . . . well, that just depresses me to no end. And when I get depressed I get . . ."

"Slightly weepy?" offered David.

"No," said Jack. "I get fast."

The mole used its squat back legs to propel itself toward Jack. Jack blurred into action, diving forward. As quick as lightning he smashed his fists straight into the star-shaped nose of the mole. It stumbled back, cupping its claws over its bleeding nose, and emitted a high-pitched squeal.

"What on earth . . . How on earth?" David was stunned by Jack's speed. "Is your dad secretly Bruce Lee? Have you been getting ninja training?"

"It's The Speed, David. We'll explain later." Trudy was sitting up but wincing in pain from her damaged shoulder.

The mole lashed out at Jack again, first with its right claw, then left, then right. Jack dodged each of the blows. He kicked out with one of his feet, catching the mole's leg and knocking it to the ground.

It sprang from the ground, its bulky gray body crashing against Jack and pressing him up against the soil wall. The mole lashed out with both claws. Jack twisted and just avoided being impaled, but the claws were now embedded in the soil on either side of Jack's neck, pinning him to the wall.

"Trudy, I could use a bit of help here. I seem to have found myself in something of a situation."

"There in a minute."

"Could you make it half a minute?"

Out of the corner of his eye Jack saw Trudy struggle to

her feet, but a second later she slumped back down again. The blood loss from her shoulder was worse than she would admit.

The mole tried to free its claws from the dirt wall for a few seconds before suddenly stopping. It cocked its head to one side as if it was thinking.

I really hope the mole isn't remembering that it has teeth, Jack thought to himself.

Unfortunately, that was exactly what the mole was thinking. It gnashed its needlelike teeth together and then pushed its mouth toward Jack's neck.

Jack reached up with both hands and shoved the mole's head away with all his strength. He could feel the hot, worm-smelling breath of the mole on his face. It snorted and his hair rippled. The little pink tentacles that made up its nose were up against Jack's face now, slimy and horrible.

What were the weaknesses of a giant mole? Jack racked his brain to see if he'd learned anything about them in his biology classes. Unfortunately, to the best of his recollection this was not something that they had ever taught in school. He decided if he survived he would write a stern letter to his headmaster explaining that they needed to revise the curriculum to include more practical matters.

The mole's teeth were pressing against Jack's flesh as he tried to hold it back. He felt something trickle down his shoulder and realized it must have broken his skin. Then without warning, the mole swayed backward and collapsed onto the ground like a sack of potatoes.

David was standing behind the mole with a spade in his

hands. There was some mole blood dripping off it. "Sometimes all the karate training in the world is no substitute for a good, solid spade," David observed.

Jack breathed a sigh of relief. "Thanks, David. Good work."

Jack and David rushed over to Trudy. She was pressing her hand against the wound in her shoulder. The bleeding seemed to have stopped, but the wound was still quite deep.

"You're going to need stitches."

"Let's go to the Ulster hospital."

"Why don't we just get Nurse Nufty at the Ministry to do it?"

Trudy shot a withering glance at Jack. "I wouldn't let her sew a tea cozy, much less a hole in my shoulder. Anyway, forget about that. David, what happened after you got kidnapped by the mole?"

David explained that the mole had brought him to the underground lair where he had discovered that the children were being forced to dig.

"But why do they need children to dig?" asked Trudy. "I mean, they have giant moles, don't they? And couldn't adults be used to run the diggers?"

"The digging's only part of why they're kidnapping us," said David.

"Then what's the other part?" asked Trudy.

"They're training us to be pirates."

"I'm sorry." Jack was sure he must have misheard. "I thought you said 'pirates'?"

"I did."

Jack and Trudy were both speechless. They hadn't

expected pirates. Although, given what Jack had seen at the start of the week, he clearly should have.

"This entire place is run by pirates," David explained. "And I don't mean those modern pirates either. I mean the classic head-scarf-wearing, one-legged, hooks-for-hands, eye-patched, 'shiver me timbers, Jim-lad' type of pirates."

"You aren't serious," said Jack.

David looked incredibly serious. "That's one of the reasons they need us. A lot of them have hooks for hands, which makes it very hard to change the gears when they're driving the excavators and dump trucks. To start off with they use us for that . . . but they're selecting the best and training us to replace the older pirates."

"How can you train to be a pirate?" asked Jack.

"They gave me a timetable."[69] David took a piece of paper out of his pocket and unfolded it. "This morning we had a class on pirate etymology—how to say things like 'yoho,' 'make him walk the plank,' and 'pieces of eight.' Then this evening I'm scheduled to have sessions on seafaring, naval lore, and singing sea shanties. I've also learned what we should do with a drunken sailor early in the morning."[70]

"Pirates," muttered Jack. "I always thought pirates were good guys, laughing, murdering, and stealing. But it turns

[69] Just because they're pirates it doesn't mean that they aren't well-organized.

[70] It is interesting to note that David never actually learned what to do with a drunken sailor midafternoon or in the evening. The instructions he received only detailed what to do with him early in the morning.

out they're bad guys, kidnapping children and digging large holes."

"And that isn't all. They've already figured out that I wouldn't be much use at driving the diggers. I uhh, might have crashed one when they gave me a go on it shortly after I got here."

"So what does that mean?" asked Jack.

"Well, because they don't need me to be able to drive a digger . . . they're doing my pirate initiation ceremony tomorrow evening." David looked ashen-faced at the thought of this.

"What's the initiation ceremony?" asked Trudy. "It can't be that bad, can it? They'll probably just take you out on a boat and make you drink a few bottles of grog."

David rolled up one leg of his trousers and showed them his right arm. Around the calf of his leg and the thinnest part of his wrist someone had crudely drawn two dotted lines with ballpoint pen.

"What are those dotted lines for?" Jack asked.

"They're going to saw off my hand and my foot," whispered David, "and replace them with a hook and a peg leg."

The thought of it made Jack feel physically sick. "They . . . they can't . . ."

David pointed across the cavern where other children were standing with crutches and eye patches. "They can and they have." Jack saw that many of the children in the cavern had already received artificial pirate limbs.

"We're getting you out of here right now," said Jack. "We can carry you up the wall using The Speed."

"Can you take everyone?" asked David.

Jack looked across the cavern—there were hundreds of captives. "Well . . . no, there are too many."

"Then you'll have to leave me. They have a roll call every morning. They've said if one of us is missing they'll kill twenty as a punishment."

"Pirates are evil," gasped Jack.

"Is that really coming as a shock to you?" asked Trudy.

"Yes!" said Jack indignantly. "I always thought they were fun. There are theme-park rides and films based on them!"

"Look, I can't leave unless all the kids here can leave," said David. "It's as simple as that. You guys get out of here, get help, and come back. But make sure you do it before six o'clock tomorrow night."

"Why six o'clock?" asked Trudy.

"That's the time set for my initiation." David nodded at the dotted line on his calf. "And if you aren't back by then, half the money I spent on my Adidas three-stripe Samba trainers will have been completely wasted."

MARTIAL ARTS/KARATE
KARATE STANCES

The standard karate stance is feet shoulder-width apart, arms with one fist clenched and one open. This was the stance the karate masters adopted when using a saw. As previously discussed, all karate masters were originally builders. Many people these days claim that the stances are based on animal positions or martial defense. In reality, they are all based on the use of carpentry tools. Which is why so many of them look like someone trying to hammer a nail into a wall. If you don't believe me, look at karate stances and then imagine them with a hammer in one hand and a nail in the other. You'd be surprised how often it works.

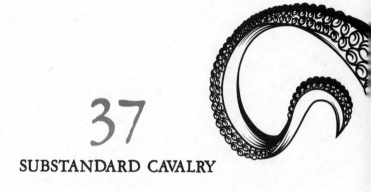

37

SUBSTANDARD CAVALRY

Jack didn't even need to pause before using The Speed to run back up the cliff wall and out of the cavern. The sad thought he used was the dotted line around the wrist of his best friend. It seemed as if things couldn't get any worse.

Once they had sneaked out of the P.E. teacher's office they headed straight to the Ministry to tell Grey what they had uncovered.

<hr />

"So how are you going to help us rescue David and the children?" asked Jack.

"Yeah," said Trudy. "We need the cavalry."

Grey sighed. "You still haven't quite got it yet, have you?"

"Got what?"

"You want the cavalry?"

"Yeah, like in cowboy movies. The cavalry rides in and saves the day."

"You are the cavalry."

"We are the cavalry?" spluttered Jack.

Trudy looked at Jack. "Pretty crappy cavalry."

"I'm not going to disagree with you on that point," said Grey unkindly. "But we Men and Women in Suits are the last line of defense. Things too odd for the police, too strange for the army, and too scary for the politicians. That's what we deal with."

"But surely you could send more agents to help us?"

"There aren't that many of us. The entire Ministry in Northern Ireland consists of less than a hundred people . . . and, well . . . things. And most of them are administration and filing staff. We might be able to have a few more front-line agents, but Cthulhu has made the bureaucracy maddeningly complicated."

"Why don't you fire him?" asked Trudy, her voice sounding barely under control.

"He's an ancient being of almost unlimited power with psychopathic tendencies. Do you want to be the one to tell him to pack up his desk and collect his last paycheck on the way out?"

"Is there no one who could help us?" asked Trudy.

"You aren't the only ones dealing with a crisis. Just at the minute we have three evil geniuses bent on world domination, a technologically enhanced virus that threatens to destroy all the world's cows, and a chess-playing computer that has reached such a level of intelligence that it wants to stop playing pointless games and audition for a television talent show. We wouldn't mind that except it really, really can't sing."

"So you can't offer any help? We don't know how we'll get the kids out of the cavern."

"We can't offer any more manpower. We could try and get you guys some equipment. Let's go and see the quartermaster."

"Incidentally, I don't suppose you have any idea why they're digging under the ground and not looking for anything?" asked Jack. "If it's pirates, I assume it might be buried treasure."

Grey thought for a moment. "It could be, I suppose. Or it might be something to do with the dinosaurs."

Grey talked to them about dinosaurs as they walked through the corridors of the Ministry to the quartermaster's store.

"I've already explained to you that the dinosaurs didn't just die out. People stopped believing in them, so the Ministry stepped in and started hiding them. They had an alarming tendency to trample schoolchildren that was becoming quite problematic."

"Where do you hide a dinosaur?" asked Trudy.

"Well, to start off with, in caves. The aquatic ones we hid in big lochs."

"Are you saying that the Loch Ness Monster is a dinosaur hidden by the Ministry?" asked Jack.

"Well, not the Loch Ness Monster. The Loch Ness Monster is something considerably more terrifying than a dinosaur.

But, generally, if you hear about a strange monster, it's just a dinosaur that's been put into hiding."

"So are all dinosaurs hidden in caves?" asked Jack.

"Well, in places like Northern Ireland they are, yes. We didn't have many dinosaurs, so there are enough natural caves and caverns to hide them in. In larger places they tend to build containment units to capture them all."

"Like what?" asked Trudy. "Don't people notice if you start digging vast underground caverns to keep dinosaurs in?"

Grey chuckled. "People notice what they want to notice. In London all the dinosaurs are hidden on the Underground tunnels. Huge stretches of unused London Tube are home to hidden dinosaurs."

"Seriously?"

"Have you ever been to London? Ever noticed that the underground trains are always being delayed? That's what happens when a dinosaur gets loose. And occasionally the tunnels make low rumbling, grumbling noises. Trains don't make those kinds of noises. Those are the kinds of noises that dinosaurs make. Low, rumbling noises. Occasionally you'll hear a high-pitched screech, but that's their mating sound. And if you hear that, it's essential that you get out of the way before you get trampled by an amorous dinosaur."

Jack shook his head. "Even with everything that's come before, this is asking too much. I just can't believe in this."

And then Grey said something that made Jack believe. "Have you ever wondered why people always say that a dinosaur was as large as a double-decker bus, or as long as three train carriages? Simple. The people who work for London transport are also the people who look after dinosaurs. So when they think of how tall a dinosaur is, they also think of public transport."

Jack was stunned. He had been thinking exactly this just a few days ago. It made perfect sense.

"Do the dinosaurs enjoy the underground life?" Trudy asked.

"They seem to," said Grey. "We make sure they're well fed and they generally just lie about all day. Notoriously lazy creatures, dinosaurs."

Jack had loved dinosaurs when he had been younger and was quite excited to suddenly believe that they were still alive. "So do dinosaurs look like they do in *Jurassic Park*?"

"They're the same shape, but they tend to be a lot brighter. They come in yellows and purples and the most brilliant red that you could possibly imagine. Some of the larger ones even come in gold and silver varieties."

Jack laughed out loud.

"What's so funny?" Grey asked.

"Well, the dinosaurs were green, or brownish green. It helped camouflage them against the trees. They would be too easily seen otherwise."

Grey shook his head. "Really? Jack, some dinosaurs are the height of three double-decker buses. Do you think that just because something large is green that you're not going to see it? If they painted buses green, would they become invisible?"

Jack admitted that the idea that something that large

could be camouflaged did seem slightly absurd. "Can I see the dinosaurs?"

"Of course you can. Once you join up in the Ministry you can be privy to all our secrets. After all, you've metaphorically signed on the dotted line."

Mention of a dotted line jolted Jack back to reality. He suddenly remembered the dotted lines around David's hand and calf. Jack felt slightly guilty. He had gotten caught up in the talk of dinosaurs and had forgotten about David. "Why did you start talking about dinosaurs in the first place, Grey?"

"I was just thinking about why all that digging is going on. Northern Ireland's dinosaurs are hidden underground in the Marble Arch Caves."[71]

Trudy's eyes widened. "Do you think Chapeau Noir Enterprises might be trying to free the dinosaurs? They could use them to try and take over the world."

"It's possible. . . ." Grey was hesitant. "But they'd be foolish if that's what they were trying to do."

"But why? Aren't dinosaurs incredibly strong and fierce?"

"They are . . . but they're also very lazy and hard to motivate, and they don't take direction well."

"In what way?" asked Jack.

"Well, if you stick out an arm pointing at your enemies expecting the dinosaur to gobble them down, you're more likely to find it chewing on your elbow. So they're of limited

[71] The Marble Arch Caves are a geopark in Northern Ireland, including stalactites and stalagmites, underground rivers, caverns, and passageways. Well worth a visit.

use as crack troops. You can get them to stampede in one direction, but that's about the most you can hope for."

"So why did you mention them?" asked Trudy.

"I just thought of the caves because they are quite near the border. And the children were being kidnapped all around the border, weren't they?"

"How do they keep the dinosaurs in the Marble Arch Caves?" asked Jack.

"Have you ever been to the caves?"

"I went with my father years ago," said Trudy. "They're full of stalactites and stalagmites."

"I suppose they told you the stalactites were made by dripping water," chuckled Grey.

"Aren't they?" asked Jack.

"The things people believe." Grey shook his head. "Have you ever noticed a shower head covered in stalactites? Or a shower tray covered in stalagmites?"

Trudy said that this was something she had never seen.

"And yet if they're formed by dripping water, bathrooms should be full of them. The stalagmites are built by Ministry craftsmen to keep the dinosaurs in."

"I've seen pictures of the Marble Arch Caves," interrupted Jack. "Those stalagmites aren't big enough to stop dinosaurs from getting out."

"They aren't meant as bars of a cage. They're more like the equivalent of a cattle grid for dinosaurs. The dinosaurs, being big and clumsy, can't get out without stepping on them. And when they step on them they hurt their feet. So they don't even try and leave."

"That makes sense," said Trudy.

"I really wish it didn't," complained Jack. "That means my entire primary-five geology project was a load of rubbish. I'm going to have to go home and rip it up this evening."

"But I really can't imagine Mr. Teach and Chapeau Noir going to all this trouble to free the dinosaurs," said Grey.

Grey pointed at the door they had stopped in front of. "Now, bear in mind, we'll have to fill out forms to get the equipment and that will be unpleasant and potentially impossible."

Jack thought he knew what Grey meant. Filling out forms was never fun. "But if we fill out the forms, then we'll get whatever equipment we want?"

"Well, yes . . . although no one has ever successfully filled out a form."

Jack felt his heart fall slightly. "How come?"

"Because the forms are infinitely long."

DINOSAURS
MATING CRY

The only thing more dangerous that an angry dinosaur is an amorous dinosaur. Therefore Ministry operatives are advised to run in the opposite direction if they hear a dinosaur mating cry.

If you have never heard a dinosaur mating cry, the sound it most closely resembles is the same sound as fingernails being dragged across a chalkboard.

This is why humans find the sound of fingers on a chalkboard so unpleasant. This was a sound of danger to cavemen versions of us from many years ago—a warning to run and hide. Therefore an ancestral memory, hidden somewhere deep in our subconscious minds, is still terrified when it hears this sound.

* * *

This also goes part of the way to explaining why the Ministry had to hide the dinosaurs in the first place. Because the sound of nails on a chalkboard sounds to dinosaurs like a mating cry, many cavemen schools had to be disbanded following a series of fatal squashings.

38

THE QUARTERMASTER'S STORE

The quartermaster's store was enormous. In fact, it was beyond enormous. With only eight letters, enormous was a ridiculously small word to try and explain just how big the store was.

For a start, the store was impossibly tall. Where the roof should have been there were several banks of fluffy, white clouds. Birds circled high above their heads. Each of the birds had miniature oxygen tanks on their backs and little plastic breathing masks strapped over their beaks.

"Is it safe to breathe the air in here, Grey?" asked Jack, doing his best not to inhale.

"Oh, yes, perfectly. The birds only need to wear the oxygen tanks for when they fly up to the rafters where they build their nests. Up there, the air is so thin that they can't breathe properly."

"That doesn't make sense," said Trudy. "Because even if the roof really is that high up, we're still under the museum, aren't we?"

"Yes, it is strange, isn't it?" said Grey. "I've never really figured out how that works."

There was a deafening crash a couple of feet away from where Jack was standing. Jack leapt into the air and his heart played a paradiddle against his rib cage.

A block of ice had crashed into the floor, causing a crater three feet wide. David and Trudy both looked to Grey for an explanation.

"Yes, perhaps I should have warned you about that."

"You think?" asked Trudy. "What was it?"

"Well, occasionally a rather stupid bird decides to fly all the way up to the very top of the roof. Up there it's so cold that their wings freeze and they turn into little birdy ice cubes. When that happens they come crashing to the ground. Nasty business. Three people have been killed by falling wildfowl this year."

"Aren't there any safety precautions we should be taking? Like, wearing some kind of a hat?"

Grey pointed to the crater the ice-covered bird had made when it had crashed into the ground. "The floor is reinforced concrete with cast-iron gratings through it for extra rigidity. The iced bird fell so far and so fast that it made a hole in that. What kind of hat would protect you?"

Jack admitted that it would have to be a pretty big hat to be of any use.

"Hasn't anyone ever done anything to make it more safe?" asked Trudy.

"One of the Ministry scientists tried. He invented a hat that was made of unusually strong metals alloys that could take any impact."

"And that saved him from falling birds?" Jack asked.

"Well, yes, but unfortunately the hat was so heavy that the first time he strapped it on he broke his neck and killed himself."

Jack and Trudy both shuddered at this piece of ghoulish information.

"That's him over there," said Grey, pointing.

Jack turned and saw a skeleton with a hat the size of a caravan strapped onto the skull.

"They didn't even take him away?" asked Jack, feeling queasy.

"No one could figure out how to undo the straps," said Grey. "And the hat's far too heavy to lift."

Jack looked up at the clouds and decided that he wanted to get out of the store as soon as possible. He couldn't help feeling that this visit to the quartermaster wasn't going to help them that much in their quest to save David.

In the center of the room there was a wide counter, and behind that there were row upon row upon row of filing cabinets. They seemed to go on forever and stretched up into the clouds.

Grey leaned against the counter in a nonchalant manner and sharply struck a small golden bell that sat on top of it.

At the sound of the *ding* a tiny man popped up from behind the counter.

"Hello, Quartermaster," said Grey.

"Hello, Grey," said the tiny man. "I thought you'd retired."

"Not retired, but not out on as many active missions these days. Anyway, breaking in a few new recruits." Grey waved his hand at Trudy and Jack. "Trudy . . . Jack, this is the quartermaster. Quartermaster, this is Jack and Trudy."

Jack and Trudy took turns leaning over the counter to shake the quartermaster's hand.

Looking over the counter, Jack saw that the quartermaster was standing on a ladder and couldn't have been much more than two and a half feet tall. But despite his height, he really wasn't tiny. Rather, he looked more squashed—like a tall man compressed into a short man.

"So what are you looking for?" the quartermaster asked.

Trudy thought. They needed something that would allow them to rescue the kidnapped children from the mine. "Some kind of grappling hook. One that pulls a rope ladder after it. And it should fire from a gas-propelled gun."

Jack was impressed by how clear Trudy was about the equipment they needed. The quartermaster didn't bat an eyelid—he had dealt with much more outlandish requests during his time at the Ministry. He nodded his head, climbed down off his ladder, and walked into the ranks of filing cabinets.

Jack turned to Grey; he had a question to ask. "Grey . . ."

"You want to know why the Quartermaster looks like a tall man squashed?"

"Yes."

"You know the way that in the Ministry things aren't always what they first appear? In the case of the quartermaster he is exactly what he looks like."

"He's really a tall man who's been squashed?" said Jack.

"Gradually squashed, yes. When I first came here he was just over three feet tall. The problem is that he keeps falling off the ladders that he uses to get to the top of the filing cabinets."

"But surely that would kill him?" said Trudy.

"Yes, it should kill him, but it doesn't. The quartermaster figured out a system to avoid dying from such long falls."

"What is it?" asked Trudy.[72]

"When he's falling he only falls part of the way at a time."

"I'm sorry?" said Jack, who really wasn't in the slightest bit sorry.

"It's like this. Say, he falls off a ladder at a height of ten thousand feet . . ."

Grey was interrupted by a sudden yell in the distance.

"*O-h-h-h-h-h-h-h-h-h-h-h-h, R-a-a-a-a-a-a-a-a-a-a-a-a-a-tsssss.*"

The yell sounded as if it was far away but getting closer.

---

[72] It is worth noting that the fact that Trudy asked this question later saves her life. You should continually ask adults questions because you never know when one of their answers will save your life. Also, adults find it really irritating if you're always asking questions. So you know . . . that's a bonus.

Jack guessed, quite correctly, that this was the sound of the Quartermaster falling off a ladder somewhere.

Grey stood still, as if he was waiting for something. Jack and Trudy decided that it was best to do the same. After a few minutes had passed they heard a slight thump. It sounded as if someone had dropped a large shopping bag onto a kitchen floor. Grey seemed reassured when he heard this and carried on with his explanation.

"Now say the quartermaster falls from a height of ten thousand feet—most people would panic and fall all ten thousand feet in one go. But not the clever quartermaster."

"So what does he do, then?"

"He falls the ten thousand feet by splitting it up into five thousand falls of two feet. Now, if a man falls ten thousand feet, he'll die, right?"

"Right."

"Now on the other hand, if he falls two feet, five thousand times, he won't die, right?"

"Okay, that makes sense . . . sort of . . . But why does he look all squashed?" asked Trudy.

"Well, even a fall of two feet subjects your body to a bit of strain. Now, if you subject your body to that strain five thousand times, then it adds up. In the end all the forces, from all the falls, all add up, and you get ever so slightly shorter—squashed."

"So every time I fall I get shorter?" asked Jack.

"Well, yes," said Grey, "but only a really, really *tiny* amount. Have you ever noticed how short old people are? That's because they also tend to fall over a lot."

"Babies tend to fall over a lot as well," observed Trudy.

"Well, exactly," agreed Grey, "and look at how short they are."

"It's not the strangest thing I've heard in the last few days," mused Jack as the quartermaster came around the corner.

He was carrying a couple of pink forms in one hand and was using the other hand to rub his bottom. Apparently even a fall of two feet hurt when you fell on your bottom.

"Here are the forms, just fill them out as best you can and then I'll get you the equipment."

Jack looked at the forms that the quartermaster had put down on the desk and then looked at Grey. Were these the legendary "infinitely long" forms? They were about the size of a notebook page and as far as Jack could tell there were only three or four spaces to fill in.

"They don't look that long," said Jack.

Grey said nothing and handed Jack his sleek black pen. It only took Jack two minutes to fill in the form requesting the grappling hook. He felt happy that the "infinitely long" form had turned out to be rather short. At the same time, part of him knew that nothing in the Ministry could be as simple as this.

"Finished," said Jack, handing the form back to the quartermaster. He was keen to get out of the store and back to thinking about how to rescue David.

The quartermaster looked at the form and pointed at something written on the bottom of it in impossibly small writing. Jack had to put his face right up against the paper and squint before he could make out what it said.

In the event of equipment being needed this year please

complete supplementary form 125jT. If equipment will be needed next year please complete form 11C1. Thank you for your cooperation.

Jack felt a sinking feeling. "I'll need the equipment this year."

"That'll be the 125jT, then," said the quartermaster, handing Jack a second form.

<hr>

Time passed. A lot of time passed. No matter how many forms Jack filled out, there was always just one more to fill in after that. Jack realized what Grey meant about the forms being infinitely long; this could go on forever. Eventually Jack noticed that he was filling out another form 125jT.

"I've already filled out this form before. Do I have to fill it out again?"

"Afraid so," said the quartermaster. "There is some duplication, but it's absolutely necessary for the system to work."

Jack realized, as he had filled out a second 125jT, that he was in a loop. He would eventually fill out another, then some more forms, then another.... There was no way out. He was trapped. He started giggling in a slightly insane way. "Forms, forms, lovely forms." He sang to himself under his breath as he scrunched them up in his hands.

Trudy went over to Jack and gently took the pen and the forms out of his hands. Jack was shaking slightly, but felt relieved that he was no longer holding any of the forms. Trudy set the paperwork on the desk in front of the quartermaster.

"We've changed our minds," said Trudy. "That equipment isn't so important after all."

"You'd be surprised how many people decide that in the end," the quartermaster said, smiling.

"How many?" asked Jack. He was still rocking backward and forward.

The quartermaster thought. "How many people give up trying to get equipment? That's a request for statistics. In order for me to give you the numbers you want I'll need you to fill in a form AAAs2W."

"Never mind," Trudy said quickly. "Grey, let's get Jack out of here."

STATISTICS
Ability to Explain Things

Statisticians will tell you that statistics are very useful for helping to explain things to people.

Of course this is not even vaguely true. Statistics tend to make things more confusing than they were in the first place. Anyone who has ever watched a children's television show will know that what really helps explain things easily is a conversation between two or more sock puppets. This is why the Ministry of SUITs has only one full-time trained statistician and six full-time trained sock-puppeticians.

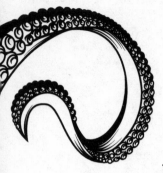

39
RETURN TO SANITY

Once out of the storeroom Jack seemed to regain his grasp on reality.

He hugged Trudy. "Thanks for getting me out of there. I don't think I'd have made it if I'd been on my own."

Trudy turned to Grey and poked him in the chest with her forefinger. "What was the point in taking us in there? What's the point in having a quartermaster who never actually gives out any equipment?"

Grey sucked his teeth before answering. "It's like this: In every workplace there is a lot of time wasting. Here at the Ministry, rather than letting important people waste their time we actually employ people like the quartermaster to waste their time for them."

"And that works?" asked Trudy.

"Surprisingly well. After a visit to the quartermaster

most people are so relieved to be doing something worthwhile that they work twice as hard as they would have otherwise."

"Any other reason?"

Grey looked around, checking that the corridor was empty. "What I told you is the official reason. The real reason is that Cthulhu..."

"Cthulhu," repeated Trudy, "the ancient and evil being with unimaginable power, the one that longs to watch the world burn and send all its people into madness and insanity."

"Yes, that Cthulhu,[73] the one that works in the filing branch. He also designed the requisition system."

"It nearly drove Jack crazy."

"Mmmm. We rather think that was Cthulhu's intention when he designed the system."

"Why doesn't someone just fire Cthulhu?" shouted Trudy.

"As I've said before, firstly, no one is brave enough to. Secondly, if Cthulhu can nearly send people insane with filing, imagine the havoc he could wreak if he was out in the world at large. Imagine what would happen if he got a job at

---

[73] Interestingly enough there really was another Cthulhu, Janet Cthulhu, who was an office cleaner and always brought cupcakes in for people's birthdays. This sometimes caused amusing confusion. It also sometimes caused people to avoid birthday cupcakes when they heard that "Cthulhu" had brought them in. They were worried they might be from the other Cthulhu and would therefore be ancient and evil cupcakes of unimaginable power, which would cause the populace of the world to descend into madness and insanity.

a merchant bank, or an arms dealer, or something like that. To be honest, it's much safer to have him here."

"Even when he nearly drives your coworkers mad?"

Grey laughed nervously. "You're exaggerating the risk. Only three or four staff go mad each year. And generally they recover after fourteen or fifteen months of rest and intensive therapy. . . . Of course, they're never quite the same again. . . ." Grey drifted off.

"Guys, I'm okay now," said Jack. He seemed to have shaken off the horror of the infinitely long forms. "But we still haven't solved our problem. How are we going to save David? How are we going to get the kidnapped children up that wall?"

Grey shrugged. "Go to the store? Buy a rope ladder? Not everything has to be amazing, you know."

"Oh," said Jack.

"If you can get us a rope ladder, Jack and I will head to the headquarters of Chapeau Noir," said Trudy. "Maybe we'll be able to find some kind of a clue there as to why Mr. Teach has been digging under the school."

"Do we really need to do that? I don't want to leave David down there for a moment longer than necessary."

"Jack, I know you're worried about David, but this isn't just about rescuing those kids. We've got to figure out what Mr. Teach is up to and stop him somehow. If we don't stop him once and for all, what would prevent him from just kidnapping more kids?"

"When did you start thinking things through instead of punching things?"

"I always thought things through," said Trudy, playfully

punching Jack in the shoulder. "It's just that before, you never thought to ask me what I was thinking."

"So how are we going to find out where the headquarters of Chapeau Noir is?" asked Jack.

"Just look it up in the Yellow Pages," said Grey. "You really should stop trying to make everything more complicated than it needs to be, Jack."

"Are you trying to tell me that evil villains list themselves in the Yellow Pages?"

"Well, of course they do. They may be evil villains, but they still need to make sure they get all their evil mail delivered."

"I'll get the address." Trudy grinned. "Go home and make up some excuse for your parents why you'll be out late tonight. I'll pick you up in a Ministry car at seven thirty."

MINISTRY OF S.U.I.T.S HANDBOOK

EVIL VILLAINS
HEADQUARTERS

A good rule of thumb is that villains almost never live in underwater grottoes, hollowed-out volcanoes, or ancient castles surrounded by gardens filled with poisonous plants. If you are a villain and you have plans of world domination, you'll draw attention to yourself if you live in that kind of flamboyant hideout. The kind of conversation that such a villainous lair will create is something along the lines of the following:

Local Policeman 1: There have been a lot of murders around here lately. Do you think it might have anything to do with that scientist fellow who moved into the old abandoned missile silo?

Local Policeman 2: Could be. He seems to have ordered a lot of equipment recently. One of his workers asked me if I knew where he could get weapons-grade uranium.

Local Policeman 1: You know, I have a bit of a hunch. I think we should go up there and check the place out.

This is the stage at which the policemen go up to the lair and get suspicious because the "coffeemaker" in the kitchen looks an awful lot like a death ray. And there are also rather a lot of dead bodies stacked up in the cellar.

Policemen pick up on those kinds of clues.

Generally, villains are a lot smarter than this. And that's a pity, because if everyone who was out to destroy the world had a flamboyant lair, we would be able to catch them a lot sooner. For example, if only the big banks shunned skyscrapers and instead had their headquarters in orbiting satellites, bases at the South Pole, Gothic castles, and enormous floating antigravity platforms, we probably would have spotted what they were up to a lot sooner. Then we would have been able to stop them before the whole financial crisis thing happened.

40

SHATTERED

It was nearly six o'clock by the time Jack got back to his house. His parents were just sitting down to dinner. Jack took up his place at the table.

"You're late," commented his father's mustache.

"Sorry, I was just helping . . . out with the . . . chess club."

"You're a member of the chess club as well now?" his mother said, surprised.

"Yes, I am . . . apparently," said Jack, who was almost as surprised as his mother was.

"Wonderful game, chess," said his father. "You know the legend is that it was invented many thousands of years ago as a way for tribes to solve their disputes without having to resort to warfare. Now, the interesting thing is . . ."[74]

---

[74] When anyone begins a sentence with "Now, the interesting thing is,"

Normally Jack would have let out a theatrical groan when his father began one of his long, boring lectures about ancient history or legends. However, this time Jack nodded appreciatively and encouraged his father to talk about chess some more. Jack's mother was suspicious at this out-of-character behavior. The reason for it, of course, was simple: The more Jack's father talked, the less Jack would have to make up lies about the chess club and why he was late.

For once it seemed to Jack that having a boring and verbose father might actually be an advantage. Jack nodded and occasionally chipped in with a "That's very interesting; so why did that happen, then?" where it seemed most appropriate.

Time passed.

"...and so you see, that's why the Russians became such masters at the game. Fairly obvious when you think about it."

Jack swallowed the last of his dinner.

"That's fascinating, Dad. Listen, I'm going over to Trudy's house tonight. Is that okay?"

"Trudy." Jack's dad smiled at the mention of a girl's name. "Is that the girl you were talking to after choir practice?"

Jack had forgotten that he had told his father that.

---

you can immediately surmise that what they are about to tell you isn't interesting in the slightest. If it was interesting, they wouldn't have had to *tell you* it was interesting. It is, however, the kind of thing that parents are always starting their sentences with.

"Umm, yes, that's her."

"Are we going to get to meet this Trudy sometime?"

Jack blushed and went a lovely shade of bright red.[75] Jack started spluttering a few words, unsure as to why he was quite so embarrassed. To be fair to Jack, it would have been difficult to explain to his parents that Trudy was not, in fact, his girlfriend but rather was his partner in a secret government agency whose job it was to investigate and stop things that were too weird for the average person to imagine.

Jack couldn't figure out a way of achieving this without causing his parents to worry about him, and so he spluttered some more. In fact, he spluttered to such an extent that there seemed to be a realistic chance of his choking to death.[76] Luckily, his mother saved him from this ignominious fate by cuffing his father around the head with a tea towel.

"Leave Jack alone. He's allowed to have a friend."

"Thanks, Mum," said Jack as he ducked out of the room.

Jack ran up to his room to think about getting changed. But what would he choose? Just what was the well-dressed

---

[75] For those of you who want to know exactly what shade Jack blushed, on a Dulux color chart his cheeks would have been considered Fire Cracker 2.

[76] Suffocation through spluttering is in fact the most common cause of dying through embarrassment. People often say "I nearly died of embarrassment," without realizing that it is technically possible. The easiest way to avoid dying of embarrassment is simply to not take oneself too seriously. If you learn to laugh at yourself, it doesn't seem so bad when other people do it as well.

burglar wearing this season? After going through his closet a number of times he came up with a pair of black tracksuit bottoms, a black T-shirt, and a black sweatshirt. It seemed appropriate.

Jack was standing outside his house when the Ministry car pulled up. He scrambled into the back beside Trudy and was greeted with loud laughter. "Why are you dressed all in black?"

"Isn't it obvious? We're burglars. We're going burglaring."[77]

"I don't think burglaring is a real word."[78]

Jack looked at what Trudy was wearing. She had on a light blue polo shirt and a pair of navy tracksuit trousers. Her hair was tied back in a ponytail.

"You don't look like a burglar."

"That's the point. I tried to dress like an office cleaner. That way if someone sees me in the offices of Chapeau Noir, they won't give me a second glance."

"Oh," said Jack. Realization dawned on him.

"Yes. *Oh.* If we're in the offices and they see you, they'll realize you're a burglar. Because you look like a burglar. In fact you could only have made it worse if you'd brought along a black eye mask and a bag marked 'swag.'"

"Sorry," said Jack. "This is my first burglary."

"It shows. Hopefully you'll improve."

---

[77] *Burglaring* is not a real word.

[78] Trudy is right about this. It isn't.

Jack was slightly disappointed when they arrived at the headquarters of Chapeau Noir Enterprises. He had been expecting a skyscraper of black glass, black stone, and silver metal. In point of fact, the building was red brick with ordinary windows and a welcoming-looking foyer.

"What were you expecting?" asked Trudy. "A hollowed-out volcano lair?"

"Well, no, but I was hoping that it would at least be a little sinister."

Jack and Trudy clambered out of the Ministry car and stood in front of the building.

"Since you're the expert, how do we get in?" asked Jack.

Trudy pulled a rucksack off her back and rummaged around in it. Jack was expecting her to take out a lock pick, a grappling hook, or perhaps a magical collapsible ladder. He was therefore surprised when she took out a clipboard.

"Follow me."

Trudy walked confidently through the office's sliding doors. She strode up to the reception desk as Jack hurried to keep up.

"We're here to check the air vents on floor eight," Trudy said to a bored-looking security guard who sat behind the reception desk.

The security guard looked skeptical at first. After all, why would a child be sent to look at air vents? "Really, look . . ." Then he caught sight of the clipboard. "Umm, okay, the elevators are over there." He pointed.

Jack was astonished and followed Trudy over to the elevators. "How did that work?" he asked her once they were safely inside one. "Is that a magic clipboard?"

"Perfectly ordinary clipboard. But it works like magic. You see, people assume that if you have a clipboard, then you also have some documentation attached to it. And they then imagine if you have documentation you must have offices somewhere. And they then imagine at the office there are lots of people working. And they then imagine that you must be a person in authority if the imaginary people at the imaginary office gave you a clipboard. So then they believe anything that you tell them. It's the power of the human imagination coupled with the authority of the clipboard."

"That doesn't sound like it could really work."

"Oh, it does," said Trudy. "In fact, I've got a survey saying it does right here." She tapped the clipboard.

"Oh. Okay then," said Jack, who found himself strangely convinced by this argument.

"Now what we need is to figure out where we want to go next."

Jack pressed the highest-numbered button in the elevator. "Up. We want to find the office of Mr. Teach himself. And the best offices are always at the top of buildings."

In one corner of the tenth floor there was an enormous office with a nameplate on the door, "Mr. Teach—Chief Executive." They could see inside the office as one of its walls was made entirely out of glass. It was sparsely furnished, with only a few filing cabinets and an enormous oak desk at the far end.

Unlike normal office furniture, the desk was made of rough, worn planks and Jack could have sworn that the decorative studs along the sides were made from barnacles.

Trudy tried the door handle. "Locked."

Jack looked around other offices and picked up a heavy glass paperweight. "I'll use this to smash a small hole in the glass wall and then we'll be able to reach inside and open the door that way."

"I'm not sure that's a great idea," said Trudy. "If we smash a hole in that window, they'll know we've been here."

Jack thought. He saw a potted plant in the corner of the office. "We can just move a potted plant in front of the hole. Then, hopefully, they won't notice."

"Do you think that'll work?"

"Do you have a better plan?"

Trudy conceded that she didn't.

Jack went over to the glass wall and looked through it. He could see the handle on the other side of the door. He aimed with the paperweight so that the hole would be right beside the handle. The paperweight made a loud crack as it made contact with the wall, which shuddered but didn't break. The paperweight hadn't even chipped the surface.

"I'm going to need to hit it harder." Jack pulled his arm back and hit the wall as hard as he could. An enormous crack appeared in the glass wall. It started spreading outward from where Jack had struck, looking like an enormous spiderweb.[79]

---

[79] Which could be an enormous web spun by an ordinary spider. Or an ordinary-sized web spun by an enormous spider. I'll let you choose.

Jack nervously took a few steps back from the wall. Trudy hid herself behind a desk. There was an ear-splitting shattering noise and the wall collapsed into a million shards of glass.

Trudy came out from her hiding place behind the desk. She dragged a potted plant in front of the pile of shattered glass. "There you go. No one will notice now."

Jack didn't think he would ever see anyone being more sarcastic than Trudy had just been. However, Trudy was not one to rest on her laurels and very quickly managed to exceed her recently set high level of sarcasm.

"So, Jack. Are you going to reach through the small hole and open the door for me?"

Jack thought she was joking, but realized she wanted him to go through with the action. Stepping over the shattered glass wall, he unlocked the office door from the inside.

Trudy walked through the door even though it would have been just as easy to step through the enormous hole where the glass wall had recently been.

"Right, we'd better hurry up and check these filing cabinets before you destroy the entire office building."

The filing cabinets were locked, but Jack smashed them open with a few blows from the paperweight. Luckily they were made of metal and so didn't shatter into a thousand pieces.

Most of the records contained nothing interesting or at least nothing that Jack and Trudy could understand. Generally they contained graphs, numbers, and incomprehensible spreadsheets.

"I don't think we're going to find anything interesting," Jack said.

Naturally enough, this was the cue for Trudy to find something very interesting indeed.

MINISTRY OF S.U.IT.S HANDBOOK

POWER OF IMAGINATION
EFFICACY OF CLIPBOARDS

Occasionally you will find yourself in a situation where someone will not believe what you are saying even if you are holding a clipboard. In this situation you should resort to putting on a white coat. People will always believe what you are saying if you are holding a clipboard and wearing a white lab coat. If you are wearing a white coat, people will believe you have some kind of science degree. At university graduation ceremonies people are given diplomas to show how smart they are. It would be much better if they were given white coats.

41

SPIN ME RIGHT 'ROUND

"Jack, look at this!" Trudy lifted a bundle of papers out of a filing cabinet and took them over to the desk.

"What is it?" he asked as Trudy spread out the papers.

"I'm not sure but I think it's a plan for where they're digging."

Trudy had spread out what turned out to be a map of Northern Ireland. It showed that Chapeau Noir Enterprises had dug around the border area where it joined onto the rest of the island.

Trudy looked through the papers. "There doesn't seem to be anything here that indicates that they're looking for gold or oil."

Jack looked through the papers himself. "Wait a minute—what do these mean? There are little dots around the edge of the map. Hundreds of little green dots."

Trudy pointed to the key of the map. "They're wind turbines. Supposedly for energy generation."

"But we know that isn't right. The wind turbines at the school aren't used to generate electricity. Otherwise they wouldn't have bothered with the new carpets and polyester uniforms to generate static electricity for lighting the mine."

Trudy was rifling through other papers. "Look at this. I think this must be an early design drawing for the wind turbines."

From the papers it was apparent that the design of the wind turbines had been based on an existing design of a ship's propeller. And the ship that the propeller had been based on was named the *Titanic*. The propeller had been altered as each blade was longer and thinner, but the basics were the same.

Trudy audibly gasped. "Do you realize what this means?" she said, turning to Jack.

Jack turned to Trudy and fixed her with a deadly serious gaze. "Frankly, I don't have a clue."

"Jack, it's quite simple. What this means is . . ."

Suddenly a voice called out from behind Jack and Trudy. "What this means is that it's the end of the road for you two."

Even before Jack turned, he recognized the voice. It was the old woman from the museum.

"Nice to see you again." The old woman smiled. "Just a pity that this is the last time anyone will ever be seeing you."

Behind her stood eight pirates. Jack wondered where all these pirates were coming from. Surely if there were this many pirates in the world, he would have noticed them before.

"You know too much for us to let you live."

"Umm, just on a point of information, I still don't really know what's going on," said Jack.

"Boys," the old woman growled, "get them."

Trudy dived into the fight with enthusiasm and verve. Jack was more reluctant. There had to be a better way to defeat the pirates other than fighting. After all, the last fight in the museum had almost ended in disaster. Violence was wrong, immature, and brutal. And quite apart from anything else, Jack wasn't very good at it.

And yet despite all this Jack couldn't let Trudy down. He needed to conjure up a sad thought immediately if he was going to survive this. One popped into his head with only minimal concentration—the time his mother had been taken to the hospital when he was six. Even to this day no one had told him what had been wrong with her. He just remembered an immense feeling of sadness. He knew that something was badly wrong, but everyone was pretending to be cheerful. But he had been six, not stupid. He knew that things weren't right. It had all worked out in the end and after a few months his mother had come home, although even to this day no one ever spoke about what had happened.

The Speed descended on Jack in the nick of time. Two of the pirates were right in front of him. They sliced at him with their cutlasses and hacked with their hooked hands. Jack desperately dived into a narrow space between the pirate's blades.

Two other pirates raced at him. He leapt up and threw a flurry of punches directly into the stomach of one. The second one tried to grab his neck, but Jack twisted away, throwing an elbow into the pirate's ribs as he did.

Jack turned to see that, as usual, Trudy was doing much better than he was. Four pirates were slashing at her, but she effortlessly ducked and dodged. One pirate brought his cutlass scything from the side, but missed Trudy and slashed across another's stomach.

Trudy stepped on the thigh of one of the pirates. Using this to get leverage, she pressed a foot on the breastbone of another and catapulted herself upward and out of the center of the pirates.

Of course, Jack couldn't just watch Trudy fight as four pirates were closing in on him. He sprinted across the room and rolled over the enormous desk. The pirates lined up on the other side of the desk. He would be safe: Whichever way they went he could go around the desk in the other direction.

Then two of the pirates went around one side of the desk, one went the other way, and one jumped up on top of the desk.

Jack realized it was obvious that this was what they would have done. He certainly wouldn't get a promotion in the Ministry if he carried on the way he was going. Of course, now was definitely not the time to be thinking about his career prospects.

The first problem was the pirate striding across the desk. Just as he was about to step off the desk and onto the floor

Jack pulled out one of the drawers. The pirate put his wooden leg onto it and it smashed through the bottom. The pirate fell over and there was a sickening *crack* as his upper thigh bone broke into two pieces. The noise made Jack retch. However, he was far too busy to consider vomiting. The three remaining pirates were nearly on him. Jack clambered on top of the desk and started kicking out at the pirates when they moved close to him. He needed to think of something fast.

Two of his kicks landed perfectly and the pirates went sprawling, but the third had managed to grab Jack's foot and pull him off balance. Jack twisted in the air as he fell. He reached out his hand and tried to catch the edge of the desk. His hand missed by inches, but his head didn't. It struck the edge of the desk with a loud *crack*ing noise.

Jack continued to fall and could feel himself blacking out. He looked across the room as his vision clouded.

Trudy had managed to floor two of the pirates who had been attacking her, but the other two had gotten ahold of her. She lashed out at them, punching, scratching, and kicking. One pirate let go and fell backward, clutching his head. The other threw her away from him.

Trudy crashed into the office window. The glass shattered and she fell through it. There was a ten-floor drop outside the window. Ten floors straight down.

Jack's vision had almost completely clouded over. He found himself thinking that he didn't really care anyway. First David had been kidnapped and now Trudy was gone. It was all over. This was his last thought as unconsciousness overtook him.

PIRATES
STORAGE OPTIONS

Many people over the years have wondered how there can be so many pirates in the world and why we don't notice them. The reason for this is simple: Pirates are very easy to store. Traditionally pirates used to be stored in hammocks. But then one day a Ministry operative pointed out that their hook hands looked almost identical to the ends of wire coat hangers.

Since then it has become de rigueur to store pirates on clothing racks when they aren't in use. This isn't cruel to the pirates, as they're used to hanging off rigging in their pirate ships. They also tend to rock backward and forward on the rails. This motion gently reminds them of the rocking motion of the sea and they find it very relaxing.

As with clothes, the hanging motion also has the advantage of smoothing out wrinkles overnight. This is why so many pirates look so youthful.

42

A P.E. TEACHER'S HISTORY LESSON

Jack opened his eyes. The light hurt. He hadn't been moved out of the office, but there were no signs of the struggle that had taken place. A new window had been put in place, the desk had been repaired, and behind it sat the annoyingly smug Mr. Teach himself.

Jack tried to leap forward to attack him but didn't move an inch. He looked down to see that he had been tied to a chair.

"I'm going to get you," snarled Jack. "I have friends."

"Yes, one of them fell out of the window, didn't she?" said Mr. Teach. "And as for the rest of the Ministry, I've escaped from their clutches more than once. I don't see why this time should be any different."

Jack was stunned. "You know what the Ministry is?"

"Well, of course." Mr. Teach stood up. With his left hand he reached to pull off his black glove. However, he didn't just take off the glove; he unscrewed the entire hand, revealing a gleaming metal hook underneath.

"You ... you're a pirate too!" gasped Jack.

"Well, quite," chuckled Mr. Teach. "In fact I am *the* pirate. I am a direct descendant of Edward Teach or, as he is more commonly known, Blackbeard. But I thought you would have figured that out. After all, my name is Teach and my company is called Chapeau Noir. Which is French for Blackbeard."

French wasn't Jack's favorite class, but he could remember some of the vocabulary. "No, it isn't. It's French for Black Hat."

Mr. Teach looked slightly confused for a minute. "What ... no ... really? Oh ... French never was my best subject."

"Moron," laughed Jack. A gleaming hook was put under Jack's chin, the point drawing blood. He quickly reconsidered how funny Mr. Teach's mistake was.

"Good idea to stop laughing. After all, soon you'll be completely at my mercy."

Jack looked down. "I'm tied to a chair here. I'm pretty much already completely at your mercy."

Mr. Teach threw his head back and laughed like a bad actor. "You haven't fathomed my plan yet, have you?"

"Um, no," Jack admitted. "If you haven't already figured this out by the fact that I'm tied to a chair, I'm not desperately good at any of this stuff."

"Then, let me explain," Mr. Teach gloated.

For some reason villains could never just tell you what

they were planning. They had to go into the whole back-story. And it was the same with Mr. Teach. He explained that he was directly descended from the original Blackbeard, who had been called Edward Teach. The original Edward Teach/Blackbeard had been a P.E. teacher.[80] Unfortunately in the American colonies there had been limited opportunities for gaining a job in physical education. The original Blackbeard had sat down and thought to himself what his skills were. Being a P.E. teacher, he was good at shouting at people, physical activities, and acts of random cruelty. Apart from as a P.E. teacher, the only other area where these skills would be useful was clearly piracy. And so the P.E. teacher had turned pirate.

Eventually the people of the colonies had gotten fed up with pirates and called in the Ministry. After a number of fraught years and many exciting sea battles, all the pirates were caught and locked up safely in Piratoriums. But Blackbeard refused to accept his fate and, with the help of an Irish pirate called Grace O'Malley,[81] he managed to escape from the Piratorium. Their escape was not noticed for several days as they had left behind some dummies in their

---

[80] Back in those days people took their names from what they did. If you made roofs you were called Thatcher, if you made horseshoes you were called Smith, and if you promised to look after people's money for them and then somehow managed to lose it all you were called Banks. Teachers were more often than not called Teach.

[81] For those who really need to know, not the original legendary Irish pirate Grace O'Malley, but one of her great granddaughters.

place. It should be noted that normally dummies of this sort are noticed immediately, given that arms and legs made of artificial materials aren't very realistic. However, dummies of pirates are much harder to spot given the fact that frequently the real pirates also have arms and legs made of artificial materials.

Blackbeard and Grace settled down, found work as P.E. teachers, and had themselves a family. However, with each generation they passed down their knowledge of piracy, in the hope that one day, one of their descendants would take to the high seas again to rob and plunder.

Since then there had been many generations of pirates born. They always decided to become P.E. teachers. It kept them fit and strong and gave them the opportunity to continue practicing shouting orders and indulging in acts of random cruelty. All the things that pirates delighted in.

Then one day one of the pirates had a brilliant idea. He was the great, great, great, great, et cetera, grandson of the original Edward Teach.

"And that pirate was me," gloated Mr. Teach. "You see, Jack, we're digging under and around Northern Ireland so it can float free."

"But that doesn't make any sense," said Jack.

"Oh, but it does. All the wind turbines we've placed around the coast aren't for electric power at all. We're going to use them to drive the country around like a hovercraft. Northern Ireland will become the world's largest pirate ship."

"So why did you need to kidnap the children?"

"Can you imagine how many people it takes to crew a ship the size of a small country? You've already met some of my compatriots. The old lady who followed you to the museum is a descendant of Grace O'Malley and Blackbeard too. And we use buried treasure to hire ourselves help like werecreatures or giant moles. But that's only a short-term measure. Even with all the buried treasure dear old great, great, great, great, great, et cetera, grandfather left us we can't afford to hire a complete crew for a country-sized frigate. And so we've been kidnapping misfit children and training them to be pirates. Most of the kids we take are losers who are made fun of by their friends. They're normally glad to feel a sense of belonging again. Being a pirate gives them a family. Of course some of them object to having their hands or legs cut off, but after the operation they normally fall in line. If they don't, we can always threaten to cut off a few more limbs."

"The people in Northern Ireland won't stand for this!"

"You could be right, Jack, but that's why I've also been building an 'enforcer.' If the people don't fall into line, either my pirates will make them walk the plank or they'll be destroyed by my enforcer."

"You're insane."

"Maybe," smiled Teach, flashing a mouth of golden fillings, "but at least I'm not unconscious."

"That doesn't make any . . ."

Before Jack could finish his sentence Teach smacked Jack across the face with his ebony cane. The world went black again.

MINISTRY OF S.U.IT.S HANDBOOK

BURIED TREASURE
Difficulty in Finding It

Technically it is impossible to find buried
treasure. When it is underground you can't find
it. However, when you dig it up it is no longer
buried. Therefore you have not found buried
treasure—you have found until-recently buried
treasure. Which is a very different thing.

43

PILLOW FIGHTS
FRIDAY

Jack had no idea how much time had passed when he came around again. He decided that he really didn't like being rendered unconscious and he would make a positive effort to avoid having it happen again.

He stood up and looked around him. He was in a small round room with dark, dolerite stone walls. The room was six feet across and was almost completely empty. He had been left lying on the floor with only a small pillow under his head and a woolen blanket thrown over him.

The door looked solid, with a small viewing hatch about five feet off the ground. There was a window in the corner of the room, but it had been boarded up with wooden planks. Jack went over and grabbed one of the planks but he couldn't budge it so much as an inch. He even tried putting both his feet against the wall and pulling with all of his might, but nothing seemed to work.

The hatch on the door opened. An ugly face with a black eye patch leered in at him.

"Let me out," said Jack.

"No."

To be fair, Jack hadn't expected it to be as easy at that.

"*Please* let me out." Jack tried a slightly different, and yet largely similar approach.

"I'm afraid you're going to be locked in there for quite a while. We'll bring you two meals a day. But no knives, no forks, only paper plates and cups. Mr. Teach was very clear on that. Nothing that you could use to escape."

Jack sighed. He had failed.

The pirate at the door spoke again. "So if you want anything, please feel free to let me know. I'll be sure not to bring it to you."

The hatch in the door closed and Jack was alone again.

He looked around the room. There had to be something, however small, that he could use to escape. He had a blanket and a pillow. Perhaps if he had been a black belt in pillow fights he could have lured the guard inside and clobbered him with it.

But the guard clearly had very strict instructions and Jack had no doubt that they included not walking inside the cell.

He could have taken the pillow out of its case and filled it with bricks. Then he might have been able to swing it at the door and batter it open. This would have been a good plan if only he had had access to some bricks.

Anyone watching Jack at that precise moment would have thought that he had decided to despair. But he wasn't despairing. He'd had an idea. He went over to the corner and lay down on the floor. He picked up the pillow and used it to cover his head and face.

Jack had no idea how long it would take to be effective but it was only a few minutes before he heard noises outside his cell.

Jack leapt up and pressed his ear to the cell door. There were two voices. One of them was the pirate guard. The other voice was deeper and more threatening.

"How did you even get in here?"

"You never mind that now. Are you going to get out of my way or not?"

"I can't allow you in there."

"Oh, can't you?" Jack heard the sound of knuckles cracking. "I know my rights. Now you've got until I count three. ONE . . ."

"I've got a baseball bat here and I'm not afraid to use it."

There was the sound of a brief scuffle and then wood splintering. "You can still use your baseball bat if you want," said the second voice. "Although if you use it now, it'll pretty much have to be for firewood or chopsticks."

"You snapped it in two!"

"Yeah, I did. Which reminds me. TWO . . ."

"You can't frighten me," lied the pirate. He wasn't fooling anyone.

"THREE."

There was a sound like a wet fish being hit by an anvil. Jack gasped when the door splintered into a thousand pieces as the pirate came crashing through it. The pirate was clearly unconscious, which had to be considered a good thing, for if he had been awake he would have been in a lot of pain. A LOT of pain.

Jack looked at the guard's face. It was red and swollen, and Jack would have sworn the nose was in a slightly different position than it had been before.

Suddenly Jack thought that there had been a total eclipse of the sun. Of course it wasn't a total eclipse. It was an enormous man standing in the doorway blocking out light from the corridor.

The man had to hold his head at an angle to avoid hitting the top of the door frame. He was six and a half feet tall and two and a half feet wide with arms that looked like socks stuffed with cannonballs.

Most disturbingly of all, he was wearing a pink tutu.

He stepped into the room so he could stand upright again. "I'm the Tooth Fairy," he growled. "We've met before."

Jack's plan had been simple. He'd put his head under the pillow knowing that any teeth left under a pillow belonged to the Tooth Fairy. He remembered that was how the Minister had lost his teeth.

He had expected the Tooth Fairy to turn up, but hadn't expected it to turn out this well. Originally he had just hoped the Tooth Fairy would have taken a message for him to the outside world. The fact that the pirate had ended up in a crumpled heap was a bonus. Jack decided he would never antagonize the Tooth Fairy.

"Hello, Mr. Tooth Fairy."

"Those teeth were under the pillow. They belong to me now." The Tooth Fairy pointed at Jack's mouth.

Jack's plan had been brilliant, but only up to a point. The pirate and the door had been the two barriers to his escape. Both had been easily dealt with. The problem was that Jack had not figured out how he was going to avoid giving the Tooth Fairy his teeth.

"Umm, about that. It was just a mistake."

The Tooth Fairy gave Jack a hard look. "Mistakes don't matter." The Tooth Fairy produced a pair of pincers seemingly from nowhere.[82] "Now, open wide."

This was not going to be pleasant. "Wait a minute," said Jack. "Can we at least put this off until later?"

"I'm a busy man. Why should I wait?"

Jack racked his brains for a convincing reason. "Look, I can't imagine you care about the fate of the people of Northern Ireland..."

The Tooth Fairy snorted to indicate that he really didn't.

"But I've just discovered that Chapeau Noir Enterprises and Mr. Teach have a plan to turn the entire country into a floating ship. And if they do that, think of how hard it would be to keep track of where the country was. And if you didn't know where the country was, how would you be able to catch people to take their teeth?"

The Tooth Fairy thought about this for a moment. "And you're going to stop him?"

Jack nodded. "I'm going to try."

---

[82] Tutus rarely have pockets. It tends to spoil the line of the garment.

The Tooth Fairy took a minute to think. "How about this: I come back for your teeth next week. For now I let you go."

"That would be appreciated," said Jack with relief.

"But just keep in mind. I'm coming back. . . ." He waved the pincers menacingly.

"I don't think I'll be able to forget. And if I do forget, I'll probably remember in my nightmares."

"Until later."

The Tooth Fairy turned to walk out the door. Jack was amazed by how hairy the Tooth Fairy's shoulders were. A tutu definitely wasn't a good look for a man of his size.

"Um, one more thing, before you go, I don't suppose you could give me a lift back to the Ministry."

The Tooth Fairy turned and growled at him.

Jack smiled persuasively.

"Don't go wasting all your smiles. Those teeth belong to me now."

Jack stopped smiling and made a whimpering noise.

TUTUS
Selection of Colors

Tutus, of course, come in many different colors, not just pink. Many people have wondered why the Tooth Fairy's was pink.

* * *

The answer, of course, was simple. He thought he would have looked stupid in a white one.

44

WHAT'S IN THE GLOVE BOX?

Jack bounded down a long spiral staircase. He was astonished to realize that he had been imprisoned inside Scrabo Tower. It was something of a local tourist attraction. A large tower on top of a hill in the middle of the countryside. It looked a bit like the kind of tower that Rapunzel would have been put in if the evil witch who had imprisoned her hadn't liked pink so much and had been working on a very tight budget.

Once outside, the Tooth Fairy pointed to a black, rusty Ford Cortina parked on the edge of the hill. Jack was fairly sure that you were meant to park at the bottom of the hill and walk up. But who would have been brave enough to tell the Tooth Fairy that?

The Tooth Fairy took a key ring out of his pocket. It was made from the tooth of a tiger, covered in solid gold. He spun the key around his finger and opened the car's doors. "Jump in, kid. I don't know about you, but I don't have time to waste."

Jack scrambled into the passenger seat and put on his seat belt. The Tooth Fairy nodded his approval. "Seat belt. Smart kid. You know how many kids lose their teeth due to a car braking too quickly?"

Jack was confused. "Your teeth can fall out if a car brakes too quickly?"

"They can if your mouth smacks into the dashboard."

"Does that really happen often?"

The Tooth Fairy reached over in front of Jack and opened the glove box. Hundreds of teeth spilled out of it, falling onto Jack's lap. "Happens all the time."

The Tooth Fairy slammed his foot onto the accelerator. He was not a careful driver. Occasionally they would come across a hiker and the Tooth Fairy would have to spin the wheel and slam on the brakes to screech and skid around them. Jack was very glad that he had worn his seat belt which, no doubt, saved him a substantial amount of dental work.

A man was waving frantically in the distance. He wore a green uniform and cap.

"I think he wants us to stop," said Jack.

"Yeah, he didn't want me to park on the hill on the way in either. Seems like he's not going to get what he wants today."

The Tooth Fairy pressed the accelerator further and the car raced toward the frantically waving man. Jack wondered at what stage the man in the uniform would stop waving and shouting and realize that his life was in danger from an almost certainly insane man in a pink tutu who was driving a black Ford Cortina.

Suddenly the man in the green cap stopped waving. He realized that the car wasn't slowing. He took several large steps to the left. The Tooth Fairy adjusted his steering so the front of the car was still pointing toward the man in the cap.

The man in the cap moved to the right. The Tooth Fairy adjusted his steering again.

"You can't run him down!" Jack shouted.

The Tooth Fairy looked at Jack. "Yes, yes I can."

"Okay," said Jack, "I said that wrong; what I meant was you *shouldn't* do it."

"That's probably true," agreed the Tooth Fairy. "But he shouted at me when I drove up the hill, and I've got a very bad attitude."

The man was now zigzagging back and forth, but it didn't do him any good. The Tooth Fairy was an excellent, if psychopathic, driver. No matter where the man in the cap ran, the Tooth Fairy adjusted the wheel so the car remained pointing at him.

Jack got ready to close his eyes. The man with the cap had given up and had stopped running. He had put his hands together and appeared to be praying now.

At the last minute the Tooth Fairy pulled the steering wheel hard to the right. The car spun in a balletic circle and stopped inches before it hit the man. The man looked around. "I'm not dead."

The Tooth Fairy leaned out the car window and punched

him in the face. "Maybe that'll teach you not to shout at people."

The man sailed through the air and landed with a thump on the ground.

"You aren't a very nice person, are you?" said Jack.

"Not particularly," said the Tooth Fairy.

The Tooth Fairy dropped Jack outside the front of the museum. "Cheers," said Jack as he leapt out of the car and ran up the steps.

The Tooth Fairy called after him. "Make sure your mum buys some soup and ice cream on her next weekly shopping trip."

Jack was puzzled. "Why?"

The Tooth Fairy held up the pincers. "Because you'll want to have food that you can eat with just your gums."

A shudder passed through Jack's body. The Tooth Fairy laughed and then roared away in a cloud of black smoke.

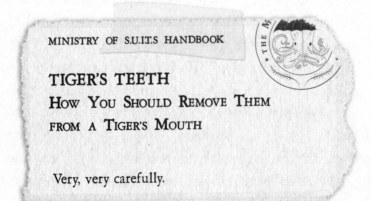

MINISTRY OF S.U.I.T.S HANDBOOK

TIGER'S TEETH
How You Should Remove Them
from a Tiger's Mouth

Very, very carefully.

45

"WE MUST DO SOMETHING IMMEDIATELY"

Jack zipped through the museum, headed straight for the Takabuti room. Once there he pressed the three fingernails on the stone hand that caused the sarcophagus to slide open and darted underground.

Jack found Grey in what seemed to be a Ministry common room. The walls were lined with leatherbound books and long velvet curtains. Ruby-red wingback chairs sat spaced across the floor.

"G-Grey, something awful's happened," Jack panted.

Grey looked up from the book he had been reading. "What?"

For a moment Jack couldn't speak. It was as if saying the words out loud would choke him. "It's Trudy," he croaked. "She's dead."

Grey looked stunned. "Then we must do something immediately."

"What?" Jack asked.

"Well, for a start we must let Trudy know."

"Huh?"

"We have to let Trudy know that she's dead. She's sitting over there having a lemonade and looking at some maps. And if she's dead, she probably shouldn't be drinking any kind of fluid.[83] She won't be able to digest it and it'll just get messy." Grey pointed to a chair across the room.

Jack turned to look and saw Trudy sitting in a chair, looking over a stack of maps. She looked remarkably lively for someone who had fallen from the tenth story of an office building. Jack coughed to try and attract her attention. Trudy looked up, annoyed that someone had interrupted her work. For a minute Trudy looked as confused as Jack felt. Then her eyes focused and she seemed to realize what she was looking at.

Trudy bounded out of her chair and launched herself at Jack. He was knocked backward with a hug of awesome power.

"Jack. It's you!"

---

[83] A good general rule of medical thumb is that if you are running a fever, it is a good idea to drink lots of fluids to avoid dehydration. However, if you are already dead, this isn't considered necessary. Most doctors advise that if you are dead you should lie very still and try not to talk to people. The not-talking rule isn't really a health-based rule. It's just that the living tend to get panicky around talking corpses.

"Trudy," Jack gasped, trying to catch his breath. "I'm fairly sure that hugs aren't meant to be this painful."

Trudy apologized for her enthusiasm and helped Jack to his feet. "I'm sorry, but we thought you'd been captured!"

"I was captured," Jack confirmed. "But I managed to free myself with a pillow."

"You must be one hell of a pillow fighter."

Jack looked solemn and nodded. "I killed three scouts at cub camp once." Jack went on to explain that he was only joking and briefly told them how he had escaped from his imprisonment at Scrabo Tower.

"But never mind me being captured. I thought you were dead. They threw you out of a tenth-floor window."

Trudy nodded. "I thought I was a goner myself for a minute. But then I remembered the quartermaster."

Jack thought back to their meeting with the diminutive quartermaster. "You mean you fell all that way two feet at a time."

"Perhaps I wasn't quite that good—you must need to practice to get to that level. I think I fell a floor at a time, but it stopped me from ending up as an omelet when I hit the pavement." Trudy rubbed her ribs as if they still hurt.

"That's amazing!"

"It isn't. It was awful. I was badly hurt and knew I wouldn't be any good to you so I ran to get help." Trudy looked ashamed of herself. "I abandoned you, Jack."

"You didn't. You did the right thing. There was no point in both of us getting caught."

There seemed to be a tear in the corner of her eye. "It was

wrong of me. Abandoning people is never right. I don't care what anyone says."

Jack knew that that wasn't all there was to it. But he also knew that now wasn't the time to pressure Trudy into telling more.

"Okay, so what do we do now? Unless we stop Mr. Teach, he'll sail Northern Ireland into the middle of the ocean. We'll all be at his mercy."

Trudy grabbed the paper that she'd been studying. "I've pulled together these maps of where kids have gone missing. Grey helped me to use the map to draw up a plan of where the tunnels are under the ground all around the island. I thought we might be able to use them to find a way of attacking."

"Brilliant, Trudy. One slight problem: I was away overnight and we've missed two days of school. Therefore I might not be able to participate in thwarting Teach's evil plans because my parents will almost certainly have grounded me."

Grey stepped forward. "Don't worry about that, Jack—it's all been sorted. I called the school and said that you had to take a few days off because your dog had died."

"I don't have a dog," objected Jack.

"Well, not anymore you don't," said Grey, irritated at being interrupted, "because he's dead. I also phoned your parents and pretended to be Trudy's father. I told them you were sleeping over. Incidentally, your father has a very impressive mustache."

"You could hear my father's mustache over the phone?"

"It is a *very* impressive mustache," Grey reiterated. "Your parents were happy enough and I sent them a car over to pick up your school uniform." Grey handed Jack his uniform. "Not that you're going to need it today."

"Of course I'm not going to need it today. Today's the day we're going to rescue David."

MINISTRY OF S.U.IT.S HANDBOOK

FALLING FROM HEIGHTS
INVENTION OF THE MODERN PARACHUTE

Many people have claimed that the first modern parachute was invented by a Frenchman called Louis-Sébastien Lenormand. This is not true. He was the first person to invent an *effective* modern parachute.

* * *

The names of the people who invented the ineffective parachutes are not recorded by history. All we know about them is that generally they were buried in very flat coffins.

46

REINFORCEMENTS

"We need reinforcements," said Jack. "We couldn't take down eight pirates at the offices. There could be dozens more underground."

"We don't have time to round any up, Jack." Trudy was shaking her head. "Every minute we waste brings David closer to having to learn how to write left-handed."

It was a stark reminder of what was at stake.

"The first thing is to try and rescue all the kidnapped children. Then we've got to destroy the digging equipment. If Teach detaches Northern Ireland from the rest of the island, then there'll be nothing more we can do."

"What about the enforcer thing he mentioned? He seemed pretty confident about that."

Trudy frowned. "That was the only part of the plan I didn't get figured out. I mean, everything else seems to have fallen into place. But I have no idea what the enforcer might be."

Jack thought hard. "Well, the only loose ends I can think of are the stolen dinosaur bones and the school boiler. Maybe it's something to do with that?"

"Maybe," Trudy agreed, "but we'll just have to deal with whatever it is when we come to it. Hopefully we'll manage."

Jack smiled. "I think we can do a little bit better than just manage. I've got an idea. Maybe we can get us some cavalry after all. Pass me the maps, Trudy."

As Jack spread the maps out across a tabletop, Grey and Trudy gathered around to listen to his idea. "Now this might be a little bit of a longshot," he confessed, "but if we can pull it off, I think they'll probably write poetry and sing songs about us."[84]

<hr />

Trudy and Jack took a Ministry car to the school. Grey had left them to work on the second part of Jack's plan.

"Do you think that the plan's going to work?"

"That's a bit like asking if the one parachute you have is going to work, Jack," said Trudy. "It's the only plan we have. So we're going to have to pull the ripcord and just accept the consequences."

"That's a cheery metaphor, Trudy. Thanks."

When Jack and Trudy arrived at the school, all the pupils and teachers had already gone home and so they easily

---

[84] They didn't. I mean it was a good plan, but it wasn't as cool as the awesome Static.

sneaked through the corridors, despite the fact that they were carrying a ridiculously long rope ladder. Trudy peeked around the corner of the boys' changing room.

"Is it all clear?" asked Jack.

Trudy nodded for Jack to take a quick look for himself. He poked his head around the corner and saw four security guards standing at the end of the changing room. They wore blue uniforms that looked like something that the army would wear if they ran fast-food restaurants. They didn't have guns on their belts, but they did have crackling walkie-talkies, handcuffs, and small cans of what Jack assumed was pepper spray.

"Okay, Jack, you're going to need to be faster than you ever have been. Think of the saddest thing you can."

Jack closed his eyes and thought. He needed to summon up something *really* sad. At first he thought of the fact that his dog had just died. Then he remembered that it had only been an imaginary dog that had died and that didn't seem so sad anymore.

Then Jack thought about the day of his grandfather's funeral. He had been seven at the time and hadn't been entirely sure what had been happening. He had known that his grandfather had died. But there was an enormous gulf between knowing the word *dead* and really understanding what it had meant. It certainly wasn't something that the death of his goldfish had prepared him for. His mother had bought him a new goldfish. You couldn't buy a new grandfather.[85]

---

[85] Actually Jack is wrong about this. You can buy a new grandfather, but the warranties on them are very short indeed.

The entire day of the funeral adults kept making jokes with him, hugging him, and calling him brave. His mother had promised him a trip to the toy store if he behaved himself.

Overall, the day of the funeral hadn't seemed that sad. But there was a moment ... when they lowered the coffin into the ground and he had looked up at his grandmother's face. She had looked so sad, and weak and alone. Before the funeral Jack would never have seen his grandmother without his grandfather hovering around in the same room. But now it was different. He looked at his grandmother that day and saw her completely differently. It wasn't the way she looked, it was more the way the grandfather-shaped hole beside her had looked.

As they lowered the coffin into the ground a single tear had rolled down his grandmother's cheek.

Jack felt truly miserable as The Speed descended on him. He didn't think anyone could have felt any sadder. However, when he opened his eyes and saw Trudy's face he realized he was wrong. Jack was astonished to see that she looked even more wretched than he felt. The single tear he had remembered trickling down his grandmother's face was running down Trudy's face. It made Jack feel impossibly sad to see Trudy, who was normally so strong, look so wretched.

"What did you think of?" Jack asked.

Trudy tried to say something, but her voice broke. She took a few seconds to pull herself together before she mumbled, "Now isn't the time. We have to save David."

Trudy sprinted around the corner of the changing rooms and blurred toward the guards. The four security guards turned to look at her. One dropped a cup of coffee as Trudy leapt up and ran along the wall before jumping onto the ceiling. She dived from the ceiling above the guards, lashing out with feet and fists. The first guard fell after three quick jabs to his jaw. Trudy then spun in mid-dive, stretching out with her feet, and kicked two of the other guards, knocking them backward. One staggered back into the shower area and fell, smashing his head on the tiles. The other crunched into a wall and slid down into a slumped position.

Trudy landed on her hands and pushed back. Flipping over the final guard's head, she sailed over him and caught his neck between her ankles. Using her speed, she continued diving forward and flipped the guard over, catapulting him into the ceiling. He seemed to stick there for a brief second before crashing to the ground. Trudy landed on her feet, nimble as a fox.

Jack had followed her down through the changing room. Although he had been moving faster than he ever had before, he still arrived a few seconds after Trudy had finished with the guards. He reached out and caught the coffee cup the guard had dropped before it hit the ground.

"I saved the coffee cup," said Jack, trying to pretend that his contribution had been important.

Trudy punched him in the shoulder playfully. Jack dropped the coffee cup and it shattered on the ground.

"I'm not cleaning that up," said Jack.

Trudy pressed the button on the globe and the tunnel to the cavern opened up. The passageway was empty.

"I was sort of expecting some kind of horrible boss monster that we'd have to battle."

"I'm pretty sure that's coming," said Trudy. "It's probably just farther along the tunnel."

"Let's not keep it waiting. I can handle a horribly murderous monster, but I'd hate it if we also made it impatient."

MINISTRY OF S.U.I.T.S HANDBOOK

GOLDFISH
Two-Second Memories

It has been claimed that goldfish only have two-second memories. Which explains why if you have a goldfish it'll almost certainly not remember to get you a birthday present.

It also means that goldfish are generally considered the most pleasant tempered of all living creatures as they don't have enough recall to bear a grudge. If you flush a goldfish down the toilet and then accidentally bump into it at a cocktail party ten years later, it won't have a clue who you are and will be interested in your name, job, and what hobbies you have.

If you meet the baby alligator you flushed down the toilet at a cocktail party ten years later, it will have chewed off your left leg before you can tell it that you are called Stephen and you work as an accountant.

47

ESCAPE

Trudy and Jack had reached the cliff edge that overlooked the cavern. Beneath them, they could see the kidnapped children still working, using mechanical diggers to shift more and more soil. It looked as if they had nearly finished.

"They can't have much more work to do."

Jack unrolled the rope ladder and they both clambered down.

They were surprised to find David waiting for them at the bottom. Jack counted his friend's arms and legs and was relieved to find them all in place, although the dotted lines remained.

"You're okay!" exclaimed Jack.

Trudy explained the plan to David. "We've got to get everyone out of here before any giant moles show up. Do you think the kids with hooks for hands will be able to climb the ladder?"

David nodded. "I think so. The ones with peg legs might struggle a bit, but we can help them."

"Okay, you start gathering them up. We'll guard the bottom of the ladder. Get everyone out and then get out yourself."

David nodded and then sprinted across the enormous mine toward groups of kids. He spoke to them briefly and then pointed toward where Jack and Trudy stood. Some of the kids ran toward the ladder, but others spread out and began telling other kids of the route to freedom.

"If one kid tells two kids, and they each tell two kids . . ." Jack thought to himself that the plan might actually work.

The first batch of prisoners had arrived with Jack and Trudy and started streaming up the ladder to freedom. Of course not all of the prisoners were children. As Trudy had figured out, the digging had been going on for decades and some of the prisoners had been held captive for thirty or more years.

Jack imagined what it would have been like to live your life underground, in the dark, with no hope of escape. He realized that if he had not joined the Ministry, a similar fate might have awaited David.

"Mr. Teach has to pay," Jack said.

"Agreed," said Trudy. "And we may get to make him pay sooner than we thought."

"What do you mean?" asked Jack.

Trudy pointed into the distance. Mr. Teach was strolling

toward them, flanked by eight of the largest pirates Jack had ever seen. Suddenly Jack realized he recognized one of the pirates, who was carrying a chalkboard! So his P.E. teacher Mr. Rackham hadn't lost his hand in a vicious rugby scrum. Like Mr. Teach himself, Rackham must have been descended from a pirate.[86]

Trudy and Jack walked toward Mr. Teach. They didn't want him to get near the rope ladder. It was vital that it was protected so the prisoners could continue escaping.

"Well, if it isn't my little friends from the Ministry," said Mr. Teach.

"We aren't scared of you, Teach," snapped Trudy.

"Please, call me Blackbeard," said Mr. Teach as he stroked his chin.

"Blackbeard Junior, maybe," laughed Jack.

"Enough!" shouted Mr. Teach/Blackbeard Junior. "You have interfered with my plans. I will turn Northern Ireland into the world's biggest pirate ship no matter what you try and do to stop me."

"Why not the whole of Ireland?" asked Trudy, who was slightly curious about this.

Blackbeard Junior pulled a face. "With fuel costs as high

---

[86] Jack was right in this conclusion. Mr. Rackham was descended from a pirate named "Calico Jack" Rackham. Calico Jack was the pirate who came up with the idea for the skull-and-crossbones flag. He was also known for having two women crew members. Because pirates may be greedy, murderous, unpleasant scoundrels, but that doesn't mean that they're sexist as well.

as they are at the moment? Do you have any idea how much power you need to drive a landmass the size of this? Anyway, if I took the whole island there would be an international uproar. If I just take the north part of the island, it'll probably be a few weeks before anyone even notices."

"That's harsh," said Jack, thinking that it was harsh... but also fair. People generally didn't know where Northern Ireland was on a map. Therefore, they wouldn't notice if someone moved it to a different place altogether.

"Eight pirates won't be enough to stop us," Trudy sneered.

"I don't intend for eight pirates to stop you, young lady. You see, I have more than a hook up my sleeve. Jack, you'll remember I mentioned my enforcer?"

Blackbeard Junior lifted a finger and pointed behind Jack and Trudy.

USEFULNESS OF P.E. LESSONS
ROPE CLIMBING

It is generally accepted that P.E. lessons are of limited use in real life. However, probably the most useless part of any P.E. lesson is being made to climb up a rope.

In real life you will almost certainly never have to climb a rope. Unless, of course, you are kidnapped and kept at the bottom of an enormous cavern, where a rope ladder is your only means of escape.

* * *

However, it is essential to stress that this is very, very unlikely to happen.

48

STEAM POWER

It took Jack some time to figure out exactly what he was looking at. And then everything fell into place at once. The missing dinosaur bones that the old woman had stolen from the museum, the boiler that had been removed from the school . . .

He was looking at the world's first ever steam-powered bone dinosaur. Blackbeard Junior's smile broadened in an annoying way.

The enforcer stood perhaps thirty feet tall and wasn't made up from the bones of any single dinosaur. Dozens of differing white bones had clearly been wired together to create the monstrosity. It had the back legs, thighs, and body of a *Tyrannosaurus rex*. Instead of the small front *Tyrannosaurus* paws it had a pair of long, thin legs that allowed it to walk forward on all fours or rear up in the air.

Its neck was that of a *Diplodocus*, thirty feet long and articulated so it could lash its head backward and forward. Its head was that of a *Triceratops* with a bony collar and a large horn sticking out of the end of its nose. To top it all, it had a long, armored tail that ended in a knobby ball. It smashed this down intermittently, leaving a series of holes across the ground.

Inside the rib cage of the bone dinosaur was the large metal boiler that had previously been inside the school. It operated the bone dinosaur's movements through a series of levers and pistons. The boiler glowed red-hot and belched oily smoke.

It was the last piece of the puzzle. Jack knew why everything had happened now. He felt oddly satisfied and terrified at the same time.

"Are we fast enough to fight a steam dinosaur?" asked Jack.

"Fast doesn't come into it," said Trudy. "It's made of solid dinosaur bone and metal. If we hit it, we're likely to fracture our fists. We've got to figure out what its weakness is."

Jack looked behind him to where the rope ladder hung. It seemed as if most of the children had escaped.

"You might beat us, Blackbeard Junior, but the children have gotten away."

Blackbeard Junior chuckled. "Doesn't matter. The digging is finished. I have control of the turbines that will sail this island wherever I want. When those children with hooks for hands see how powerful I am they'll realize that being a pirate is better than being a passenger."

"And what about the people who aren't pirates?" Trudy spat at him. "They'll fight you."

"Oh, really? Let's just see what happens when I sail us to the North Pole and leave us there for a few years. Or maybe I'll sail us into the middle of a hurricane. People will obey me, or they will face the consequences."

Jack was beginning to realize that Blackbeard Junior was so insane that his plan might work.

"And if anyone tries to attack me, they'll have to face my steam dinosaur. You also need to keep in mind that we'll be sailing the seven seas. No one will be able to find this small country—so there'll be no help from the outside world."

Trudy turned to Jack. "If your plan is working, Grey should be here by now."

Jack glanced at his watch. "We don't know how accurate those maps were. It might take him a little longer than we thought. You reckon we can hold off a bone dinosaur for five minutes?"

"I reckon I can avoid a fatal squashing from a steam-powered bone dinosaur for five minutes," Trudy said with a smile.

They took up elaborate battle stances with their arms outstretched and fists clenched.

"Do you know karate?" Jack whispered to Trudy.

"No," Trudy whispered back.

"Then why are we standing like this?"

"I have no idea."

The steam dinosaur crashed forward onto all four legs and swung its neck and head at the pair, trying to knock them over. Like an Olympic athlete Trudy twisted and performed an effortless high jump, clearing the neck vertebrae of the steam dinosaur.

Jack was a second behind Trudy and knew that he wouldn't clear the obstacle as easily. Instead he ducked and slid through the dirt, missing the *Triceratops* collar by mere inches. The dinosaur reared onto its back legs and lashed out at Jack with a bony foreleg. The sheer size of the dinosaur leg caught him and sent him hurtling across the room.

Jack crunched into a soil wall and fell to the ground. He was conscious, but barely. He watched across the room, knowing that if they were going to survive, Trudy was going to have to save the day.

The steam dinosaur aimed a second leg at Trudy. As the leg swung she leapt onto it and grabbed it with both hands. The steam dinosaur seemed to be confused, as Trudy hadn't gone sailing through the air like Jack had. Using the dinosaur's momentary hesitation, Trudy clambered up the leg and swung herself onto the rib cage.

The dinosaur used its long, articulated neck to turn its head and look at its own rib cage. Trudy dangled on the outside, holding on to a large rib bone with a single hand. The dinosaur's head swayed on the neck and then lunged toward her. Trudy scrambled up, using the rib cage as a ladder. She only just avoided getting impaled by the enormous nose horn as it tore a shred off her shirtsleeve.

Trudy's hand slipped inside the rib cage and touched the red-hot steam boiler that was powering the bony monstrosity. She swung backward, barely hanging on with her one unburnt hand.

"Why don't you give up?" shouted Blackbeard Junior. "He'll get you sooner or later."

The dinosaur lunged toward Trudy again with its long bony *Triceratops* horn.

"Watch out!" croaked Jack. He summoned all his strength, stood up, and started to run toward Trudy and the dinosaur.

Trudy caught sight of Jack running. "Run the other way, Jack—I've had an idea!"

Jack was confused. What kind of idea had Trudy had that would necessitate his running away? And anyway, how could she possibly have an idea that would defeat the steam dinosaur—that would take an explosion!

Luckily, although neither Jack nor Trudy had brought anything that would explode with them, the steam dinosaur had . . .

Trudy was still hanging on to the rib cage of the steam dinosaur as it turned its head. The dinosaur used its incredibly flexible neck to attempt to impale Trudy on its horn.

The horn was less than a foot away from Trudy's body when she deliberately let go of the rib cage. She fell fifteen feet straight down, but more importantly, the steam dinosaur's horn kept moving straight on, through its own rib cage, puncturing the boiler inside.

There was a massive *CARUMPH*[87] and the boiler exploded in a blaze of oil, smoke, and fire.

---

[87] I think I've got that right. Explosions are notoriously difficult to spell.

Literally a few seconds after Jack had been running toward the steam dinosaur he found himself being blown away from it. He choked on smoke, and the heat of the flames on his face caused him to scramble blindly backward. First he was deafened by the roar of the burning air; then he heard a sound like a thousand xylophones being dropped from a helicopter. Fragments of bone were falling on the ground around him. The steam dinosaur had been destroyed. It had been more than destroyed—it had been blown into a thousand tiny fractures.

Jack tried to get to his feet but fell back down instantly. His right ankle had twisted under him and he felt rods of pain shoot through his leg. Jack grimaced and bit his lip. He turned back to where the steam dinosaur had been and saw Trudy lying half-unconscious and bleeding. A shard of dinosaur bone had gone straight through her shoulder. Considering she had been wounded in the shoulder by a mole only a few days ago it definitely wasn't a good week to be Trudy's shoulder.

Jack's world darkened. He looked up to see that Blackbeard Junior was casting a shadow over him.

"You've destroyed my steam dinosaur. No matter. I only built it to see off anyone who tried to stop me and it seems to have done that when it exploded."

Jack should have felt more triumphant, but his shoulders sagged and the only thing he really felt was tired.

Blackbeard Junior kicked Jack's ankle. Jack's face contorted in pain. "Why did you do that?"

"I used to be a P.E. teacher, Jack. So I'm pretty much pure

evil." Blackbeard Junior laughed to himself. "And you folks at the Ministry would put me in a Piratorium, if you caught me. So you have to expect a little bit of gloating."

"Well, what if we didn't? What would you do then?"

Blackbeard shrugged. "Kill people. Steal treasure. Sink boats. Just normal piratey things, I suppose."

Although Jack felt that this sounded less evil than the kind of things that the average P.E teacher did, he still knew he had to stop Blackbeard Junior. "So what happens now?"

"Do you see the digging equipment over there?" Blackbeard Junior indicated a range of machines, excavators, trucks, and drills. "Do you see the large black tube in the middle?"

Standing in the middle of all the modern construction equipment was something that looked like a relic from a bygone era. It was an enormous cast-iron tube fifty feet high. It flared out slightly at the top, where a long wire was attached. Jack traced the length of the wire with his eyes. It ran down to the ground and across the floor of the cavern and finished in Blackbeard Junior's hand.

"What on earth is that?" asked Jack.

"It's beautiful is what it is. It's the world's largest gunpowder cannon. I call her *Queen Anne's Revenge* after Great, Great, Great, Great, Great-Granddad's old ship."

Jack should have been formulating a plan of escape, but as usual, his curiosity was making him focus on entirely the wrong issues. Instead of thinking *Can I stand and run?* he was far too interested in Blackbeard Junior's cannon.

"Is it pointed at the ground?"

Blackbeard Junior winked. "Bright lad—it is indeed. And

it's loaded with a cannonball stuffed with explosives. When I light this fuse it'll burn to the cannon and set it off."

"You're going to shoot the earth? You really are insane."

"Not at all. The explosive cannonball will cause a series of shockwaves to spread across the ground. As the shock waves move they will become more powerful and faster. When they hit the edge of the country they will rip it free from the final few pieces of land that hold Northern Ireland in place. And then the reign of the greatest pirate ship in the world will begin!"

Blackbeard Junior turned to walk away. Jack realized it was all over. Trudy was unconscious and he could barely stand. The Speed was of limited use when you couldn't even get yourself into a vertical position. Grey was nowhere to be seen with the reinforcements.

They had come so close to winning, the children were freed, Blackbeard Junior's plot had been exposed, and Trudy and Jack would only have had to smash the earthquake cannon to be victorious. However, there was little chance they could achieve that now.

Jack looked at Blackbeard Junior, who was struggling to light the fuse. It was difficult to strike a match when one of your hands was a hook. The matches dropped and spilled on the ground. Blackbeard Junior glared at Jack as if daring him to say something.

Jack didn't say anything. But the look had made him decide to do something. Even with a twisted ankle. Even with eight pirates and Blackbeard Junior to fight. Even with the odds impossibly stacked against him, Jack wasn't going to give up.

From somewhere far away he heard a deep rumbling noise. Was it Grey with the cavalry? Maybe if he could just delay Blackbeard Junior for a few more minutes.

Jack slowly rolled over onto his knees.

Blackbeard Junior looked up from the matches. "What are you doing, boy? It's over; give it up."

Jack shook his head and pushed up. His ankle felt like it had a dozen red-hot skewers stuck though it. But he could do this. He could do it for David, for Trudy . . . for Grey . . . maybe even a little for Cthulhu and the Misery.

"It isn't over, Blackbeard Junior. It isn't over until you kill me. And if you know anything about the Ministry, you know that one determined operative using The Speed is more than a match for eight mangy pirates."

The mangy pirates looked slightly disgruntled at being described in such disrespectful terms. Mr. Rackham clacked his pincer in an indignant fashion.

"You reckon you can beat eight pirates, lad?"

Jack was pretty sure that even if his ankle had been broken he wouldn't have been able to beat the eight pirates with their hooked hands and cutlasses. However, it was something that he certainly wasn't going to admit to Blackbeard Junior.

"I reckon I can. You fancy giving up? I'll go easy on you."

Blackbeard Junior wobbled his head from side to side as if he was weighing his options. "The thing is, lad, it's a kind offer. But I'll be getting on with lighting the fuse here. Lads, finish the pip-squeak off."

The eight pirates, led by Mr. Rackham, advanced on Jack.

BEING SAVED
In the Nick of Time

Many people ask what the key skill for a Ministry operative is. Probably the most important to practice and cultivate is "being saved in the nick of time."

Of course, there isn't actually any other way to be saved than in the nick of time. If you get saved *before* the nick of time, then you weren't really in danger and so it doesn't count as being saved. However, if you get saved *after* the nick of time you probably haven't been saved and therefore all that anyone can do is order a wreath and inform the next of kin.

Therefore, if you are being saved, it is essential that you try and arrange it to be as close to the nick of time as possible.

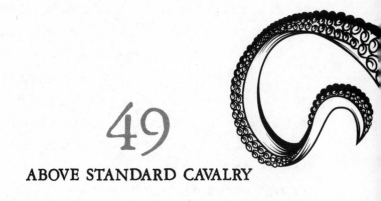

49

ABOVE STANDARD CAVALRY

Blackbeard Junior had somehow managed to get a match stuck to the end of his hook and was attempting to strike it against the edge of a matchbox.

Jack could still hear the rumbling noise close by. Although it didn't seem to be getting any closer—were Grey and the reinforcements lost in a nearby passage? He needed some way of signaling them so they knew which direction to take. However, with the eight pirates advancing on him it didn't seem as though he would get the chance.

"I never liked you, Jack," sneered Mr. Rackham. "You were awful at rope climbing." Rackham dropped the chalkboard that he normally carried and drew a cutlass with his one good hand.

And then Jack had an idea. He knew how he could signal Grey. The idea made him feel elated; however, he focused on how sad he would be if the pirates killed him. How sad he would be to never see Trudy again. How sad he would be to miss future adventures with the Ministry. The Speed descended on him and, with fire burning through his damaged ankle, he sped toward the pirates. The Pirates could barely believe their eyes[88] as Jack streaked toward them.

Jack dived and rolled before anyone could stop him. He reached out and grabbed the chalkboard Rackham had dropped. Blackbeard Junior lit the match and applied it to the fuse, which started to burn toward the cannon. "Got her lit, lads!" he bellowed. The pirates let out an enormous cheer.

"Bon voyage, Jack. Me and the crew will be going topside now. I'm afraid the two of you don't have tickets. I imagine you'll be blown to smithereens when the cannon goes off."

Jack looked at Blackbeard Junior. "Just one more thing." Jack dragged his fingernails across the chalkboard. The screeching noise echoed loudly across the cavern, setting everyone's teeth on edge.

Blackbeard Junior seemed puzzled. "Well, it's a very unpleasant noise, but we're still going to leave you here until the cannon goes off. So I don't . . ."

The screeching sounds of Jack's fingernails on the chalkboard were still echoing around the cavern.

". . . think that you should be . . ." Blackbeard Junior was interrupted in his gloating by the low rumbling noise getting louder—it was beginning to blot out the echoing

---

[88] To be perfectly accurate, some of the Pirates couldn't believe their eyes, while others couldn't believe their eye. A lot of them had patches.

chalkboard screech. Blackbeard Junior looked around but couldn't figure out where the rumbling was coming from. He strode back over to where Jack lay. The pirates stayed where they were and chattered nervously.

"What on earth is that?" Blackbeard Junior asked. "What's that noise?"

Ignoring Blackbeard Junior, Jack squinted into the dark of the cavern and saw something that made him want to cry with happiness.

"It's my friend Grey . . . with the cavalry."

Jack pointed into the darkness. Blackbeard Junior turned to look. His jaw dropped.

There are many amazing and beautiful sights in the world. Northern Ireland has the beauty of the Giant's Causeway and the picturesque North Coast, America claims the awe-inspiring size of the Grand Canyon, London has the architectural gem of the dome of St. Paul's cathedral, Paris has the industrial engineering masterpiece that is the Eiffel Tower.[89] These are all wonders of the world and amazing to behold. However, none of these stunning sights could have filled Jack's heart with as much joy as what he saw coming lumbering through the enormous cavern.

Dozens of fully grown dinosaurs. *Stegosaurus*, *Tyrannosaurus*, *Triceratops*, *Diplodocus*, *Iguanodons*, hovering *Pterodactylus*, *Velociraptor* weaving in and out between the feet of their larger companions. And many, many others.

[89] Although we can all agree that it would be better as the Eiffel Roller Coaster.

And the colors! Bright reds, silvers, gold and orange, vivid purple. It was a veritable rainbow of dinosaurs.

"This isn't possible!" yelled Blackbeard Junior. The dinosaurs did not seem worried about whether people thought they were possible or not; they kept thundering across the floor of the cavern getting nearer and nearer. Blackbeard's eight pirate henchmen started shuffling their feet nervously.

Jack decided it was time to get out of the way as the dinosaurs were close to full stampede mode after being excited at hearing what they assumed was a mating call. While Blackbeard Junior was distracted by the oncoming dinosaurs Jack managed to stand and hobble his way over to Trudy.

The bone splinter was still embedded in Trudy's shoulder, but he was relieved to see that it had stopped bleeding. It was right in the same spot where the mole had hit her earlier, but on the bright side it meant that she would have only one scar. When she woke up Jack was fairly sure it was going to sting a bit.

Jack hauled Trudy over to the relative safety of the alcove and helped her into a sitting position.

"Trudy? Are you okay?" He had to speak loudly to be heard over the sound of dinosaurs stampeding across the enormous cavern.

Trudy's eyes flicked open. "Okay? Am I okay? What kind of a question is that? I've got a piece of dinosaur in my shoulder. Of course I'm not okay."

"What I meant was . . ." Jack trailed off when he realized that (a) he wasn't really sure what he meant and (b) even if he had been sure what he meant, now was not the time to start an argument about it.

"Has Grey arrived yet?"

Jack looked over at the thundering herd of dinosaurs. Blackbeard Junior had placed himself between the dinosaurs and the enormous cannon. The other pirates had decided that their best option was running and screaming and occasionally getting trampled by a dinosaur.

The dinosaurs kept on running. Jack could now see that Grey was riding on the back of a particularly large purple *Brontosaurus*, urging it onward with his umbrella.[90] Grey also seemed to be carrying an iPhone connected to a set of Sonos speakers out of which was blasting Wagner's "The Ride of the Valkyries."

"I think you could most definitely say that Grey has arrived."

"Your plan worked, then?" Trudy smiled.

"It seems so. Obviously Cthulhu agreed to use his evil powers to destroy the stalagmites at Marble Arch caves. Grey seems to have managed to have the dinosaurs stampede quite effectively."

"And the map?" asked Trudy.

Jack shrugged. "I think they might have gotten a little lost. But I managed to get a message to them using this." Jack held up Mr. Rackham's chalkboard.

"But you don't even have any chalk," said Trudy, confused.

Jack thought about trying to explain to Trudy how he

---

[90] The dinosaur's name was Bernie. But that's just a coincidence.

had remembered Grey saying that a dinosaur mating cry was a high shrieking noise. But then he thought better of it, and decided there would be time later for full explanations.

〰〰〰〰〰〰

The dinosaurs were almost directly in front of Blackbeard Junior now—the other pirates had fled long ago. Blackbeard Junior threw his hands up in the air and roared at the dinosaurs to stop. It was a ridiculous thing to do. For a start, dinosaurs, as has previously been stated, don't respond well to instruction. Once they had started stampeding they clearly weren't going to stop until they came to something they couldn't trample. Additionally, even if they had understood what Blackbeard had been saying, they were moving so quickly that they wouldn't have been able to stop if they had wanted to.

The knee of a *Diplodocus* crashed into Blackbeard Junior's chest and sent him sailing through the air. He smacked into the ground but then was almost immediately hit by a *Tyrannosaurus*'s tail as it ran past him. That sent him spinning and twirling until he was trampled by a dozen *Velociraptors*, their claws tearing his flesh. For a second it looked like he was trying to get to his feet, but a passing *Stegosaurus* knocked him over. As he fell his hook hand caught on its spiked tail. It hooked tight and Blackbeard Junior was dragged along as the *Stegosaurus* ran into the distance.

Blackbeard Junior was not the only thing to suffer from the dinosaur's trampling. The enormous cannon named *Queen Anne's Revenge* had been stamped and smashed into flat little pieces. Even if the fuse was still alight somewhere, it certainly wasn't attached to the cannon anymore.

As the dinosaurs passed where Trudy and Jack were, Grey stood up on the back of his purple *Brontosaurus*, paused for a few seconds, and then leapt off, performing a double somersault before landing neatly.

"Dinosaur surfing," said Grey. "I imagine it'll be all the rage at the next Olympics."

"That was the most amazing thing I've ever seen," said Jack.

Grey raised one eyebrow. "Keep in mind that it's only your first week on the job. It will get weirder."

Jack laughed.

"But Blackbeard Junior got away." Trudy frowned.

Grey put a reassuring hand on Trudy's good shoulder. "Sometimes the bad guys do get away. The important thing is that we foiled his plan. Everyone is safe. The cannon is destroyed and the prisoners freed."

"But won't he be back?" asked Trudy.

Grey shrugged. "Blackbeard Junior? Yes. Or someone like him. There'll always be some maniac planning to do something awful and spoil the world for the rest of us. But we'll be here waiting."

"The Ministry of Strange, Unusual, and Impossible Things."

"The Men in Suits," agreed Jack.

"And women!" Trudy pointed out.

"Quite," said Grey. "But now I think we ought to get you to a hospital. You appear to have a shard of bone sticking out of your shoulder. It looks painful."

"It does look painful. About the same level of pain that I experience when you punch me in the shoulder," agreed Jack.

Trudy looked at Jack and balled her fist. She raised herself up to punch him in the shoulder, but luckily the pain of movement caused her to pass out. Jack looked at her unconscious form. "Sometimes I wish she could be like this all the time."

Grey carefully put his hands under Trudy's shoulders and nodded for Jack to take her feet. "We'll take her to the Ministry and get the medics to fix her up."

Jack remembered Nurse Nufty with a leg where her arm should have been. "Grey, how about we just take her to a regular hospital instead."

"A very sensible suggestion, Jack. A very sensible suggestion indeed."

OBJECTS
Ease of Being Trampled by Dinosaurs

Objects generally fall into two categories. Category A is objects that can be trampled by a dinosaur. Category B is objects that *can't* be trampled by a dinosaur. There are very few objects which fall into Category B (jumbo jets, skyscrapers, etc.)

People are almost always Category A objects unless they are really very fat indeed.

EPILOGUE

TIDYING UP

Despite the fact that Northern Ireland had come close to destruction, Jack was amazed at how easy it was to tidy up the loose ends.

―――――――――

Jack and Grey had managed to get Trudy up the rope ladder and found David waiting for them. "Are we all saved?"

"Pretty much."

"Did you capture that pirate bloke?"

"No, he got caught up on a dinosaur and was dragged away. No idea where he is now."

"Dinosaurs?" asked David.

Jack thought that finally curiosity had gotten the better of David.

"There was a really good documentary on dinosaurs last weekend on BBC. Did you see it?"

Jack decided not to react to how calm David was about everything that happened. No matter how strange things got, David was always going to be a little stranger.

The freed children all went back to their families. Of course no one was told that they had been kidnapped as part of a plot to try and create a floating Northern Ireland. The Ministry ensured that a story was spread that it had been an illegal gold mine. Missing hands and legs were explained away as mining accidents. The story was preposterous, but it was more believable than the truth. People would believe the most ridiculous things as long as you didn't ask them to think too much about it.

Of course some people asked awkward questions about why the kidnappers had all continually talked about "pieces of eight" and why their children had been forced to learn sea shanties. But in the end they stopped asking questions. After all, the idea that there were pirates in the world was... strange, unusual and, well... impossible. Most of the stories the kidnapped children told were passed off as post-traumatic stress disorder.

The next day in the paper a story appeared saying that Mr. Teach, the chief executive of Chapeau Noir Enterprises, had gone missing while flying his personal jet. Jack had a feeling that Blackbeard Junior would be back. A man capable of cutting an island in two wouldn't be defeated so easily by a runaway dinosaur.[91]

---

[91] Even I couldn't tell you what happened to Blackbeard Junior. However, it wouldn't be hard to believe that a certain little old lady, a direct

Trudy got her shoulder fixed at the Ulster Hospital. The doctor was a friend of Grey's and agreed to write up the operation as being due to a dog bite. Trudy's arm would be sore for months afterward, but she quite liked the scar. "Scars are your body's way of letting people know that you have interesting stories to tell," she told Jack.

Trudy seemed to enjoy coming to school in a sling. Rumors about what had happened to her abounded. Some people said she had gotten into a fight with an Olympic medal–winning boxer. Other people said that she had crashed a stolen car.

Jack and Trudy were summoned to the Minister's office and both awarded medals at the Ministry for foiling Blackbeard Junior's plot.

"You both deserve these," said the Minister as he placed the gold medals around their necks. "But keep in mind the work of the Ministry is best kept mostly secret. Don't go around showing these medals to everyone."

Jack frowned. "What's the point in having a medal if you can't boast about it?" he asked.

Grey took the medal from Jack and unwrapped it. It was just chocolate covered in tinfoil. He took a bite of the medal and handed it back to Jack.

"Really? Chocolate? Like the gold coins you get at Christmas."

---

descendant of Grace O'Malley, might have found him still attached to a dinosaur and helped him to escape. Of course that is nothing more than conjecture.

The Minister nodded. "Interestingly enough they based the idea for those coins on our medals, not the other way round."

"Chocolate medals. That's a bit of a swizz."

The Minister shook his head. "Not at all. They taste lovely. If you need to hide them in a hurry, you can just eat them. Makes perfect sense."

"Do you have any medals?" Trudy asked Grey.

"In the past I got a few. Maybe a dozen or so. Hard to keep count when you just eat them."

⁂

The next week at school Jack and Trudy sat together on a wall.

"The weekend seemed really quiet," Jack observed.

"Quiet's nice sometimes," said Trudy as she looked down at her sling.

David walked across the playground and said hello. "Hey, Jack, there's a guy in the school office looking for you."

"Oh yeah? Who?"

"Didn't catch his name," said David. "Big man, wore a tutu, was carrying a pair of pincers."

Jack's face turned white.

But that's another story . . . .

CHOCOLATE MEDALS
RECORD FOR WINNING MOST MINISTRY MEDALS

The bravest man in the Ministry won over thirty thousand medals. He was one of the best-ever operatives.

Unfortunately he was forced to retire as he got too fat to work in the field after eating all his medals.

ACKNOWLEDGMENTS

I'd like to thank Gemma[92] and Holly,[93] the best work colleagues I've never met.

[92] Gemma, how proud of me are you that I've managed this entire acknowledgments without using a footnote (apart from this one, obviously)? And you said that footnotes were "becoming like a sickness with me."

[93] Holly, what do you think of this as an acknowledgments section? I'm planning to wait until Gemma is busy with something else and then I'm going to jam in a whole lot more footnotes.

**THANK YOU FOR READING THIS
FEIWEL AND FRIENDS BOOK.**

The Friends who made

THE **MINISTRY** OF **SUITS**

possible are:

JEAN FEIWEL, Publisher

LIZ SZABLA, Editor in Chief

RICH DEAS, Senior Creative Director

HOLLY WEST, Editor

DAVE BARRETT, Executive Managing Editor

KIM WAYMER, Production Manager

ANNA ROBERTO, Editor

CHRISTINE BARCELLONA, Associate Editor

EMILY SETTLE, Administrative Assistant

ANNA POON, Editorial Assistant

Follow us on Facebook or visit
us online at mackids.com.

OUR BOOKS ARE FRIENDS FOR LIFE